T0279168

PRAISE FOR NINO CIPRI

"These stories . . . excel in a kind of subtle startling,
like meeting unexpected ripples in a mirror. Its last and most
accomplished story, 'Before We Disperse Like Star Stuff,'
is absolutely wonderful in every respect."
—*New York Times Book Review* on *Homesick: Stories*

"These stories are so deliciously queer and
dark and playful; Cipri is a treasure."
—**Carmen Maria Machado,**
National Book Award Finalist and author of
Her Body and Other Parties, **on** *Homesick: Stories*

"A riveting first collection that announces a major new talent
unafraid to embrace the beauty of the mysterious. Uncanny,
gorgeous, unyielding, original, and unforgettable."
—**Ann and Jeff VanderMeer** on *Homesick: Stories*

"Nine speculative stories capture the most universal parts
of humanity through an organic and refreshing take on the
paranormal . . . they'll all haunt readers long after the book is
closed. A beautiful, sometimes haunting, always inviting and
inclusive collection about life, love, and the paranormal."
—*Kirkus Reviews* on *Homesick: Stories*

"*Finna* is a book of fantastical impossibilities and biting
commentary on the perils of capitalism. But it's also a heartfelt
exploration of two people moving apart, only to be forced
together in the most nightmarish of circumstances."
—**Mark Oshiro, #1** *New York Times*–**bestselling,**
award-winning author of *Anger Is a Gift,* **on** *Finna*

★ "Cipri hits all the right notes in this fantasy novella packed with action and emotion. Part horror, part humor, and all heart, the story uniquely showcases two queer protagonists dealing with their own emotional separation while also being forced to work together."
—*Library Journal*, **starred review, on** *Finna*

★ "Cipri continues to mix queer characters and anti-capitalist themes with energetic, bouncy prose. Highly recommended for readers looking for sf with queer protagonists."
—*Booklist*, **starred review, on** *Defekt*

ALSO BY NINO CIPRI

Homesick: Stories
Finna
Defekt

Dead Girls
Don't Dream

Nino Cipri

HENRY HOLT AND COMPANY
NEW YORK

Henry Holt and Company, *Publishers since 1866*
Henry Holt® is a registered trademark of Macmillan Publishing Group, LLC
120 Broadway, New York, NY 10271 • fiercereads.com

Copyright © 2024 by Nino Cipri. All rights reserved.

Our books may be purchased in bulk for promotional, educational,
or business use. Please contact your local bookseller or the Macmillan Corporate and
Premium Sales Department at (800) 221-7945 ext. 5442 or by email at
MacmillanSpecialMarkets@macmillan.com.

Library of Congress Cataloging-in-Publication Data
Names: Cipri, Nino, author.
Title: Dead girls don't dream / Nino Cipri.
Other titles: Dead girls do not dream
Description: First edition. | New York : Henry Holt and Company, 2024. |
Audience term: Teenagers | Audience: Ages 14–18. | Audience: Grades 10–12. |
Summary: When seventeen-year-old Riley is murdered in an occult ritual,
the witch's daughter Madelyn resurrects her in an attempt to break the cycle of
violence and escape the horrors of Voynich Woods.
Identifiers: LCCN 2024010690 | ISBN 9781250791405 (hardcover)
Subjects: CYAC: Magic—Fiction. | Dead—Fiction. | Forests and forestry—Fiction. |
LGBTQ+ people—Fiction. | Horror stories. | LCGFT: Horror fiction. | Novels.
Classification: LCC PZ7.1.C564 De 2024 | DDC [Fic]—dc23
LC record available at https://lccn.loc.gov/2024010690

First edition, 2024
Book design by Mallory Grigg
Printed in the United States of America

ISBN 978-1-250-79140-5
1   3   5   7   9   10   8   6   4   2

For all of us looking for wonder
in the deep, dark woods

CHAPTER ONE

Riley cursed as her leaky pen dribbled out a blob of ink, smearing and staining the tips of her fingers.

"What happened?" Sam, her little sister, asked. She craned her neck around to look, and the temporary tattoo Riley was drawing on Sam's shoulder smeared even more.

"Don't move," she said. "You're messing it up."

"*You're* messing it up," Sam replied. Which was bratty, but also true. Sam had asked for a death's-head moth, because that was just the kind of ten-year-old she was, and while Riley wanted to be a tattoo artist someday, all she had to practice with right now was a permanent marker and a squirming kid.

They were sitting behind the counter—an old, angled desk that Uncle Toby had found on the side of the road, hauled back, sanded, and refinished—in the Roscoe Mysteries Museum and Tour Center. It seemed like a fancy name for an unfancy operation, run out of an old barn off Route 31. The exhibits were in former horse stalls, hand-painted, dusty, and cobwebby. No livestock had lived here in decades, but a faint animal smell—hay and musk and manure—lingered anyway.

One of the tourists here for Toby's Sunday evening tour, who'd been taking in the exhibit about Camille Voynich, looked over at them disapprovingly. Riley forced herself to smile. Uncle Toby was technically paying her to watch the museum and check people in. But the tourists mostly sucked, or maybe Riley was just exceptionally awkward and unfriendly.

"Did you . . . have a question?" she asked. This guy had ridden up to the old barn on a road bike that looked like it had cost more than Uncle Toby's truck. Nothing had managed to impress him yet. When he didn't ask her anything, or say anything, or do anything but stare at her like a bug, Riley added, "My uncle says that Camille Voynich's disappearance started the, uh, modern myth cycle about Voynich Woods."

"I'm fine," he said shortly, turning back to the portrait of the Voyniches that had run in the *Roscoe Independent*. The two parents looked dour, if well-dressed. Their older daughter, Lillian, stood at her mother's shoulder, staring at the camera with a tight little smile. Camille was seated between her parents, dressed in layers of white, lace at her throat and covering her hands and wrists, long dark hair lying in a braid across one shoulder. Riley had always thought that she looked destined to be a ghost.

"Dickhead," she whispered under her breath, mostly for Sam's benefit.

They were right in the thick of Roscoe's meager tourist season, with the fall foliage about a week or two before its peak but the early autumn warmth not yet chased off by the gray rains. They'd gotten a good number of people for the tour: the aforementioned cranky bicyclist, a family of four with varying degrees of Boston accent, a retired couple who'd had to leave their enormous RV on the shoulder of the road because the parking lot was too small, and a couple of middle-aged women who were definitely plotting out some kind of podcast episode about Roscoe and Voynich Woods.

"This looks like a kid drew it," the dad from Boston scoffed, holding up one of the prints of Roscoe's Witch of the Woods. Riley had, in fact, drawn that when she was fourteen, a little too obsessed with both Voynich Woods' mysteries and drawing creepy women with long hair obscuring their faces. It was exquisitely embarrassing that Toby still sold art she'd made years ago.

"What's the difference between a forest and woods?" the mom from Boston asked. She seemed bored, half watching her kids touch everything in the little gift shop with fingers stained from the ice cream they'd been eating. "Why's it called one instead of the other?"

Sam piped up, "It has to do with tree density. If the majority of the area has tree canopy, then it's a forest. If it's less than that, it's a wood. It's technically a forest now, but when it was named, they called it a wood because the logging industry had cleared away a lot of the trees, and—"

"Uh-huh, that's super," the mom said. "Kaylin! Don't put that in your mouth!"

She pulled the geode out of her kid's mouth, wiped it hastily on her shirt, and put it back on the display. Riley wished that literally any of the monsters in her uncle's museum were real, and that she could feed people to them.

"I have a question," one of the podcast women said, looming up suddenly in front of the desk. She was wearing what Riley could only assume was merch for her podcast, a T-shirt with the words BAD THINGS AND GOOD PEOPLE above a chalk outline of a body with a bright yellow smiley face. "Why isn't the wall of missing people complete? There are some names I'm not seeing on there."

She said it loud enough that the other tourists turned to

look at her. The adults, anyway. The kids were now driving the crystals around like they were toy cars.

More than any other kind of tourist, the ones who claimed to know more than Uncle Toby were the worst.

Sam went stiff. Riley didn't look up from the nearly complete moth she'd drawn on Sam's shoulder, but she did squeeze her sister's arm. "We only include people who conclusively went missing inside Voynich Woods," she said quietly.

"But what about—"

"Not everyone who's ditched town gets added to the official list," Riley said. She tried to sound bored instead of angry. She didn't look at the wall, at the ten black-and-white photographs that stretched from 1938's Camille Voynich—the most famous of the missing, and the one who the woods were named for—to 2018's Amy Macready. She didn't think about whose photo wasn't there. "Some people just leave."

"Official list according to who?" asked the other podcaster lady.

"That would be me," Toby said, finally coming into the barn. "Though I'm more of an unofficial historian. But literally nobody else wants this job, so."

He said it lightly, timed to get a laugh, and it worked, dispelling the tension that Riley had created by being her usual charming self. She was ready for tourist season to be over.

Riley pointedly went back to her drawing, tuning out anything else that the two podcast ladies asked as they crowded up to Toby with questions. She put a few finishing touches on Sam's death's-head moth, comparing it to the picture she'd pulled up on her phone. Not bad, she decided, for permanent marker on someone who hated sitting still. She took a quick photo and turned her phone around to show Sam.

"Nice," Sam said. "Kinda smeared."

"You're sweaty," Riley told her.

"*You're* sweaty. And you stink," Sam replied.

Riley capped the marker and said, "All teenagers stink. Give it another few years and you're gonna be even worse."

"Gross," Sam announced, and Riley shrugged. Couldn't argue with it. "You should offer to give the tourists fake tattoos."

"Maybe in a few years I can give them real ones. Roscoe Mystery Museum, Tours, and Tattoos."

Toby must have been half listening, because he looked over and grinned at her before going back to his conversation with the podcast women. He had promised to pay for a tattoo for Riley's eighteenth birthday, on the condition that she never, ever tried to give herself one in her bedroom again. (It had gotten infected, the little snake she'd tried to press into her skin with a sewing needle and some nontoxic ink. In retrospect, not her smartest decision.)

"It's wild," one of the podcast women said, loud enough to break Riley's focus. "How beautiful and timeless this place is, but how there's this dark history threaded through it."

"Oh my god, like the caves—" said her friend.

"Yes! Just like the cave system under the woods! Beauty all around you, but below your feet . . ." She trailed off meaningfully.

"I can see you've already done some research," Toby said. "Have you heard of the Witch's Well sinkhole?"

He was in full tour guide mode as he started talking about karst geology and the area's caves: a big, friendly smile, a hint of "aw, shucks" swagger, and a gentle country twang to his voice. Not how people in Roscoe talked—which was nasal and fast, syllables scooped out of words—but how outsiders might expect them to speak. Riley and Sam called it the Redneck Professor persona. It had been weird to see Toby slip into it the first couple of times; their mother's brother had always been kind, but he had no idea how to interact with the two nieces he found himself caring for whenever Mom was arrested or in rehab. It got channeled into long, uninterrupted speeches about topics he was perpetually researching for "the book." Riley didn't know what the book was about, exactly, only that it seemed to include local history, cryptids, and ghost tales, sure, but also the Wabanaki Confederacy, the eugenics movement in New England (and the importance, in general, of remembering ugly history that made you feel bad), and all the failures of the state that led to the local opioid epidemic. She didn't know how all those things fit together; she suspected Toby didn't know either, and maybe that was why the book never seemed to be finished.

Toby led the tour group out of the barn, having smoothly transitioned into his talk about myths and stories from the Western Abenaki tribes. Once he got them ushered out, he leaned back in the doorway. "You two good?" he asked. "It seemed tense when I came in."

"Podcast lady said there's missing people we left off the wall," Riley said.

"She's right, though," Sam whispered.

Riley didn't realize how tightly she was gripping the marker until her hand cramped. She shook it out, opened her mouth to argue that Mom hadn't disappeared into the woods, but into the night with an arrest warrant in her name. Then she thought better of it: Why spoil a nice day with the one thing she and her sister would never agree on? "Sam, we're not going to talk about it for some random lady's podcast. She came up to us like she was about to accuse us of a conspiracy."

"I'll keep her away from you two. Or do you want to skip the tour? Stay home?" Toby offered.

Riley looked at Sam, leaving it up to her.

"We'll go part of the way with you," Sam said. "Then we've got plans."

This was news to Riley. But Sam never had the same misgivings about Voynich. She loved the woods, loved the stories that Toby told about them, and the monsters and missing people that were basically in their backyard. She'd only been five years old when she and Riley came to live with Toby, and she treated the creepy-ass woods behind their house like her own personal playground.

"Still on the hunt for the Wishing Tree, huh?" Toby asked.

Riley's eyes slid over to the exhibit about the Wishing Tree. The story went that there was a big tree, hidden somewhere in the forest. If you came to it with pure intentions and left a gift—a coin, a nail, a ribbon, depending on what you wanted—it would grant you a wish. It was one of the first exhibits that she had helped Toby put together; they'd sketched the outline of a tree on a piece of plywood, then painted it with acrylics that the high school had thrown out after cutting all the art classes because of the budget.

Riley could hear Toby's voice in her head, the lecture he gave: The earliest evidence came from journal entries of a logging foreman in 1830, who referred to the Wishing Tree like it was already an established myth in the woods his men were clearing.

It was probably older than Roscoe, but nobody had ever seen it or taken a picture of it. Some people called it the Witch's Tree and claimed that it had hosted dark, unholy sabbaths.

"Whistles?" Toby asked.

Riley pulled the silver whistle on its chain out of her shirt. Sam did the same with her whistle. With the spotty reception in the woods, it was more reliable than a cell phone.

"You remember the rules?" he prompted. He'd learned at some point that he couldn't keep them out of Voynich Woods. The forest butted nearly right up to the fields beyond the backyard, and Sam was particularly enamored with the woods and the creatures it supposedly hid, while Riley tended to chase after her. So he instituted rules: Always carry whistles, never go alone, always come home before dark, and if anyone calls your name, don't answer them.

The last one wasn't a rule found in most survival manuals.

Sam gave a thumbs-up, and Riley nodded.

Outside, the Boston dad grumbled loudly about wasting daylight, while the bicyclist was telling the podcast ladies about a tour he'd taken of a ghost town down in the south of the state. "Much more professional," he said.

Toby pasted his tour guide smile back on and said, "Guess we shouldn't keep them waiting."

◆ ◆ ◆

It was a beautiful day to be outside, crisp and autumnal, sunny enough that Riley was hiking in only a sweater. Toby stretched out a hike up the mountain that Riley could cover in thirty minutes into a nearly two-hour tour, from the old gatehouse down at the entrance to watching the sunset at Dyson Pond, a picturesque spot with a clear view of the mountains and Roscoe's downtown—if you could call the tiny collection of shops and empty storefronts that. Roscoe had never been much of a town, had only become less of one as time went on. The tourists that Roscoe did attract came for Voynich's monsters and missing, and the strange history of an ostensibly beautiful place.

"There are a lot of ghosts in Voynich Woods," Toby said now, more than an hour into the tour. "The oldest one has been called a lot of things, but most of us locals call her . . . the Dead Girl."

A round of snickers, and Toby smiled. "Yeah, we get real creative around here.

"Most ghosts that people see don't show a lot of signs of death, exactly, just a certain . . . unearthliness. The Dead Girl gets her name from her looks, which are very gruesome. But she's also the friendliest supernatural entity in these woods. The story goes, if you're lost and call out her name near a body of water, she'll come to you, and if you're lucky, she'll lead you to where you need to go. Some stories say to call her name three times, some say five times—"

"Wait, what's her name?" one of the tourists asked. They always asked. Toby smiled again; last week, he'd taught Riley all about the power of the mysterious smile. The two of them had practiced while her little sister Sam held up numbers to judge them like it was the Olympics. She'd kept docking Riley points for not being enigmatic enough.

"Nobody knows," Toby answered. "But if you're brave

enough, you can try your luck guessing it when we get to Dyson Pond, which is one of her favorite spots."

Toby started ushering the group farther up the path. One of the podcast women lingered until she could walk with Riley and Sam at the back of the group. "Loving the hike. And all the stories your dad knows—"

"He's my uncle," Riley said. She pulled Sam to her side, wanting to physically wall her off from this woman's questions.

"Must be nice having family close by," said the woman. She spoke crisply, like she was recording right now. "Are you all close?"

Riley hated questions about her family, especially from strangers. Even when said strangers weren't obviously snooping, what was she supposed to say? That one of her parents was in Holy Cemetery and the other had skipped town after violating her parole conditions?

"I guess," she said, trying to channel "off-putting, sullen teenager" as much as possible. She glanced over at Sam, who was doing her best to avoid the woman's curious gaze, and then at Toby. He'd stationed himself at the head of the group, while she and Sam had lingered at the back. The other podcaster had occupied him, and from what Riley could hear, was talking his ear off about poor Amy Macready, the last "official" disappearance in Voynich Woods.

"You probably figured out that we're here for research purposes," the woman said.

"You should talk to Toby, then. He's the guide." Riley could feel her shoulders pulling in. Did the woman not notice Riley itching to flee this conversation, or did she not care? "Like, the one who knows stuff? I'm not—"

"It's good to get multiple perspectives." The woman

gestured to her T-shirt. "I don't know if you've heard of our podcast—"

"Nope," Riley said.

"Oh, well, we do a mix of true crime and supernatural—"

"Don't really like podcasts," Riley interrupted. "They're pretty boring, you know? Like, why would I want to listen to two random people get excited about some person who died like twenty years ago?" She paused for a second, then said, "No offense. I'm sure your podcast is cool."

Riley was aiming for maximum psychic damage. She'd practiced this tone on teachers, classmates, neighbors, anyone who made a habit of prying. One teacher had turned such an incredible shade of red that Riley wondered if she'd managed to literally burn him.

It completely bounced off this woman, who laughed and said, "I certainly like to think so!"

Apparently, the tone wasn't as effective if you didn't already know Riley—didn't already pity her and expect her to act like a little lost waif.

"My journalistic instincts have been telling me that there's a more interesting story here," the woman continued. "Not the official mysteries, or even the cryptids—they're just flavoring, you know? But beneath it, there's some real tragedy here. A local police officer gave us an interview—"

Riley didn't hate easily—she didn't like the power that it gave other people. Hating someone felt like an open invitation to squat on valuable real estate in her brain, and she'd given up enough of it already. But she could feel herself starting to really hate this person and her podcast.

"And he was saying that there are plenty of junkies and

lowlifes who have gone missing too, but that they never earn as much media as a nice grandmother like Amy Macready. Do either of you have any experience or opinions about that? A quote for the listeners?"

Sam abruptly turned around before the woman finished. Before Riley could grab hold of her, Sam had slipped off back down the trail, ponytail bouncing against the nape of her neck.

"Sam!" she called.

"What's wrong with her?" the woman asked. From the front of the line, Riley saw Toby looking back at her, eyebrows furrowed. He must have seen Sam run off. She tried to send him a telepathic apology for the one-star review he was about to get on Tripadvisor.

Riley turned back. "Are you recording this?" she asked.

The woman squared her shoulders. "I would never record a minor without consen—"

"Here's my quote," Riley spat, just loud enough for her to hear, but not the other tourists. "Fuck you. Enjoy your tour."

◆ ◆ ◆

Voynich Woods was a weird place: creepy and claustrophobic, beautiful and not to be fooled with. Somewhere you went if you were in the mood to feel unwelcome. Voynich Woods always seemed to be waiting for you to put a toe out of line.

It took Riley about fifteen minutes to reach the fork in the path. She turned in a wide circle, eyes alert for any movement or scrap of color that was out of place. She'd grown out of believing Toby's rule about not answering if you heard someone call your name in the woods, but Sam was a staunch believer. It wouldn't do much good to call her name.

A throat cleared behind her. Riley flinched so hard she nearly fell over, then turned to the source of the sound.

"Hi, Mr. Bancroft," she said.

If Mr. Bancroft had a first name, Riley had never heard it. He was a lanky, narrow-shouldered man, his skin rough and reddened from years spent working outside in every kind of weather. He was Voynich Woods' ranger, although the only badge of authority he had was a vest with a name tag, and a hunting rifle in case any bears or coyotes got too close. He'd been there longer than Riley had been alive; Toby said he couldn't remember Voynich Woods not being watched over by him.

"You haven't seen Sam, have you?" she asked hopefully.

He stared her down, unblinking even as he leaned over and spat out a thin stream of tobacco between his teeth. "Recreation area closes at sunset," he said, which was what he always said. Voynich's "recreation area" was the only part of the forest with maintained paths; everything else was technically private land, belonging to whoever was left of the Voynich family. "Anyone caught in the woods after that will be prosecuted for trespassing."

Riley generally only knew how to deal with adults if they were family, teachers, or tourists, and Mr. Bancroft was none of the above. It didn't help that he hated teenagers in general and that he was unfriendly to her family in particular. "I know," she said. "Sam does too, she just . . ."

He made a show of checking his watch. "Sunset's in thirty-six minutes, officially." He always spoke like he'd clenched his jaw for so long that it had stuck that way.

"I'll have her out before then," said Riley.

He nodded to the path on the left. "She wandered off that way. I'll whistle if I see her."

"Thanks," Riley muttered. She was going to string Sam up by her toes. She was going to tell Toby to block YouTube at home. She was . . .

Comforting herself with fantasies of revenge that all involved Sam being safe, Riley took the looping path up the mountain. Hopefully Sam hadn't ventured too far off the path. She pushed forward, calling out specific threats as time went on and Sam didn't reappear.

"You have ten seconds to get out here before I tell Toby to change the Wi-Fi password!" she shouted. The evening chorus of birds was silenced by her sudden shout.

For years, Riley had had recurring nightmares about opening her eyes and finding herself deep in the forest, knowing it had trapped her. She would be walking, unable to stop or turn around or even slow her steps, and the trees would seem to get taller. Or she'd be shrinking, along with any chance of her ever leaving.

She clutched the whistle around her neck but didn't put it to her mouth yet. Three short blasts meant trouble, meant *help me*. Ranger Bancroft was a weird, grumpy old man, but he'd come if he heard her whistling. He'd probably arrest her for trespassing when he did, but that was dropping farther down Riley's list of things to worry about.

"Five seconds," Riley announced. "Four. Three. Two—"

"Wait, wait, Riley!"

Riley opened her eyes to glare down at her sister, who had appeared on the path in front of her. "Don't scare me like that, Sam," she said. "You know you can't be in the woods by yourself."

"I have my whistle," said Sam, pulling it out of her shirt.

Riley pressed her palm to the matching one she wore. Maybe she'd get a whistle as her first tattoo, she thought idly.

"Whistle won't actually keep you from getting lost," she said to Sam. "Just make it a little likelier that Mr. Bancroft will find you and arrest you for trespassing."

"Come on, we need to get to the Obelisk before sunset," Sam said. She grabbed Riley's hand and started towing her off the path, through the underbrush, into a glade where the forest floor was green with ferns and moss. Golden light was slanting through the trees, and she could see the burning sun through their trunks, hovering above the horizon.

"Do you want to talk about what that podcast lady said?" Riley asked.

Sam shrugged and kept walking.

"I told her to fuck off, if that helps."

Sam smiled, just at the corner of her mouth, and Riley decided that made any forthcoming one-star review worth it. Toby would probably agree. This was just what being the older sibling was about.

They continued walking for a while, Riley starting to sweat as they climbed upward.

"So, the lore says—" Sam started.

"Oh, the *lore*? You mean the old rednecks who hang out at Dunkin' Donuts all day?" To be fair, they had good stories, if you liked absolute nonsense. Sam took after Toby, in that she loved it.

"The *lore*," Sam said, "says that to find the Wishing Tree you go to the Obelisk and turn east, with your back to the setting sun. But I was thinking, the sunset isn't always directly west, you know? It's like, a little off." Riley had taken that unit in fifth-grade science as well, so she nodded along. "It's only directly west on the spring or fall equinox—"

"Which is today," Riley said.

"I know," Sam said smugly. "So today's when we're going to find it, when our shadows face directly east."

Nobody knew when the Wishing Tree had last been seen; the location had never been found, which made it as much of a cryptid as the Dead Girl or the Witch of the Woods. Sam was determined to succeed where many tourists and at least two ghost-hunting shows had failed.

The Obelisk was a very fancy local name for an unfancy landmark, a big slab of granite that had been a lot more imposing before a good chunk of it cracked off during one volatile spring. They'd stopped taking the tours there, since it was a steep hike for a not particularly thrilling rock. The story Toby had always told about this rock was that a man had challenged the devil to a wrestling match, and when he'd won, he'd asked for a boon. He'd asked to live forever, and the devil had smiled at him, before turning him into the stone.

Sam must have been thinking about Toby's story as well, because she said, "There are a lot of stories about the devil in the woods."

Riley nodded. "Toby says that most of the stories aren't talking about, like, Satan. Just a kind of trickster."

"Mrs. Lafontaine says there are definitely Satanists in the woods."

"She also says that government agents bathe in stolen children's blood." Mrs. Lafontaine had never been one of Riley's favorite neighbors, even before she went full conspiracy theorist. During the pandemic, she'd started hanging handmade signs along the road in front of her fields, replacing them anytime someone threw them in the creek or shot them full of holes. The ones out there now said DEMOCRATS . . . MORE LIKE . . . DEMON CULTS?

They rounded a turn and came up to the Obelisk, its lumpy not-quite pyramid shape looming up through the tree trunks.

"Why would the devil grant wishes?" Sam asked. "I thought that was what the tree was for."

Riley shrugged. "Maybe the tree belongs to the devil. Maybe it got tired of meeting people face-to-face. Maybe the tree is like, the devil's secretary."

Sam giggled over that. They walked in silence for a little while before Sam asked, "What would you wish for?"

Riley thought of Toby's stories about the Wishing Tree again. You left coins to wish for good fortune, iron nails to right a wrong done to you, a pair of shoes for children, a candle for better health, and a strip of cloth with a name on it, if you wanted that person to love you. Nothing that Riley wanted fit into those neat categories. She wanted to learn how to tattoo people, even though she found the idea of permanently changing someone deeply unnerving. She wanted to get out of Roscoe, but the idea of leaving Sam and Toby made her feel dizzy with anxiety. She was almost afraid to want things; like if she tried to grasp them, they'd somehow be taken away from her.

"I don't know," she said. "What would you wish for?"

"To know where Mom is," Sam said immediately. "To bring her home."

Riley clenched her jaw. Of course Sam wished that. Why wouldn't she? She barely remembered living with Mom, and Riley had done her best to shield her from the worst of it.

Riley knew her mother's likeliest whereabouts were in a nameless grave somewhere, or—not objectively worse, but more hurtful to think about—that she was living under a different name in some nowhere state to avoid getting arrested. Either Anna Walcott was dead, or her daughters were dead to her.

"I'm gonna check on the other side of the Obelisk," said Sam, with no clue that she'd emotionally kneecapped Riley.

"Cool," Riley said, and let her go.

On some instinct, she looked up at the sky. Clouds had gathered overhead, thick and gray, making it seem even darker. Just yesterday had technically still been summer. But the wind blowing down the mountain felt like autumn, chilly and damp, pulling leaves off the trees. Riley could imagine the glade with a carpet of bloodred leaves on the ground, her breath turning foggy as it left her. But *imagine* was too weak of a word; Riley worried that if she closed her eyes, that was what she'd see when she opened them. Like her body was trying to tell her something that her mind couldn't accept yet.

"Riley!"

The voice was faint, far off to Riley's left instead of farther up the path. Damn it. Sam must have gone ahead.

Riley wasn't stupid, and she knew that going off the path made it a whole lot likelier that she'd get lost. Apparently, Sam had not learned the same lesson, despite all of Riley's and Toby's efforts. She stepped off the path with a sigh and followed, all too aware of the fast-falling darkness. Shadows seemed to swallow up the dim spaces between the trees, stretching eagerly into places where they had no business being.

She caught sight of something moving out of the corner of her eye. A long length of ribbon that had been tied to a tree, sun-faded to a light yellow. As she looked, she saw other scraps of fabric.

They were attached to a wolf tree.

She'd found the phrase in one of Toby's many history books. White settlers in this part of the country had leveled the forests for farmland, and when they realized that the thin topsoil didn't produce much, they brought the forests back to log them. But smaller, controlled. Tamed. They took down the old, sprawling trees, not for wood, but because they wanted the room and the sunlight for more profitable trees. The logging companies called those ugly unprofitable oaks and hickories and maples "wolf trees" because they were like wolves preying on a flock of sheep, stealing resources away from a nice, tidy forest that could be clear-cut every twenty or forty years.

This wolf tree towered up, bigger than any others in Voynich Woods. Riley wasn't even sure what species it was. Its roots rose out of the ground and spread out in a roiling mass. There were glints of metal where silver coins had been hammered in. Iron nails bled rust down onto the bark, and bits of cloth, bleached and tattered from the weather, fluttered amid the branches. Generations of people had carved letters and sometimes full words into the gray bark. Shoes were up there as well: rotting leather boots and sneakers, lonely pairs of baby shoes.

Not just any wolf tree. The Wishing Tree.

Riley heard a distant rumble of thunder. The wind had picked up, bringing the smell of rain with it. The first of the autumn storms, signaling the end of summer and the beginning of winter.

Riley found her eyes drawn to one branch hanging nearly at

eye level. No coins or nails in it, no ribbons or cloth. Instead, caught in the fork of the branch was a silver heart-shaped locket.

Riley's imagination was doing the thing it liked to do, crafting the worst possible scenario and dumping adrenaline into her body to prepare to fight or flee. The locket was bait, and a deadfall trap would open the second she touched it. Or the tree would open a horrible, sideways mouth and devour her.

The stupid anxiety fantasies weren't working like they were supposed to. She could feel adrenaline filling her system, feel cold sweat gathering in her armpits and palms, but she was rooted in place.

Riley reached out toward the locket. She felt like her mind had been split in two. Part of her was reaching for the locket, and part of her was watching herself reach like she was one of those stupid girls in a horror movie, screaming, *WHAT ARE YOU DOING?* inside her head.

She forced herself to take a step back. Then another. She didn't have to do this. She could turn around, find her way back. Or use her whistle—that was smarter. Sam would find her, Mr. Bancroft would find her.

Only, when she looked down, the locket that she'd seen hanging from a branch was in her hand.

Why was it in her hand? She couldn't remember grabbing it. She wanted to fling it away, but she felt a sort of free-floating anxiety; what if the tree, or whatever lived in it, thought throwing it away was disrespectful? Or what if throwing the locket away woke something that until now had been sleeping?

A twig snapped behind her.

The sudden impact took her off her feet, and that was all she felt at first: the bright burst of pain as something hit her on the side of the face, followed by the heavy slap of her body hitting the ground.

She remembered, with sudden vividness, the time a robin had flown into a window of her mother's apartment. She'd run to get Mom, who had looked at the bird, winced, and said, "Well, let's make sure it's comfortable," in such a way that told Riley the bird wouldn't survive. She'd picked it up so gently, cupping it in her calloused palms, and laid it in a shoebox full of old kitchen towels.

Riley lay there, the pain in her skull so heavy it pinned her to the ground, staring up at the man who had hit her. Tall enough to fill up space like a freestanding wall, wearing a black mask with a gold sun embroidered over the face. It caught the warm light of the dying sun, gleaming amid the darkness in the trees. The mask was beautiful, looked handmade and expensive.

She crawled backward away from the man, who watched her, head cocked like some curious beast. He still had a rock in his hand, and Riley pawed at the ground without taking her eyes off him, trying to find something she could use as a weapon.

There was a hand in her hair suddenly, and a horrid, pinching pain on the side of her chest.

"You won't scream, will you?" a second person behind her said in a hoarse whisper. "I hate it when girls scream."

When Riley looked down, the handle of a knife protruded from her ribs. A red stain was spreading out from it.

She thought distractedly of her old nightmare, walking through Voynich Woods, shrinking as the trees grew taller. She'd never been able to remember how she'd ended up in the woods in those dreams, why she'd go there alone. She believed it was a warning to do everything right: carry a whistle, stay on the path, go home before sunset. If Riley followed the rules, she'd never be one of the people on those missing posters.

If she followed the rules, she'd never end up like her mom.

The red stain had spread across her shirt and sweater, sodden fabric sticking to her skin. She watched as the knife was pulled from her, the pain multitudes worse than when it went in, like the blade was dragging against bone. She opened her mouth to scream, but the hand released her hair and was slapped over her mouth. Red started spreading across her vision as well.

Riley hadn't noticed before, but the wolf tree was dead, empty of leaves, its many branches bare except for the tokens that people had left. Riley tried to focus, but her mind kept returning to the robin and its vivid red breast. Small and still in the shoebox, it had seemed so fragile. She'd run her fingers gently over the bright feathers on its chest before she realized it had stopped breathing. It would never brighten another winter.

The knife went in again, and color bloomed on Riley's chest. Riley opened her mouth, but no sound came out. There were shadows in her vision, abstract patterns of darkness like tattoo ink. The lines of darkness were growing thicker, tangling together. The light was getting cut into tinier pieces, eaten away.

She would have to bury the robin before Sam woke up, and later she would tell Sam the bird had gotten better and flown away. Riley had always—

She—

"Sam?" she whispered, right before the last bit of light was devoured.

◆ ◆ ◆

INTERLUDE: THE WOODS

Excerpt from *Bury the Echo:*
A Local Historian's Perspective on
Folklore, Forests, and Other Important Stuff,
or So I'm Telling Myself (Working Title),
by Toby Walcott.

In the ten years or so that I've been running tours of Voynich Woods, countless sightseers have compared it to a fairy-tale forest.

Voynich survives as one of the last old-growth forests in the state, and the Northeast in general. It feels like a place that humans haven't touched, though that's a lie; people have been living in and around the forest, the mountains, and the valleys for millennia. Western Abenaki tribes have lived here for hundreds of generations, and the town of Roscoe was chartered in 1761. The forest survived industrialization and the logging boom and bust, as well as a brief and failed attempt at becoming a resort destination. It thrived through the Depression, with plenty of bootleggers traveling through the forests. It even managed to survive the last few housing booms, when real estate developers were snatching up chunks of land for a thousand McMansion subdivisions.

Voynich Woods endures.

If it feels untouched by humans, then Voynich

Woods does feel touched by something else. Devils, witches, ghosts, a wish-granting tree, feral children, strange beasts—it's more than just aesthetically correct to call it a fairy-tale forest. In stories, the forest stands in opposition to the safety net of civilization: known versus unmapped, dark versus light. We don't know what lives there. We might not want to know. But we can't seem to stay away from it. Some go into the woods to take a shortcut. Some go to find their fortune, or to ask for the impossible. And some go to escape. Even believing that the woods are filled with monsters, and maybe especially because of that.

Parents—or any of us adults who have a set of impressionable ears following us around—we pass down stories about travels into, and hopefully out of, the woods. Because stories are maps our children can follow: Here are the safe paths and the unsafe ones; here are the wonders they might lead you to, and the horrible dangers as well.

In Roscoe, we all grew up under the story of Camille Voynich. One night in 1938, the eight-year-old girl and her seventeen-year-old sister, Lillian, went into Voynich Woods—though they weren't yet called that. Only Lillian came out, claiming that the devil had taken Camille.

Such a story might have been accepted even fifty years earlier, when Roscoe was mostly a collection of logging camps and churches masquerading as a town. But by 1938, Roscoe was trying to remake itself as a modern resort town, with hiking trails and lodges catering to the rich from Boston and New York. And the Voynich family was instrumental in that: rich transplants from New Jersey who'd bought out the remaining acres of forest when the logging companies went broke. They built trails and cabins, even made plans to bottle Roscoe's spring water as a health tonic. They considered themselves scientists, of a sort: the sort that peddled "water cures" and eugenics as the answer to modern ills, but still big believers in rationalism and applying the scientific method (though mostly to other people).

When their youngest daughter disappeared, "the devil did it" was not an acceptable answer, even when it came from the girl's sister.

And maybe especially coming from her; Lillian Voynich was the child of her mother's scandalous first marriage, and supposedly her family left New Jersey after Lillian was caught carousing in Atlantic City a few too many times. There are rumors that she was either institutionalized or hospitalized for a time, but I haven't found any evidence as to why.

But Lillian's remains the only story we have, and to her credit, she never changed or recanted it. No trace of little Camille was ever found. Few signs of *any* of the missing were ever found. Voynich Woods—so named for the little girl whose bones, presumably, are still somewhere within them—refuses to be sensible, modern, *knowable*. It doesn't divulge its secrets; it just invites you in to find them, if you can.

Lillian came to Camille shaking like an aspen leaf, pale as the November sky. The devil had come to Lillian in the woods and promised her all kinds of things. Riches, any husband she could choose, power the likes of which no mortal could imagine. She refused him, of course. But now she was convinced that one of his witches—and everyone knew that the woods had its witches—would come after her. Sneak through her window, yank her out of her bed, and carry her off into the night.

"Sleep with me," she begged Camille. "Share my bed. Make sure I don't let in anything that means me harm."

No sister would refuse such a request, even if Camille didn't believe her about the devil. Lillian had always been given to fancy and flights of imagination, enough that Mother said her mind was infirm, and Father had arranged for her to stay in a hospital and have some kind of procedure done. Camille wasn't quite brave enough to ask what kind of procedure, or how was it supposed to have helped. Lillian only seemed stranger, angrier after she came back, more given to sulking and daydreaming.

Camille promised Lillian now that she would share her bed that night, though nothing would happen, and nobody would come.

Nothing knocked at the window. It was Lillian herself who lurched out of bed, nearly knocking Camille to the floor. She stepped over her sister, her nightgown falling around her calves.

Camille called her name, softly so it wouldn't wake the household. And when her sister didn't hear, Camille pushed herself to her feet to follow.

"Lillian," she hissed. "Stop playing! This isn't funny!"

Lillian always liked such tricks: a little mean, but obviously meant to test that one cared for her. Camille thought again of that hospital stay, the crescent-shaped scar on the curve of her belly, the way Lillian haunted the edges of rooms when their parents were in them. She never played such tricks on them; they had staunchly refused to play along.

Lillian's gait was strange and stiff, her eyes tightly closed. She went down the stairs, through the hallway and kitchen, and let herself out into the back garden. She did not respond to her name or to attempts to lead her back to bed. Camille knew that waking a sleepwalker could curse them to a twilight life, half-asleep and half-awake for the rest of their days. And what if this was the devil's work, as Lillian had said? So Camille followed her.

God help her, Camille followed her down the garden path, past the well house and the orchard, into the forest proper. Followed her all the way down into the dark, and she was never seen again.

CHAPTER TWO

Madelyn had timed her breaths to the *tick tick tick* of the grandfather clock in the dining room. She sat alone at the big table, waiting for her mother to arrive or for the clock to ring out the hour. In for five ticks, hold for five ticks, out for five ticks. Sometimes she held her breath for longer, as if that might make time move faster.

Dinner was strictly from six thirty p.m. to seven thirty. This was the third night in a row that her mother had left her sitting there alone. Hunger gnawed at her stomach. All around her, whispers filled the empty house. That was the other point of the breathing game: Listening to the clock made it easier to ignore them.

Five ticks, then another five, then another five. Hold and repeat.

The whispers were telling her it was time. The storm raging outside meant it had happened again.

There was a tree in the forest that her mother took her to sometimes. It was hung with all kinds of little treasures: coins and ribbons and pages torn from books, and her mother couldn't get too close to the tree itself, but she needed those treasures. It was safe for Madelyn, though. She gathered up those little treasures, which seemed to burn and writhe in her hands with magic. Sometimes, something called her name, but her mother always told her to ignore the voice.

Her mother called the thing in the tree Generous, when she said anything about it at all. Madelyn had learned more from her mother's silences about it, the negative space that surrounded it. Generous was old. Generous protected them. Generous had something called a covenant with her mother, and that was why she could use the coins and ribbons and shoes to make the wards that surrounded their house, and other magic besides.

Sometimes, Generous was hungry. And it was her mother's job to see Generous fed.

Madelyn could always tell when it was hungry; a cold electricity moved through the forest beyond her mother's house. She could feel it at the very edge of the wards, goose bumps prying up from her skin, the fine hairs rising on the back of her neck. Inside the house, constant whispers would rise to a staticky roar in her head, warning her. About what? She wasn't sure. Sometimes she remembered a dark space where she went when she was bad. Sometimes she had nightmares about her mother standing above her, crying and disappointed.

Madelyn looked across the dining room at the clock. The glass face was warped and stained, but she could see that it was 7:26. Four minutes left. The rain kept falling against the window. The whispers swelled, faded, swirled together. There was an ache under Madelyn's scars that rose and fell with them.

The whispers never resolved into real voices. She wasn't even sure they were speaking *to* her, or if it was just a conversation among themselves that she couldn't help but overhear.

She could go, Madelyn told herself. She could go to the

TV room, pop in one of the DVDs of her favorite show, *HMS Broomstick*. She could recite the dialogue along with the characters, imagining what it would be like to be a rich, glamorous witch on a seemingly never-ending cruise with her sisters. There would be ship comedians that were the reincarnations of minor Babylonian gods and a buffet with food that someone would slip a love potion into.

It was the only TV show that her mother approved of, so it was the only one that Madelyn watched. She thought sometimes that she remembered TV shows that weren't on ships, or about witches, but her mother insisted it was the only show that they watched. Madelyn wished that magic was a little closer to what she saw in *HMS Broomstick*.

Madelyn looked at the clock again: 7:27. She was stupid for waiting. Her stomach grumbled, and the ache under her skin burned, as if it realized she was its captive audience. She pressed down on the scars that stretched across her forearm, trying to silence the pain.

Don't be stupid, she told herself, trying to make herself move. *Just leave. Get up and—*

The front door slammed, and Madelyn shoved her seat back into place at the table. Straightened her posture, fixed her face into a friendly (but not *too* friendly) smile, and put her hands into her lap. The ache redoubled where she had pressed down, but she forced herself to ignore it.

Madelyn listened carefully to the sounds her mother made, trying to ascertain her mood. Car keys hit the bowl beside the door, but not too loudly. A sigh accompanied the light thumps as her mother took off her shoes. A whisper of wool as she hung up her coat. She sounded a little tired, maybe, but not angry. Madelyn unstiffened a little, forced her hands to stop clutching at her thighs, and waited.

"It finally feels like fall out there," Mom said. Her voice was soft; Madelyn sometimes thought it felt like cashmere against her skin, even when her mother was furious. "There's that chill in the air. I was so sick of the heat."

Mom came into the dining room and stood behind Madelyn's chair, resting one cold hand against her shoulder. "First of the autumn rains tonight. It almost feels like we should celebrate. My favorite season."

She squeezed Madelyn's shoulder, just a shade too tight.

"Mine too," Madelyn said. It was a lie; she preferred spring. Fall meant that winter was coming, and it would be months stuck in the house with her mother.

"I know," said Mom. Squeezed Madelyn's shoulder again, then traced her finger against the long scars that crisscrossed Madelyn's nape. Madelyn fought down a wince as the ache sharpened at the touch, spreading across her shoulders. "You're the most beautiful thing I ever made, Maddie. Have I told you that lately?"

Madelyn couldn't remember the last time she had said it, but it was something that her mother loved to tell her.

Mom had brought the smell of outside in with her, as if the cold, damp wind had followed her into the house. There was another smell on her too—a tinge of iron beneath the smell of rain. Madelyn looked down at the hand on her shoulder. Brown grit under her mother's nails, crusted in the creases of her knuckles. It could have been mud. Madelyn knew it wasn't.

A sick weight pulled at her stomach, and the whispers rose up like a gale. That was what had the whispers so agitated: why the rain was falling in its particular frenzied cadence, like some-one had yanked this storm out of the sky. Why the last time she'd gone to Generous's tree, she'd felt a sort of heavy, hungry atten-tion on her.

The clock suddenly chimed, startling them both. Mom laughed.

"I guess I lost track of time. I missed dinner?" She looked at Madelyn, as if just noticing that she was sitting at one side of their dining table. "I'm sorry, sweetheart. I'm not very hungry, are you?"

Madelyn shook her head.

"That's all right, then," Mom said. "I'm so tired, I might go to sleep early. It's been an awfully long day. You know how to fix something yourself if you need to, right?"

Madelyn nodded. Their cupboards were bare. When she'd been younger, Madelyn had sometimes been surprised by feasts that her mother prepared: cucumber sandwiches and cakes and tea in delicate cups, a roast chicken with potatoes. She'd watch Madelyn eat with fascination and pride. She hadn't made a meal like that in a long time, but Madelyn was still expected to wait for family dinner.

Mom clasped her shoulder again; her touch was light, but Madelyn was pinned in place as Mom leaned down, her auburn hair falling down around her, and kissed Madelyn's cheek right over one of the scars. The pain that lived under her scars, which had settled down into a dull ache, suddenly flared up, and Madelyn had to suppress a wince. Her mother did not like for Madelyn to flinch away from her affection.

"Can I go outside in the garden?" Madelyn asked softly.

Her stomach was clenching painfully, the whispers rising like a tide, hissing danger at her. Something had gone wrong.

"Don't stay out in the dark too late," Mom said. "Things are . . . unsettled out there tonight."

Mom bumped her forehead against Madelyn's. The pain under Madelyn's skin flared again, pressure building until it felt like her scars would split open, and the whispers rose up, rushed voices tripping over each other. Madelyn measured her breath against the clock until her mother's footsteps faded up the stairs. Then she stood, grabbed her jacket from the hook by the door, and forced herself to walk calmly out into the back garden.

She could feel it immediately: the unsettledness that her mother had talked about. The day had been clear and bright, but a sudden storm had blown in, squatting right over them, in no hurry to pass over the mountain. The storm had subsided to a drizzle, but leaves and broken branches littered the lawn, and the trails had turned into slick mud. The voices around Madelyn swelled, like they were trying to shout through a door when they normally whispered. Something had happened.

There was a break in the trees where a rocky outcrop stood, providing a view all the way down into Roscoe. The sun had set a while ago, and the yellow streetlights were flickering on down in the town, and on the western edge of town, she could see flashing blue and red lights. A police cruiser was making its way through the streets. She wrapped a hand around a thin birch tree and leaned out, tracking its progress as it turned onto the county road that curved along Voynich Woods. Maybe it was something else, Madelyn thought desperately. Something routine: a fight, teenagers vandalizing something, a rowdy drunk. But the cruiser pulled onto Voynich Drive, where she could only see glints of light through the trees that lined the road. The police only did that when someone was officially missing.

Blood under her mother's nails. Full moon tonight, though it was hidden behind a thick wall of clouds. The voices chorusing all around her.

Years ago, when her mother still took her down into Roscoe, she'd seen a missing poster taped to a store window. Mom tugged her away and squeezed her hand in warning anytime she started to ask about it—to ask why the lady that she'd seen in the forest hadn't come home.

Sometimes, because the forest gives us so much, it takes something back.

You mean someone, Madelyn had said.

I mean, her mother had replied sharply, *that there's a balance to be paid and a covenant to keep.*

She used that voice that meant the conversation was over. Mom hadn't taken her into town since then. She wasn't sure how long ago that had been.

Madelyn looked back at the house. All the lights were off, and the windows reflected the darkness back at her, showing nothing. She could go back inside. Take a bath, maybe. Rewatch Season 3 of *HMS Broomstick.* There was one episode where main characters met their opposite selves from another universe when the *Broomstick* crossed the Bermuda Triangle: mischievous, debonair men who wore blue and black instead of white and pink. She had imagined meeting her own opposite: a boy with no scars, who walked in silence, who lived in the world instead of in a house set above it.

Would that boy go back to the house? Back to his mother (who would never hurt him) and watch a TV show about Madelyn's life? How boring that show would be: just a scarred-up girl who knew something bad would happen to her, and let it because she was too scared to defy her mother.

Madelyn hated how long it took to move, even after she'd made her decision. Hated her own weakness.

The old orchard was at the far end of the garden, on the border with the forest itself. It was overgrown, and the gnarled apple and pear trees tangled their branches together overhead. Her mother had set up little watchers at the very limits of her property, and in the crook of one tree stood a coyote skull with a bird's nest filling its jaws, a handful of tarnished old rings left there like eggs. But this ward only looked outward, into the trees and away from the orchard. Madelyn's stomach turned at the smell of rotten fruit rising from the ground, as she found her way to the old well, half-buried under brambles.

She shoved off the thick slab covering it and looked down into the deeper darkness.

"Jane," she whispered down into the well. "Jane, I need your help."

The fire under her skin was maddening now, and she wanted to peel her skin back from her bones. She called Jane's name again, once, twice, three times, and let the heat build and the pain sharpen until it split the scar under her eye. Hot blood coursed down her cheek and fell into the well, and she could have cried from relief.

Twin lights blinked open in the darkness below her. A pale hand snaked out and pressed to the surface of the water, then pushed through: long, broken fingernails, mottled gray skin, whitish bone poking through. The other hand followed, then arms, then a face with lank, dripping hair.

From far away, you might not notice anything wrong about Jane. She had dark brown hair that hung down her back and around her face, obscuring her eyes. She wore a gray dress that seemed old-fashioned, with a round collar and long skirt, a man's coat over it, and scuffed leather boots.

Madelyn didn't have—or particularly want—the luxury of distance. Besides, she knew monsters that looked mostly normal, like her. Or beautiful, even, like her mother. Jane's gray skin, her claws, her teeth, none of that scared her.

"Police are at the gatehouse," she whispered. She knew her mother couldn't hear her, not from all the way up in the house, but she couldn't make herself speak any louder. "Do you know what happened?"

Someone's lost, Jane said. Her voice was distorted, deeper and rougher than a human voice should be. There was a rumble underneath it, like a waterfall. *Lost and alone. Alone and cold. Cold and de—*

"Don't," Madelyn said. But the truth was clawing under her skin, behind her eyelids.

Dead, but not gone, said Jane. *You can still help her. Save her. Save yourself. Unless you're okay being stuck here?* she asked.

Jane was her first friend, and still her only friend. She'd only known how to be alone or with her mother, until one day, she was down in the orchard and heard the strangest voice singing. It warbled like a radio underwater, and she tracked it to the old well.

When, like today, she'd shoved the cover off the old well, the singing cut out when a shaft of sunlight pierced the black water.

"Hello?" she'd called out. Quietly, of course, and after quickly looking to make sure her mother wasn't in earshot. "Are you still there?"

There was an episode in Season 4 of *HMS Broomstick* where someone had fallen down a well, and it had been a very harrowing twenty-one minutes while the rest of the crew tried to get them out, with a lot of complaining about what a well was even doing on a cruise ship to make everyone laugh when they wanted to cry. So Madelyn had asked, "Do you need help getting out?"

No, said the voice. *But I think you do.*

Madelyn had pondered that. There had been a time when she could leave, right? And a time when her mother would take her into town. But she couldn't remember when that had been. And now, she didn't even allow Madelyn to leave the property, not with the watchers screeching out anytime she tried to sneak past. Her mother's gaze had taken on such weight.

Thinking about it had made the scars across her chest and throat hurt, so she stopped thinking about it.

"How did you get down there?" she had asked. "How did you get past the watchers?"

I can travel the water's ways, the person had said. *Your mother's magic can't see it.*

"Could I travel that way too?" Madelyn had asked.

Jane had floated to the surface of the water then and let Madelyn see her, see all of her. She'd seemed surprised when Madelyn didn't run at the sight of her, and only said, *It won't be pleasant. And it won't be easy. You might not like where you end up.*

"I don't like where I am," Madelyn had said, a truth she hadn't realized until she spoke it aloud. After that, it was easy to go with Jane.

◆ ◆ ◆

She never remembered what she saw when Jane took her through the water's ways. She came out of them with a gasp, like waking from a nightmare. There was a sense of horror, that she'd seen something awful, but it always faded. When she had asked Jane, the dead girl was noncommittal. *The water takes its toll,* was all she said about it.

Now, she climbed up from the banks of Dyson Pond and followed Jane. The muddy path narrowed under their feet, then disappeared, and they had to maneuver between barren branches and the sprawling fingers of tree roots.

The Wishing Tree stood alone in a clearing. Squat little flowers, corpse-white, grew in a ring around the clearing's edge. Odd; it wasn't the season for wildflowers.

Madelyn had been raised not to fear the woods, nor the things that walked in them. But she'd always been afraid of the Wishing Tree. Her mother took her there to gather Generous's treasures, but she wouldn't get close. Madelyn always came away safe and unharmed, but it never stopped feeling like she was taking her life into her hands. Every time she saw it, something way down inside her most animal parts whispered, *Get away from this place, it's not safe.*

Now, amid the coin-flecked roots, there was an open grave.

The animal part of her had been right. "That's it, right?" she asked Jane, nodding to a rectangular hole dug into the dirt.

Jane nodded solemnly. Gravely, you might say, if you were Jane, who loved terrible jokes.

Madelyn cautiously walked forward until she could crouch beside the grave; all the voices were silent, which was somehow more unnerving than if they had been shouting. The scent of blood clawed at her throat. Down in the dirt, there were scratches all along the edges of the grave, as if someone had tried to claw their way out and gotten sucked in anyway. She lay her fingertips gingerly into the gouges in the clay. They fit. Hands about the same size as hers had made them.

Jane, who hadn't followed her, reached down and yanked one of the flowers that circled the clearing. The flower had almost no stem, just dark roots that trailed down, leaking an orangey sap. As Madelyn watched, the roots seemed to twitch like a spider's legs.

Jane shoved the flower whole into her mouth and chewed on it. *Riley Walcott. That's her name.*

"I need some light," Madelyn said. "Is it safe?"

Jane looked around. The temperature of the air suddenly dropped. Jane's hair and dress moved, though not in the same direction as the suddenly shifting wind. *They're searching for her, but they won't find this place.* She looked up into the Wishing Tree's barren branches. *Nobody finds this place unless they're called.*

Madelyn pushed the sleeves of her jacket and sweatshirt as far up her arm as they could go. She let the pain thicken and coalesce under the scars around her knuckles until it split them open, and let out some of her magic.

She'd been able to make things grow, once. Flowers were easy. She could reach out to them, in her mind, and . . . nudge them. Pull energy from one place and put it somewhere else.

Her mother had hated it. This was before the scars, before she started having nightmares about the basement. Before the whispers in her head and the pain locked under her skin, twisting and turning restlessly until it forced its way out.

The skin of her hand flared like a match, then started to burn steadily. The fire felt like a warm, living glove on her skin. The pain under her skin abated; the whispers softened, as if satisfied. Madelyn leaned down, trying to keep herself steady in the slippery mud.

And there she was. Riley Walcott, according to Jane.

Her body was mostly covered in a white cloth, but a single hand lay bare, half-closed with its palm up, catching odd raindrops as they fell. Madelyn reached down and gingerly peeled back the cloth. A big, nasty bruise spread across Riley's face, crusted with dirt and blood. She peeled the sheet back a little more, trying to assess the damage, and immediately regretted it.

Riley had a hole in her chest, a grave that mirrored the one she'd been buried in. And like Riley's grave, it looked like something had been buried inside her. Madelyn couldn't make out the details and didn't want to, but she could see the glint of metal.

She wanted to gag. It seemed like a violation to look: something she had no business seeing, even if Riley didn't know she was there. She flipped the sheet back over her.

"Now what?" she asked Jane.

Jane's eyes were focused on something that Madelyn couldn't see.

Now you bring her back.

"Me?" she asked. "I can't do that. I—No. Can I?"

Flowers were one thing. Flames were another. What Jane was suggesting was way beyond either of those.

Jane didn't argue with her. She just stood there, waiting implacably.

"What if I mess up? What if I can't fix it?"

Jane looked pointedly down at the grave. *It would be hard to make things worse for her.*

Maybe, but Madelyn worried that she'd accidentally find a way.

Jane turned and looked at her. *You don't like where you are, you said.*

"I don't."

And you want to be free.

That was harder to answer. What was *free*? What did it look like? The chorus of voices spoke over her doubts, though, and she answered for them. "Yes."

Maybe if she was free, they would be quieter.

I can't break the cycle. I can't bring her back. I can find anyone in the woods, I can go anywhere you call me, but . . . Jane trailed off. It was disconcerting to watch, like whatever was tethering her to this place, this time, had suddenly stretched to the point of snapping.

"I can bring her back," Madelyn said.

She had talked herself out of so many things. Her mother had taught her, over and over, not to trust her instincts; told her that she was unreasonable, suspicious, paranoid, that her mind was too easily tainted or influenced. It was thrilling, for once, to move purely on instinct, no time to second-guess herself. She tried to pick up Riley's hand and realized there were roots coming out of her skin, anchoring the dead girl into her muddy grave. She pried Riley's arm up from the mud, wincing as the roots snapped and broke.

"Riley Walcott," she whispered. "Come back."

The fingers twitched, like they were beckoning her. When Madelyn shut her eyes, she sensed something surrounding them: a web with Riley in the center. Threads of magic, running all through this clearing, that were keeping her here.

And somewhere in the web, something was watching them. That same presence Madelyn had felt before, full of simmering rage and hunger. The thing her mother was afraid of, the reason she never got too close to the tree—unless, it seemed, she was burying a dead girl amid its roots.

They were running out of time. Madelyn tried to make her voice stronger, surer. "Riley, get up."

More of her scars split open. One across her shoulder, another inside her cheek, splashing blood across her tongue. A third across her knuckles. "Riley, it's time to *come home*."

Riley's eyes were open, staring, dead. And then they were focused on her.

CHAPTER THREE

On the day her mother disappeared five years ago, Riley woke up somehow already knowing she was gone, that Mom had never come home. Her bed was neat and obviously undisturbed. There were no clothes on the floor, no scatter of loose change, no lingering smell of cigarette smoke or the perfume she used to cover it.

It wasn't the first time Riley had woken to her mother's absence. She could still remember the first time, when she was eight and Sam was about one; she'd woken up to Sam crying in the middle of the night, standing up in her crib and bawling. No Mom in sight. Riley had warmed up a bottle for her, then pulled her blankets into the other room and slept in her mother's bed. Mom stumbled in a few hours later, loud enough to wake her, but at least Sam kept sleeping. Mom stood in the doorway watching Riley watch her, then turned and went to sleep on the couch.

But that was *before*. Anna Walcott had promised her eldest daughter that *this* time she would stay sober if it killed her, and Riley had believed her. She'd needed to believe her. So despite the dread curdling in her stomach, she scrambled the one egg left in the empty fridge and gave it to Sam with some toast for breakfast. She said Mom had left early for work but would probably be home for lunch. At lunchtime, Riley used the last of the bread to make mayonnaise sandwiches for her and Sam, and told her that Mom must have gotten the time wrong, but she'd be home for dinner, probably with McDonald's as a surprise. At seven, she decided to walk with Sam to McDonald's and pay for dinner with the emergency cash that Toby had given her the last time she'd seen him. It wasn't much, maybe sixty dollars, but she'd wanted to refuse it, to say, *We won't need it, she said this time it was for real.* But having faith in her mom was new, so she took it and told herself she'd give it back to Toby at some point, since she'd never need it. The cash lived in an ugly box that Sam had made in kindergarten art class, decorated with cutout pictures from old magazines, beads, and smears of glitter that still shed on Riley's hands. The kind of thing kids were supposed to bring home to their parents, but she'd brought it to Riley. Riley kept the money in there alongside the fancy art markers and pens that Toby had given her for Christmas, kept the whole thing tucked away between her mattress and the wall. Hiding money and anything valuable from her mom was a deeply ingrained habit.

But when Riley pulled out the box, there was only a ten-dollar bill and a handful of loose change rolling around next to the markers. Riley stared at the crease across Alexander Hamilton's face and tried not to think about anything. Just squash every thought like a Whac-A-Mole game, so she wouldn't have to wonder when her mother had found the emergency cash, or imagine what she'd bought with it. Ten dollars and change was still enough for dinner, and that was what mattered.

At McDonald's, Sam picked at her food, leaving a mess of half-chewed chicken nuggets and cold, crumpled fries that made Riley want to scream a little, thinking of their empty refrigerator.

"When's Mom coming home?" Sam asked.

Beneath the table, Riley dug the tips of her nails into her palms. "I don't know," she admitted.

"Can we call Uncle Toby?"

"No phone," she said. Mom had had to cancel Riley's phone plan when it got too expensive, though she'd promised it was temporary. The next paycheck had to go to rent and groceries, but the one after that—

"We could ask to use someone's here?" Sam said.

A couple of weeks before, Mom had told Riley that she was on her last chance with her caseworker at the Department of Children and Family Services. "They're looking for an excuse to take you and Sam from me," she had said. "And I don't know what'll happen to the two of you if they find it."

"Nah. We'll wait a little longer," she told Sam. "It'll be okay."

She braced herself for an argument, maybe even a full-blown tantrum. But Sam just nodded.

They went home and they waited, rewatching movies they'd borrowed from the library until they both fell asleep on the couch. Riley blinked awake after midnight. Mom still hadn't come home.

That was it: She couldn't negotiate with her mother's absence anymore. Couldn't keep waiting. She woke Sam up ("Mom's back?" were her first words, and Riley had had to shake her head).

Riley's phone was still inactive and useless, so they'd have to walk to the all-night gas station a mile away. She bundled Sam into a winter coat, then lifted her on her back and tied an extra blanket around her, because the temperature was hovering around 25 degrees. Her sister's weight sat heavy on Riley, bent her forward. She thought of pictures she'd seen of child workers and war refugees. It never occurred to her to leave Sam behind.

Riley knew that she couldn't think too much. She couldn't think about what would happen to her and Sam, and she absolutely could not think about what had happened to her mother. If she started to think, she would panic. If she started to panic, she wouldn't stop. She could only think about putting one foot down after the other.

She locked the door behind her and turned to start her slow, laborious journey. But instead of the county highway on the outskirts of Roscoe, Riley found herself among the tall, gaunt tree trunks in Voynich Woods.

Oh. *Oh.* This was a dream, and a familiar one: having to relive the whole stupid day when her mother left them, only something would go wrong. She'd talked this out in therapy years ago; the dream was her brain returning to an important moment in an attempt to integrate trauma, blah blah blah.

The only thing to do was walk, just like in real life. The only way out of this particular nightmare was through it.

She hadn't been walking for long when someone spoke her name.

"Riley," her mother whispered behind her.

She hadn't heard anyone approach. There was nothing, and then there was her mother's voice, which she hadn't heard in . . .

Two versions of herself were laid over each other: Riley at twelve, whose mother had been gone twenty-four hours, anger and fear tangled together into a knot in her throat. But she was also seventeen, hadn't seen her mother in five years. The anger and fear had calcified, a stone she had to keep swallowing.

Because her mother was dead. Wasn't she?

That was the thing she could never say to Sam. Anna Walcott had been a broke single mom on welfare, with probation and court-ordered therapy for addiction; fifty dollars stolen from her oldest daughter might get her a bus ticket to Boston, maybe New York City, but it wouldn't buy her a whole new life. The local cops didn't have a great track record for solving cold cases, but if there'd been something to find, they would've found it by now, right?

All the missing people, starting with little Camille Voynich and ending with her mother, weren't together hanging out somewhere. There was no magical portal in the woods, no fairy ring or magical cave from which they'd eventually stumble, like Rip Van Winkle waking from his twenty-year nap.

"This is a dream," Riley said, an accusation under the words like a knife up her sleeve.

"Something like that," said Anna Walcott. "I missed you, Riley. Turn around and let me look at you."

She shifted her weight to turn, then stopped herself. She didn't want to look at her mother. She didn't want to pretend that this was real, because when she woke up, she'd be left with all the rage and sadness and none of the momentary happiness.

Toby had some videos of Anna, old low-res ones taken

on a digital camera when Riley's mother was still a young woman in search of a good time—not happy, exactly, but not worn thin and threadbare by years of struggle. Early after her mother's disappearance, Riley would watch those videos sometimes, try to melt the stone in her chest just enough to breathe around it again. She'd stopped at some point; the old videos had lost their magic. They made her feel worse instead of better. Numb.

She pulled that numbness around her now. Armor. Dug around until she found her anger and pulled that close to her as well. "Then you shouldn't have *left*," Riley hissed. "And if you wanted to come back, you should do it in the real world. Not a stupid-ass dream."

Then she forced herself to start walking again. Luckily, she was on a wide path in the woods, level and packed. Sam was still sleeping on her shoulders, and Riley tried to shift her weight into a more comfortable position.

"Is that what you want?" her mother's voice said. "A life where I stayed? Where you had the family you should have had?"

A few months before she disappeared, Mom had picked her up from school in a Jeep Wrangler that Riley had never seen before, Sam in a booster seat in the back, and punk music blaring from the speakers. Mom had told her it was a new holiday: Mermaid Day. You celebrated by driving to the ocean and spending the night on the beach. She'd bought them junk food for the hours-long drive to Portsmouth. They'd made a bonfire and ate s'mores for dinner, had a three-person mosh pit to the Distillers as the sun set, and then bedded down in the car, exhausted from a beautiful day.

But something had shifted during the night: The breeze coming off the water was cold and smelled oily, and Riley's stomach hurt from all the sugar she'd eaten. She and Sam had slept badly, the air in the car was cold and damp, condensation fogging the windows. Sam had a nightmare that was so bad that she'd peed in her sleeping bag, and Mom had broken into tears while cleaning her up. And then—

Riley shied away from the memory, angry at her mom for making her think about it.

What did Riley want? She wanted to be left the *fuck* alone. What came out was, "I want to go home."

She heard someone take slow, considerate steps toward her. "Do you? Everything in the universe that you could wish for, and that's what you want?"

The voice . . . didn't sound like her mother anymore.

"Where *is* home?" the voice asked. "Your uncle's house, where you were taken in like a stray cat? The moldy apartment where your mother abandoned you? Why can't this be home?"

The thing behind her now felt as tall as the trees around it, as wide as the side of a barn.

Riley had stopped walking. She was still carrying Sam, gripping her sister's legs around her waist tightly. What would Sam do if she woke up?

"You're carrying your home with you, Riley," the creature behind her said. It was closer to her now, close enough that she could feel its breath against her neck, smell loam and rot wafting from it. "A heavier burden than you'll ever admit to yourself, isn't it? What would you do if you could put it down?"

Riley shut her eyes, trying to remember how she'd gotten

here. This was a dream, but she couldn't wake herself out of it. She tried to retrace her steps—

"Riley," the sly voice whispered to her. It drew her name out like a caress. "I could give everything you've dreamed of, if you just tell me what that is. Freedom, right? Escape? A place in the world where nobody knows you, nobody looks at you and sees your mother."

Riley saw it, as clear as she saw the trees surrounding them: herself, a couple of years older, moving confidently through a busy city street. Tattoos printed up her arms and over her exposed chest like armor. Nobody looking at her like she was just another exhibit of tragedy or monstrosity in Toby's barn. Distant, removed, and untouchable.

"I can give you that," the voice promised. "Just set your burden down."

Riley hissed through her teeth. "That's my sister. She's not—"

"You'll have to leave her behind eventually," the thing said. "I'm just offering a way to skip all the dramatics. Just let go."

Riley wasn't stupid. This had to be a trap of some kind. "What happened to me?" she asked. "How did I . . . I was in the woods. I saw—"

She remembered blood bright red on her chest, and then she could only think, absurdly, of robins, the dull gray of their wings and the cheerful orange of their breasts.

Her gaze searched through the trees around her, hoping she'd spot an escape. Instead, she found another pair of eyes staring back at her. A child, younger than Sam, staring at her from behind a tree. Wide-eyed, with dark, tangled hair. Fear in her eyes, looking at whatever stood behind Riley. The child shifted, and Riley could see two long, deep wounds that lay over her front. One ripped open her throat, while the other tore down the center of her chest. All around the edges of that terrible wound grew tiny white flowers. An iron rod pierced her chest, and smaller pieces of iron pierced her hands.

Riley put a hand to her chest to pull her whistle out of her shirt. Three short blasts meant, *Come find me. Come save me.*

She felt something else instead, flat where the whistle was round, engraved instead of smooth. She was wearing a locket shaped like a heart, finely engraved with a pattern of flowers and vines, but old and tarnished, grimy against her fingers.

When she looked up again, the child was closer. She was staring at Riley with deep, fathomless eyes.

"Riley," the voice said. "We're running out of time. She's found you. I've made this offer twice, and I'll make it once more. What do you want?"

It would be so easy, she thought. *To let go.* To stop struggling toward an uncertain dream, to have it gifted to her instead.

"I want to go home," Riley said again. Even though it was true, it hurt to say it.

The creature, when it spoke again, sounded as if it were smiling. "The old covenant, then. A wish, a secret, and a boon."

"What? What's a coven—"

"Because if you don't want to set your burden down, maybe you wouldn't mind if it became just a tiny bit heavier? A fair exchange to get what you want. A way home."

The voice was her mother's again, warm and rough from a decades-long smoking habit. She spoke in Riley's ear, and she smelled like tobacco and amber perfume and sweat, the way she would after a long shift. There was no slur in her voice, no brittle anger, no stress. It promised adventure, the same way she'd declared it Mermaid Day on the way to the beach. *We're getting out of here,* her mother had said. *Nobody's gonna stop us.*

The locket was still in her hand. Riley squeezed it against her palm and nodded. "Take me home."

Something scratched at her skin. Thin, spidery vines were peeling up from the locket, searching through the air and grabbing onto her. She felt them pierce through the fabric of her shirt, pierce her skin. She tried to pull the locket away, but the vines were burrowing through her flesh, into a deep, horrible wound across her chest. How had she not noticed it? How had she forgotten the knife wedged between her ribs?

The trees around her were fading into a thick, oppressive darkness. The weight on her back—Sam's weight, as she'd carried her through the night to find home—was gone. Now there was a weight on her chest, *in* her chest. She'd fallen backward at some point, in pain and panic, and she could feel the vines spreading inside her, piercing through her flesh and pinning her into the dirt. It *hurt*, needles under her skin— but wasn't she dead? Things shouldn't hurt if you weren't alive to feel them.

The pain was a promise, then; she was not dead, at least not yet. The thing that had spoken in her mother's voice had offered her a way home, but she still had to find it.

You can handle pain, Riley told herself. *You're strong. Isn't that what everyone always told you? How strong you were, to deal with your mom for all those years? You hated it, but you knew they were right. So prove it.*

She could sense that she didn't have long; she wasn't alone

in the darkness. Something was trying to pull Riley back, keep her here in this in-between place.

It didn't matter. What mattered was getting home. Riley's fingers groped forward until they caught hold of something: the thinnest of threads, but when she pulled on it, it held. The darkness didn't want to let her go; she had to wrench herself away inch by agonizing inch, roots and tendrils pulling until they snapped.

When she opened her eyes again, Riley was back in Voynich Woods. For a second, she wanted to cry: all that pain, and she was still in the nightmare. But then she realized she could breathe again, she could feel her soaked clothes sticking to her skin and shivers wracking her body. She was awake and somewhere else, somewhere *real*. She was alive. Or something close enough. So she did the only thing imaginable: She screamed.

She hadn't noticed someone was holding her hand until they tried to pull away. A figure stood over her, lit by an orange flame. A stranger with wide eyes and scarred skin, a girl about her own age. Skinny, upright, holding some kind of flickering light in her hand that spilled out of her cupped fingers.

Riley put up her hands to fight, but stopped at the sight of roots emerging from her arms. She scratched at them, yanking them out. They pulled at her skin, leaving open wounds on her forearms that oozed something too thick to be blood. It was like the darkness she'd escaped from had found passage inside her body and was bursting out of her now. It didn't seep like normal blood but curled up out of her skin, reaching intently through the air like shadowy tendrils. A bass note of panic kicked in Riley's chest. *Thrum.*

"Um," a voice said. "Riley?"

Blood was smeared along the girl's fingers, dripping down the back of her palms, and Riley remembered bright red staining her chest, pouring out around the handle of a knife.

Fear, thick and putrid, coated her tongue. Anger riding its coattails, urging her to strike before the girl tried anything else.

Riley grabbed the girl's wrists and squeezed. The scars across the girl's forearms turned white, the blood lurid against her skin.

"Was it you? Did you do this to me?"

Was that her voice? It sounded so strange.

"I—I—"

You could tear her apart, a cool, distant voice inside her said. *Like tearing the petals off a flower. Loves me, loves me not—*

The iron tang of blood in the air was the only warning Riley got before the girl's arms erupted in blue and yellow flames. A flash of agonizing pain; Riley shrieked and pulled away while the girl scrambled back. She and the girl stood and stared at each other, wounded and wary.

Kill her, that voice said, and Riley found herself in full agreement.

She started to rush forward, but suddenly it felt like she'd run straight into a wall. She stumbled back and would have fallen if there weren't a small, thin, gray hand twisted around the collar of her shirt.

The hand belonged to a corpse: gray and patchy skin, empty eyes, lips chewed away to expose long, yellowing teeth. The smell of rot and pond scum rolled off her in waves.

Calm down, the dead girl said. Her voice was inhuman, somewhere between a waterfall strong enough to crack stone and the fragile warble of a song under water. It tripped a breaker somewhere in Riley's brain, and she was falling again. First forward into the dead girl's bony arms, and then into unconsciousness. Honestly, it was a relief.

◆ ◆ ◆

The second time opening her eyes went better. She was beneath the trees of Voynich Woods, which still rustled with falling rain. The damp air was cool and clammy against her skin, and she held up her hands. No roots in her skin. She let herself, for one hopeful second, believe that it wasn't real: the man in the mask, the knife, the—the dream of being dead. A covenant. A wish, a secret, and a boon.

She sensed a presence nearby and sat up fast. The same girl was sitting on a fallen log a few feet away. She seemed taller than Riley but scrawnier, with a hoodie pulled over her head. Greasy red hair spilled out of the hood, catching in the wind. Her sleeves were rolled up, and Riley spotted more of those long scars that she'd seen before They spread from the knuckles up the forearm, then disappeared under the sleeves.

"Hi," the girl said. "My name is Madelyn. Are you . . . I'm not going to ask if you're okay."

"Am I dead?" Riley asked, suddenly remembering a story she'd been assigned in English a few years ago, about a freaky vision some guy had in the moments before being hanged. Maybe this was all her dying neurons firing off the second before her demise.

"Not anymore," Madelyn answered.

That was not super comforting. Almost the opposite, actually. Riley sat up a little straighter, trying to remember all the stupid advice that counselors had given her over the years. How to deal with the unexpected or the anxiety-inducing. Deep breathing wasn't going to solve her problems, but it couldn't hurt, right? But feeling her body, counting each finger and each toe, grounding herself in physical sensation, drove home how *wrong* she felt. Her breath was thick and slow, her skin was cold, sticky with something that probably wasn't tree sap, and her heart, there was something wrong with her heartbeat—

"Do you remember what happened to you?"

She did. Most of it. More than she wanted to.

"Sam," she said. She started struggling to her feet, because oh, shit. *Sam.*

"She's okay," the stranger said hurriedly. "It was only you. Down in there."

She's safe, a voice said—a terrible, hoarse, warbling voice.

Riley looked, and saw something with gray skin and long, straight brown hair peeking out from behind a tree.

"That's Jane," said Madelyn. "Or that's what I call her. Like Jane Doe? It was kind of a joke."

Water took my name, Jane said. She came out from behind the tree. Water dripped from the bottom of her dress and the strands of her hair, darkening her boots and the ground below. She had no lips, just rows of pearlescent teeth emerging from shredded skin. No eyes, just an absence. Not even a socket or skin. It was like looking down into a cave.

Riley was talking to Toby and Sam's favorite story about Voynich Woods—the Dead Girl who wandered its trails.

"I guess it's not that funny if you think about it," Madelyn finished weakly.

She got home safe, said Sam's favorite ghost. *I made sure of it.*

Riley started to stumble to her feet. "I need to go home."

"Wait," Madelyn said. "I don't know if that's a good idea."

"I don't care what you think," Riley said, too exhausted to be anything but blunt. "I don't know you. I don't know what happened or why you're here or—"

Madelyn held up her hands. "Just look down, okay?"

Riley reflexively looked down, prepared to see blood, dirt, whatever slimy shit she'd dragged herself through. Her shirt was torn, and at first she thought Madelyn was nicely trying to tell her that her boobs were hanging out. Which, who even cared right now?

But then she caught sight of something beneath the torn fabric. She pulled it gingerly apart to look.

A ragged rectangle of skin was missing from her chest, nearly two handspans wide, stretching from her collarbones to the swell of her breasts. The edges were horrifyingly neat, bloodless, a lipless mouth caught mid-scream. The muscles were missing, carved away like a human anatomy doll, and her ribs seemed not to be made of bone and meat, but a black, half-solid ooze. Riley couldn't stop herself from running her finger gently along the edge of the gaping wound. A jagged pulse reverberated against her touch, off-rhythm and alien. There was nothing beneath it, no blood, no heart, nothing that seemed alive at all. It was . . . empty.

She was empty.

There was no pain. Someone had taken off her skin, opened

her up, infected her with this, this substance, and she didn't feel any pain from it at all. Her head throbbed where she'd been hit, and her hands where she'd scraped them, but she felt nothing from the thing that should have killed her.

Because it *had* killed her, she realized.

"I think you're going into shock?" Madelyn said.

How can I be going into shock when I'm—

Riley cut off the thought. "I need to go home," she repeated, because *home* still felt real, though nothing else did. It was a handhold; a mile marker and a compass, something she could orient herself to. Maybe the only thing. Once she was home, she could figure this out.

What *had* happened?

The nausea hit her without warning, and she stumbled a few steps away before her stomach heaved. The taste of mud and bile filled her mouth.

She looked up sharply as she heard a zipper being pulled. Madelyn was wriggling out of her jacket, then unzipping the black sweatshirt she wore beneath it. She held it out to Riley.

"To cover it up," Madelyn said. "You probably have enough to explain to them without adding . . . that."

The sweatshirt didn't smell particularly clean, and Riley inhaled the scent of woodsmoke and skin as she put it on. The fabric was warm, though—warmer than she expected, like Madelyn had pulled it from a dryer five minutes before.

Riley noticed that the scars she'd first noticed earlier ran up Madelyn's arms and curved over her shoulders. Madelyn must have felt her staring and slipped her jacket back on.

Riley opened her mouth to say goodbye to the worst-ever fever dream, she hoped, or maybe to ask for directions back to Roscoe. What came out instead was, "I don't want to be a mystery to solve."

She'd grown up steeped in all the mysteries of Voynich Woods. She recited them for tourists all the time, the monsters that had been spotted, the children and tourists who had disappeared into it. Mysteries existed only to be dissected, flattened into gossip and stories for tourists. All Riley wanted was to escape Roscoe, escape the place where she'd never be more than Anna Walcott's girl, *and isn't it a shame what happened to her?* She'd just started to ramp up to escape velocity, and now she was a fucking episode of *Scooby-Doo*.

"I'm sorry," said Madelyn. "Maybe we should talk more tomorrow? I guess it's been a . . . big day."

"A big day?" Riley repeated. Going to the county fair was a big day. Your first day at high school was a big day. "Fuck off," she said.

"We can talk more tomorrow," Madelyn said diplomatically. "I can come find you."

Or not, Riley thought. "How do I get out of here?"

Jane volunteered to show her the way out of the woods. Riley thought of all the stories about the Dead Girl of Dyson Pond, the cheesy little display of her in the barn. She only appeared to the lost, and seemed to always frighten them back onto the main path. They walked in silence, and Riley's last view of Madelyn caught her with hunched shoulders, staring after them.

"Jane," she said, because even if this was one long and stupid hallucination, she might as well get some details for Toby's museum. "How long have you been like this?"

Long time, Jane answered. *Long enough to stop keeping track.*

Toby would hate that, she thought. He wanted details. Measurable things. He got tired of all the vagueness surrounding the stories of the things that lived in the woods. Sam, on the other hand—

Jane suddenly stopped, turning her face up to Riley's. *It was your sister's voice you heard?* the Dead Girl asked. *Calling your name?*

Riley nodded, wary of Jane's sudden interest.

Love like that shouldn't be used to hurt. But it always is.

Riley was about to ask what in the cryptic hell any of that was supposed to mean, but the darkness in Jane's eyes seemed to spill outward, catch her up in it like a wave tugging down a swimmer. When she snapped out of it, she was standing on a dirt path. She could hear the highway and see scant streetlights through the trees. *I can find my way home from here,* she told herself, and wondered why something rang hollow in that thought.

INTERLUDE: THE MISSING

Excerpt from *Bury the Echo: A Local Historian's Perspective on Folklore, Forests, and Other Important Stuff, or So I'm Telling Myself (Working Title)*, by Toby Walcott

About 600,000 missing persons reports are filed every year in America. The number sounds unimaginably high; picture the whole state of Wyoming and a few counties bordering it disappearing. But most of those people are found quickly. Only about 90,000 of them stay missing for more than a few days.

Going missing in the woods is a different story than in a city or a small town, and it's nothing like the dramatic reenactments true-crime shows love to make. Private land, like Voynich Woods, doesn't have the resources of a national or state park: There are no dedicated search and rescue teams, no tracking dogs unless they're brought in from out of town. The response is coordinated between the two-person local police force and the county sheriff. In practical terms, that means four guys with a couple of dozen volunteers searching 7,500 acres of dense forest—almost twelve square miles, with few trails once you're past the public recreation area.

Officially, ten people have gone missing in Voynich Woods in the last century. That may not seem like a lot, but that's about the same number of cold cases the Grand Canyon has, despite attracting a tiny fraction of its visitors. The first was Camille Voynich herself, who disappeared in 1938. Georges Bouchard, a surveyor for a pulp and paper company, disappeared during a hunting trip with his sons in 1941. Seventeen-year-old Nathalia Hansen left to use the bathroom during a picnic in 1959 and was never seen again. In 1967, a draft dodger named Ralph Ware was making his way to Canada via back roads. He camped illegally in

Voynich and disappeared. An eight-year-old Boy Scout named Lyndon Roach vanished during a hike in 1972. In 1983, Malika Archer was on a road trip with friends. They pulled over to stretch their legs and lost sight of Malika nearly immediately. A local poacher named Anton Levesque disappeared in 1990, though his rifle was found leaning against a tree. Grace Santiago, a middle-schooler, was lost on a school field trip in 1994, though half the town still thinks that her father kidnapped her after a nasty divorce. Alyssa Nguyen, a thirty-year-old mother of two, vanished in 2009. Amy Macready, a local grandmother, disappeared while walking her dog in 2018. (The dog was found, and locals say that it refused to step foot in the woods afterward—but as far as I know, it was adopted out before anyone actually tested that.)

That's the official list of Voynich's disappeared, the one that's kept on a bulletin board in the local police station, or trotted out on listicles like TEN SUPER-DUPER CREEPY PLACES YOU COULDN'T PAY US TO VISIT. And there are *official* explanations for why these *officially* missing people have never been found. The area is known for quick-changing weather and sudden storms. Geologically, the bedrock is soluble marble and some limestone, littered with caves and sinkholes, some of them large enough to earn names like the Witch's Well. Aquifers and snowmelt streams drain into these caves, taking plenty of detritus—including human remains—with them as they flow underground.

Unofficially, everyone in Roscoe knows someone who just stopped showing up to classes at the high school, or their job at the grocery store, or the Narcotics Anonymous meeting at St. Anne's. This got worse at the height of the opioid epidemic, which seemed to yank handfuls of people off Roscoe's streets. Some reappeared in rehab or jail or the county morgue, and others didn't.

You'd think that with all these missing people, Voynich Woods would be overrun with ghosts. But we only have the Dead Girl, named for her terribly decayed appearance. Plenty of people believe she's the ghost of Camille Voynich, and to be fair, they're both young, female, and dead. But every account of the Dead Girl has her leading people out of the woods. Which makes me wonder—or maybe just indulge in wishful thinking—if she's somehow the product of *all* the missing in Voynich and Roscoe: official and unofficial both. That they're working together to make sure people come back home.

What had Lillian done? Only beaten the devil at his own game.

She didn't seek out the devil without a plan. The stories of the Wishing Tree and dark deals in the devil's woods, told to her by the locals her parents hired to build their ridiculous spa, offered a guide: first, that outwitting the devil was quite possible, and that it was usually done by a mix of pluck, cleverness, and careful planning.

She was ready when the devil appeared at the Wishing Tree. The stories had all been clear on what it offered: a wish, a secret, and a boon.

Her plan went awry almost immediately; she had planned to ask for her parents to die with an altered will, leaving their combined fortune to her. Instead, when the creature that called itself Generous asked what she wished for, the words were yanked out of her. "I want a child."

"Done," said the devil.

"Not yet!" she amended. She was seventeen, and she had other plans. "In—in five years."

Generous wore a hooded cloak that obscured most of its face—not black or red, which Lillian would have assumed to be the normal costume of the devil, but a deep green. The hood shifted enough for her to see Generous smile at the correction.

"How . . . ," she started to ask. "How will it happen?"

"Is that the secret you want?"

"No," Lillian said, and had to grind her teeth in frustration. "I want to know how to work my will on the world. Force fate in my favor."

Generous smiled wider and showed her how to take the little offerings in the Wishing Tree—the coins, the keys, the lockets, the ribbons—and use them as a locus for power: to bind, to ward, to control, to make illusions, even to create life of a sort. The trick was in melding together varying elements, particularly life, death, motion, and stillness, giving and taking, all of it fueled by the dreams and desires left in the objects people had hung on the tree.

"And your boon?" asked Generous.

"Let me think on it," she replied. Could it see she was lying? If it did, it gave no sign.

It took her months to sketch out the trap, to start laying it around the Wishing Tree. She scattered bindweed seeds through the clearing, knowing that they would choke out the other undergrowth. She buried ribbons and chains in patterns radiating out through the tree, braiding them into a web that covered the clearing.

Finally, she was ready. She only needed Camille to anchor it all in place.

It wouldn't have worked if she didn't love Camille; if her sister were not the brightest and most beautiful thing in her life; if Camille hadn't loved Lillian just as fiercely.

It wouldn't work if it didn't feel like Lillian was cutting out her own heart and burying it under the Wishing Tree. When it was all done, she left an offering of her own: a silver locket, engraved with the flowers that Camille was named for, clasped around her ruined throat.

Generous met her in the clearing. It must have noticed her damp skirts, the dirt and blood underneath her nails. But it didn't comment on her appearance, only asked if she had decided on her boon.

"My sister," Lillian said, and then had to pause, choking on the words. When the fit passed, she told Generous, "My sister is sleeping beneath the Wishing Tree. I ask that you go and wake her up."

Did Generous know what she was doing? Again, it gave no sign of anger or disappointment. It didn't refuse her. It made its way past her, careful footfalls between the roots of its tree. Sometimes Lillian caught sight of hooves beneath its long green cloak, as one would expect from a devil, but other times, its feet looked human—dirty and bare of shoes—or bird-like. Sometimes there was nothing beneath that cloak besides moonlight or mist, but she could always hear Generous's approach; it was solid and real, but never one thing or another.

She felt it when the binding took hold, and the trap she'd built in the clearing snapped shut around Generous. She heard the scream—rage, hurt, grief—rock through the woods, and believed it was Generous: the scream of a creature who has been cheated, beaten at its own game by someone not beholden to its rules.

CHAPTER FOUR

The police lieutenant hung up the phone, over which Riley had heard Toby's voice in shrunken sounds of panic and then relief. He looked back over his desk at Riley. "Your uncle is coming to pick you up," he told her.

She nodded. "Thanks," she said. Her voice sounded distant, even to her own ears. She kept Madelyn's sweatshirt zipped up to her chin, and a musty-smelling wool blanket tugged tightly across her shoulders.

It wasn't even ten o'clock. It felt like it should be so much later.

Lieutenant Harvey made eye contact with Sergeant Bajrovic, who had brought Riley into the station. The sergeant had picked her up; Riley had come out of Voynich Woods on the other side of town and walked for maybe thirty minutes before a patrol car roared past her. Its brake lights went on immediately, dyeing the whole road red. She considered running, but the only place to run was back to the woods, and she decided she'd take her chances with Roscoe's two-person police force.

Riley had felt her palms start sweating the second she stepped through the glass doors into the police station. It didn't matter that she'd done nothing wrong; it was like she feared it on a molecular level, an epigenetic anxiety from all the times her mom had been brought here.

This was also where she and Sam had ended up the night Mom disappeared. The same copies of *Highlights* magazine and *Garden & Gun* were sprawled in the waiting room. Same bulletin board of missing persons—*the official list*—and another wall with local outstanding warrants.

And the same cops. Lieutenant Paul Harvey had watched her mother turn from a rebellious teen to a repeat offender. Sergeant Mina Bajrovic had actually grown up with Anna and Toby Walcott, graduating the same year. Mom had always hated Harvey, who'd been busting her since she was a teenager carrying a joint in her backpack, and had a tense relationship with Mina, a former friend who was now the one with a badge.

Sergeant Bajrovic sat in the chair next to Riley. "Before Toby gets here, do you want to change?" she asked. "I've got a spare set of clothes about your size."

"No," Riley said hoarsely. She made an effort to put some life into her voice. "I'm fine."

"Maybe a shower?" Bajrovic offered. "All that mud can't be—"

"I'll shower at home."

They all sat in silence for an uncomfortable amount of time.

"So," Harvey said, after another nervous glance at Sergeant Bajrovic. "Do you . . . want to tell us what happened? We can wait until your uncle is here if you want. A caseworker from DCFS is coming too."

Riley looked up at that. "Wait, what? Why would you call DCFS?"

"They called us," Harvey drawled. "Once they heard you

were missing, they asked us to keep them updated, so they're sending someone over to check in with you."

Riley couldn't imagine anything she'd rather do less than check in with one of the overbearing snoops from the Department of Children and Family Services. Riley had come to really hate the agents who were supposedly in charge of her well-being. Her mom had lost custody of her daughters at the worst of her addiction, and they'd stayed with Toby for a while until she got it back. When she disappeared, DCFS moved on to hounding Toby; he was fine as an emergency guardian, but a single gay man in his thirties who ran a cryptid museum didn't fill them with confidence. Toby had hired a family court lawyer and fought for permanent custody so nobody had to worry about Riley and Sam ending up in foster care. He was still paying off the legal fees, and while he never said anything about it, Riley couldn't help but wonder if she somehow cursed whoever took care of her.

"Why don't you start at the beginning?" Harvey said. "Just tell us what happened, so we have it on record."

"Is Sam okay?" Riley asked. Jane had said she made it home, but—

"She's fine," Sergeant Bajrovic said. "She got back, she's all right. But we're trying to figure out what happened, okay?"

"Yeah, it's strange for someone to come back from the woods. New one for us," Harvey said. At Sergeant Bajrovic's look, he shrugged defensively. "I'm just saying. If this was a regular occurrence, her uncle's tours wouldn't be nearly as interesting."

"Thanks?" Riley said. Harvey was always showing up to their tours with a cousin or old college buddy in tow, proud to show off Roscoe's dirty laundry to out-of-town friends, especially when he could add his own color commentary to stories of the missing.

Tell them what they want to hear. Can't you see what they want from you?

That thought wasn't hers. It didn't originate in her brain, or wherever thoughts came from. It felt like a message in a bottle, buried in silt for who knew how long before bubbling up in her mind.

Shut up, she thought back at it. *And fuck you.* Something had crawled into the back of her throat and was squatting there. She put her hand to her neck, as if she could feel whatever was in there from the outside. *Stupid,* she told herself. Until whatever was under her fingers moved.

She yanked her hand away so fast that she banged it on the desk, and both of the officers jumped.

"Uh, are you—" Sergeant Bajrovic started to say.

Riley did not want to answer any questions about whether or not she was okay, so she didn't wait for the sergeant to finish her question.

"Sam ran off while we were doing a tour with Toby," Riley explained shakily. "She, you know. Wants to be YouTube famous for cryptids."

"Trying to find lampmouths again?" Harvey's tone was too intimate, too knowing. He leaned in toward her like a kindly grandfather, understanding but more than a little patronizing. "Always been my favorite local legend. I saw one when I was your age. Weirdest thing, like a little lightbulb hanging off thin air. And you're looking at it so hard, trying to understand what you're seeing, that the teeth don't catch your attention until . . ."

Trust Harvey to interrupt her statement with one of his own stories. *He wants to be important,* she thought. Roscoe was *his* town, and even if it was a tiny, ugly kingdom, he felt a sense of ownership over it. She could see it on him.

And Bajrovic? Well, she wanted to help. How many times had Riley's mom said that? Though she never made it sound like a good thing. Mom hated being helped, or maybe she hated *needing* help more.

A knock interrupted them. Riley's heart jumped, thinking it would be Toby. But instead, there was an unfamiliar white woman with long auburn hair standing in the doorway. She looked rich. You could always tell rich rural people apart from trash like Riley's family; their boots were always new instead of being forced to survive winter after winter. And it was obvious their winter coats hadn't been inherited from a relative or a coat drive at the church.

"Hi there," the woman said, and even her voice sounded rich to Riley. Like she spent most of her time talking about, like, caviar and real estate development. "My name's Ivy. I'm from DCFS. Is this a bad time?"

Nobody ever has a good time at the police station, Riley thought. She didn't bother to say anything, because *is this a bad time?* from rich people wasn't so much a question as a warning that your bad time was about to become worse. She'd learned that much from corralling tourists for Toby's tours.

"Not at all, Ivy," Harvey said. "We're waiting for Riley's guardian to pick her up."

"So, Riley. It sounds like you had a little adventure tonight?" Ivy said, smiling like it was a joke. Riley's name sounded crisper in her voice, two separate syllables where most people in town swallowed it down to one and a half at most. "I cannot tell you how relieved I was when Lieutenant Harvey here said you'd been found."

"Uh, thanks," Riley said. "Me . . . too?"

Ivy smiled kindly at Riley's underwhelmed answer and said, "May I sit?"

After some shuffling, she sat next to Riley at Harvey's desk, and Sergeant Bajrovic leaned against the wall. Her smile, if anything, grew wider, and Riley had to struggle to summon up a smile back for her. Ivy's niceness felt like it had teeth, was designed to chew you up and swallow you.

"So what were you doing in the woods in the first place?" She unpacked several manila folders stuffed with papers onto the table in front of her.

"My uncle leads tours in Voynich Woods."

Ivy shuffled her notes. "The, ah, ghost and monster tour?"

"It's a great tour," Sergeant Bajrovic said. "Really educational."

"It's about the local lore surrounding Roscoe and Voynich Woods. Ghosts, the Witch, old myths, that kinda stuff," said Riley.

"Ghosts and witches? And that's educational?" Ivy asked. She was still smiling, but skeptically now.

"She's underselling it," the sergeant said. "It's great. Her uncle's basically the entirety of Roscoe's tourist industry."

"Ah, right, you live with your uncle," Ivy said. She flipped through some papers. "Where are your parents, dear?"

A hush fell over the room.

"Isn't that in your notes?" Riley asked.

"Somewhere, probably," she said lightly. "I'm not the most organized, unfortunately."

Was Ivy actually this unprepared, or did she just want to see what Riley would say? It didn't matter, ultimately. Riley couldn't seem to unclench her jaw enough to give any answer.

Eventually Harvey said, "Her father died in, what was it, 2008? Anna Walcott did a runner five years back when her boss found out she'd been skimming cash off the till at the Purple Pig."

He'd *accused* her of stealing. Nothing had been proven, really, but it was hard not to read guilt into her running off.

When Riley looked up, Ivy was staring directly at her. It felt like someone had snapped a bass string in her chest. *THRUM.* For a second, in her periphery, she saw faint dark veins rise up in her vision, and she quickly looked away. She took deep breaths until she was sure that shadowy tendrils weren't going to shoot out her eyeballs or something. What the hell was that?

"So, you live with your uncle," Ivy continued. "And went on a walking tour with him. Why go off by yourself? What were you trying to do?"

"My sister, Sam. She wanted to look for the Wishing Tree." *Wolf tree,* Riley thought, and pressed her fingers into the wool blanket until they ached. It had only been a few hours ago, but it felt like weeks had passed. "One of the tourists was kinda . . . weird, so she ran off, and I went to track her down. I saw Ranger Bancroft and he told me—"

"Funny," Ivy said. "He said he didn't see you."

That stopped Riley cold. "What?"

Sergeant Bajrovic cleared her throat. "When your uncle called and said you were missing, Ranger Bancroft was the first person we asked. Said he'd been in the gatehouse the whole time, never saw you. Didn't know you were missing until Sam found her way home."

"No, I saw him, he told me that Sam went . . . ," she said, and then—because the skeptical looks on their faces hadn't changed—added, "Why would I lie about that?"

"Why would he?" Sergeant Bajrovic asked, but mostly to herself.

"Nobody's accusing you of lying, Riley," Ivy said quickly. "But it sounds like you might be a little confused?"

"I'm not *confused*," Riley said, but she could hear the shakiness in her voice. She was *so* confused; she'd prepared herself for skepticism, maybe, even to be accused of lying, but not over the least impossible part of her story.

Ivy gave Riley a sad little smile, tucked up into corners of her mouth. "I hate to ask, but with things how they are these days—well, you know better than most, Riley."

Riley knew what was coming next. Ivy set a plastic cup with a lid on the desk. Riley had seen little cups just like this: passed across the table to Toby after he'd taken over custody, usually during a surprise home visit. Before that, in her mother's hands at parole meetings, or right in this very station once or twice.

"Uh," Sergeant Bajrovic said. "That's not . . . I'm sure—"

"Given Riley's former home environment and the circumstances of how she got lost, as well as the fact that she was technically trespassing, the department has decided a drug test is a reasonable request."

"This is . . . irregular," Bajrovic said, but she sounded hesitant. "We normally don't test minors—"

"I'll be asking Mr. Walcott to take a test as well," Ivy said brightly, like that made it better.

It took everything Riley had not to throw the cup at her face. "I'm not my mom."

"That you are not," Harvey agreed. His voice was light, but his shoulders were tense. "Haven't cussed us out or tried to steal anything even once."

"You don't have to do this, Riley," said Sergeant Bajrovic. She stood up straighter, pulling out some of that cop authority. "Nobody can force you to take a test without a warrant."

Harvey looked uncomfortable, but Ivy wasn't fazed. "That's true," she allowed. "But not cooperating during an assessment does make it more likely that an open case will be filed."

She said it like it was out of her hands, like some invisible power in the sky opened investigations, not her.

Ivy turned her smile at Sergeant Bajrovic for the first time since they'd all sat down. "Besides, if there's nothing for Riley to hide, what's there to worry about?"

Riley remembered how awful it had been when DCFS was investigating her mom. She wanted to spare Sam from that.

"I'll piss in your goddamn cup," she said, snatching it off the table.

"There's the famous Walcott spirit." Harvey laughed. Nobody else did, and he cut himself off with a fake cough.

"Thanks," Ivy said. "And I'm sorry for the inconvenience. I just want to make sure you and your sister are safe."

She waited for Riley to respond, but Riley had nothing else to say. What a goddamn joke.

Weirdly, she wished for a second that she could tell her

mom about this. *Not only was I killed in some fucked-up ritual and brought back from the dead, but DCFS is piss-testing me to make sure I wasn't on drugs when I died.* Her mom always laughed more the worse things got, and Riley wanted to imagine she'd laugh at this as well.

"Mina," Harvey said. "Can you show her where the bathroom is?"

"I know where it is," Riley said, getting up.

She didn't realize that Sergeant Bajrovic had followed her, until her arm snaked out to slow Riley down. Riley flinched away from it, keeping a tight hold of the blanket around her shoulders.

"Riley, hold up," the sergeant said.

"I can find the bathroom myself," Riley said. "Can you go warn Toby when he comes in? He won't want Sam to see him get tested."

"I can call a public defender for you," she said, ignoring her request. "You don't have to take this test."

Riley rolled her eyes. "They don't work family court. Shouldn't you know that?"

A blush spread across Bajrovic's cheeks. It made Riley glad in an ugly way, to share some of the mortification around. Was this how her mom had felt all those times she'd wound up here?

The sergeant stopped in front of a single-stall bathroom and knocked on the door. (Who did she think could be in there? It was only her and Harvey in the station.) She waited a moment, then put her hand on the doorknob. Before she opened it, she turned to Riley. Sergeant Bajrovic pressed her lips together and said, "I just wanted to say, I'm sorry about your mom. I knew her in high school, a little, and—"

"You were friends," Riley said. "She still had pictures of you."

She wasn't sure why she said it, only that her mother was obviously on her mind. Mina Bajrovic had been friends with her and Toby, and Riley had found stashes of old digital photos of the three of them all through high school. Mom in her ever-present black eyeliner and spiky pixie cut, Toby hiding in baggy sweatshirts, and Mina looking clean and pressed between them. Riley had been born during what should have been her mother's senior year, and Mina was in plenty of her baby pictures. It irked Riley that in her new life as Sergeant Bajrovic, that same girl would shrug off her family's friendship. Downplay it.

"We were," Sergeant Bajrovic said. "I wasn't sure if she would have—it doesn't matter. I'm sorry about what happened to her, and glad that you—"

"Didn't wind up the same way?" Riley said, a sneer wrinkling her face. If this woman was so sorry about what happened to Anna Walcott, why hadn't she stuck around to help? And what did she expect from Riley now—forgiveness? Understanding? Sure, Riley understood. Anna pushed people away, stole from the ones who stuck around, wasted second and third and fourth chances. Sam didn't remember; Riley had made sure to shield her from it, as much as she could. It would have been nice if just one other adult besides Toby had done the same for her.

She waited for Sergeant Bajrovic to answer, but she seemed taken aback by Riley's annoyance, her unwillingness to play along. Anna wasn't a cautionary tale to Riley; she was her mother. Riley wasn't here to deal out forgiveness on her mother's behalf.

"Can I go pee in my cup now?" Riley asked.

The sergeant pushed open the door to the bathroom. Riley shoved past her, then slammed the door shut and locked it. She looked at the little plastic cup and wondered if they could tell you were dead from a urine sample.

◆ ◆ ◆

Sam's eyes were so wide that they were the only thing Riley saw when she came back: the brown irises nearly swallowed by pupil, the whites glaring in the cold fluorescent lights. Her eyes swallowed everything, including Riley. Then Riley got grabbed in a bone-squeezing hug, Toby on one side and Sam on the other, and was spared the sight of her sister's stare.

"I'm okay," Riley said. She was terrified for a second that the goo would start emerging from her skin. Sam was crying, big tears and loud sobs, holding on to Riley with panicky tightness. She tried to focus on the familiarity of her family's hug, but even that felt strange, like their skeletons were trying to press right through the skin. "I'm okay," she said again, trying to shove the panic down. She couldn't breathe until Toby released her, but even then, Sam refused to let go of her. She sat in Riley's lap like she was a little kid again, rocking back and forth.

Mina must have warned Toby about the drug test, because Toby slipped off with Ivy for a couple of minutes after Riley finished telling her story for a second time. She heard a noise, got turned around, had misplaced her whistle somewhere. She didn't bring up Mr. Bancroft again, and neither did anyone else.

"It was my fault," Sam said quietly while they waited for Toby to come back.

Riley nudged her sister's shoulder. "It was not."

"I wanted to look for the Wishing Tree. And I made you come with me, because the l-lore says—" Her lower lip was trembling, and she was looking at a spot on the table as she stammered.

"Sam, come on," Riley said. "I'm fine."

Sam didn't answer her, and Riley felt—it was hard to say. It was hard to look at Sam, misery in all the lines of her body. Riley wanted to comfort her, but she didn't know how. She didn't want to talk about it, think about it, remember any of it.

She'd never been all that "in touch with her feelings" or whatever; she was more than a little convinced that feelings were actually justifications for stupid choices, decided on after the fact. *Why did you do that? Because I was angry.* But she'd been to enough therapy to know where feelings were in her body, the sensations they brought. She could feel the greasy residue of shame in her gut, rage's bright crackle behind her eyes. But her body had turned strange, and her feelings felt even stranger.

After he came back from his own drug test, Toby couldn't seem to meet Riley's gaze. The silence in the room was solid as bricks, like a wall was being built between her and Toby in real time. It dwarfed her by the time they finally signed all the paperwork that allowed Riley to leave. Harvey and Bajrovic both shook Toby's hand, and Toby pocketed the pen that he'd been using to sign everything. He always did that: stole pens from banks, the school, everywhere. "Let's go, Rye."

Was he mad at her? He couldn't be mad. But looking at Toby, she couldn't shake the feeling that she was watching a stranger. Or maybe she was the stranger now.

Sam had fully conked out while they processed the paperwork mountain—Riley recognized a stress nap when she saw one—so Riley hoisted her up carefully, trying not to jostle her awake. Toby helped her get Sam buckled in, then took his time getting settled into the driver's seat, fussing with the seat belt unnecessarily. Riley could feel the anxiety scratching up her spine to claw at her brain.

Toby didn't turn on the car, and they sat for long, agonizing seconds until he asked quietly, "Will you tell me what happened?"

"I already told—"

"I know what you told them," he said, pointing at the police station. "I also know that . . . that what we tell the police, or our parents—or guardians or whatever." He took a deep breath. "It's not always the whole story, because we don't think we can trust them with it."

Riley imagined telling him the parts that she remembered, and the horrible blanks in between. It wasn't that she didn't think he'd believe her. He'd grown up next to Voynich Woods and made half his living by telling stories about the impossible shit that happened there. But she thought of what she'd told Madelyn: *I don't want to be a mystery.* Toby had built his life around the strange things that happened in Voynich Woods. She couldn't stand the idea that he might look *at* her and think only of what had been done *to* her. Try to figure it out, understand it, measure it, make it small enough to fit into an exhibit in their barn. Or worse, he'd find the Wishing Tree himself: find whoever it was who had done this to her—if something happened to him, she thought shakily, if he got hurt, what would happen to Sam? Her mother was an addict of one kind; Toby was obsessive in his own way. He wouldn't see the hole in her chest and not ask any questions. She had to deal with this herself. Like always.

"I was stupid," she said. "Turned off the path because I thought I heard something, fell and hit my head, and . . ."

Toby reached for her shoulder, and Riley flinched away from him, terrified something would blast out of her skin again. That the thing in her chest would crawl out of her. "Don't!" she said, curling away from him, into the door.

Toby looked horrified; he pulled his hand back and wrapped it around the steering wheel.

"Sorry," he said, face turned to the window. He shook his head a few times, then faced front again. He must have taken her silence as the end of the conversation, because he turned the car on. Riley fumbled with numb fingers to get her seat belt on. They got onto the highway, silence thick and hard between them.

CHAPTER FIVE

"Up."

A single word was enough to yank Madelyn from sleep, at least when her mother spoke it. It must have been early in the morning, not quite dawn; there was just enough light in her room to see her mother's pale skin and paler nightgown, practically glowing.

"Mom?" she said cautiously. She'd come home after finding Riley and seen low light still on in her mother's room, visible beneath the crack in the door. She'd crept into her own bed, exhausted but too excited to sleep. She must have dozed off eventually, though, to be woken like this.

Her mother snatched the thin blankets off Madelyn's legs. She was wearing a tank top and a soft pair of shorts beneath them, and she jerked her legs up, feeling exposed. The cold made her scars stand out, lurid and ugly.

"You're filthy," Mother said. "Didn't you wash up before bed?"

She hadn't, too afraid that the noise of the shower would wake her mother, who would come in to find out why Madelyn had been out so late.

Does she know? Madelyn thought, thinking of her meeting with Riley in the woods. *She has to know. She must see it on me, like the dirt.*

"I must have forgotten," she said slowly.

"Up," Mother said again, and Madelyn scrambled to obey her. "We're going to get you clean."

Madelyn walked forward on numb feet, following her mother through the halls. At one juncture, they both paused. Turning right would lead them to the stairs down to the living room, and eventually down to the basement.

Run, Madelyn told her legs. She always did, and like always, they refused to obey her. They just stood there, in an agony of waiting to see which direction her mother would take.

They went left, to the second-floor bathroom, and a whispered sob of relief escaped her before she pressed her lips together. Mother didn't acknowledge it.

The bathroom, like the rest of the house, was old and showed every year of its decay. Mold and water stains crawled across the ceiling and up the walls, and the tiles underfoot were chipped and discolored. It was long and narrow as a closet, and it seemed crowded in there with two people. Her mother turned on the bathtub faucet, and it groaned and sputtered before water started flowing into the scuffed porcelain tub.

"You're shaking," her mother said. Madelyn forced herself to be still.

"It's cold up here," she lied, though it was cold throughout the house.

Her mother simply looked at her, like Madelyn was a book she was struggling to read.

"Stop hunching," Mother said. "You look like you want to hide."

Madelyn hastily straightened under her mother's gaze. The

whispers took up the word and repeated it like a command: *hide, hide, hide.* But Madelyn knew better.

The trick, she had learned, was to ruthlessly squash down her desire to hide or cover herself—any part of herself—from her mother. It had become easier each year; she could sense her mother's interest and sharp focus on her fading a little each year as she became less of a child. That was what Mom really wanted, she knew: a little girl to take care of. Someone who would let Mom be her whole world and never care what lay beyond the wards and watchers that she set around the perimeter of the property.

Mother picked up Madelyn's hand. Madelyn held herself carefully still as her mother examined the torn cuticles and the chewed nails. She'd always been prone to little acts of self-destruction, picking at herself until she bled, then pressing on the wounds until blood welled up in fat little beads.

"This is why the scars won't heal properly," Mother said. "They wouldn't look so ugly if you just left them alone."

"Sorry," Madelyn whispered, barely audible over the spitting faucet and groaning pipes.

Mother sighed. "After everything, the best I could do is a patchwork daughter. Might as well call you Frankenstein."

"Frankenstein was the doctor," Madelyn said, the words coming out before she could stop them. "Not the creature."

Her mother squeezed her hand, tightening slow as a vise until Madelyn could feel her bones grind against each other. "When did you read that?" she asked, then answered herself. "*You've* never read that. We don't have it in the house."

Madelyn had a clear memory of picking it out of one of the downstairs bookshelves. A red, leather-bound hardcover with gold lettering embossed on the cover. *Frankenstein; or, The Modern Prometheus*, by Mary Shelley. Her hands were smaller in the memory, and unscarred.

"You're right," she said. "I don't . . . I don't know where I saw it."

Her mother snorted. "It doesn't matter. Are you saying I'm the real monster here?"

Yes, Madelyn thought. And it must have shown on her face, because her mother suddenly yanked Madelyn's hand forward. Madelyn was caught off-balance and toppled over the lip of the half-filled tub, crashing into the wall first before falling into the water. She tried to struggle up, but there was a hand on her chest, shoving her back down. The water forced its way up her nose and into her mouth, tasting like dirt and rust. She could hear the dull thud of her heart in the water, the gurgling coughs that were ripped from her throat as she choked.

Her scars throbbed, wanting to unzip and spill out blood and magic. But before she could, the hand pressing down her chest was gone. She shot up, dragging in air and retching out water.

"Maddie?" her mother said. Her voice was dull, distant.

She flinched when her mother touched her, then flinched again, bracing for her to be angry that her daughter would shy from her touch. But her mother's hands were soft, and her voice was sad and sorry, dripping with concern.

"Did you slip?" Mom asked. "You must have slipped. These floors are so—Are you okay?"

You pushed me, Madelyn thought. But she was still in the tub, still choking out thin breaths. *You almost drowned me.*

"I'm okay," she rasped. She opened her eyes. Mom was

looking at her with genuine worry in her eyes, and something Madelyn wanted to believe was regret. Her nightgown had been soaked with bathwater, and it clung to her bony knees as she knelt by the tub.

"I'm . . . ," Mom echoed, and Madelyn held her breath, wondering if her mother was about to apologize, and if so, why that terrified her even more. Madelyn had long since separated the different aspects of her: Mom and Mother. Madelyn hated Mother, though she at least was truthful. But she wielded the truth like sharpened scissors, cutting down to the bone. She loved Mom but couldn't trust her. She blew up like summer storms, then fell into dangerous melancholy. Madelyn couldn't make the mistake of thinking that one was less dangerous than the other.

"You know I love you, right?" Mom asked. "I love you so much. And I'm so scared you're going to shut me out. It happened with my mother when I was your age, and she . . ."

A shadow crossed her face, and Madelyn, not wanting her mother to fall back into her anger, said quickly, "I know, Mom."

"It's only us, Maddie," Mom said. "Only us in this terrible world."

She plucked the wet strands of hair off Madelyn's face, then cupped her cheek. Her thumb pressed right against the ridge of scar tissue. "You're the most beautiful thing I've ever created," she whispered.

Why couldn't her mother be one thing? Why couldn't she just hate Madelyn, and Madelyn could hate her? Why couldn't Madelyn be strong enough to . . .

She didn't even know how to finish that thought, what she could possibly do with the strength she wished for. She wished she didn't crave these moments of softness and love from her mother, hold them close to her chest like they would keep her warm when her mother's mood went cold and angry again. Mom patted her cheek, smiling, and stood. "I'll go make breakfast. Don't forget to clean up after your bath, okay, Maddie? This floor is so slippery when it's wet."

Mom pressed a kiss to her fingers, then her fingers to Maddie's cheek, before slipping out of the room and shutting the door softly behind her. Madelyn sat back in the tub, still dressed, and listened to her fading footsteps.

She had a clear memory of being seven or maybe eight. She had picked a dandelion that had gone to seed, and her mother had tried to snatch it out of her hand before she could send the seeds flying with a quick breath to spread across the lawn. The seeds had dislodged as her mother tussled with her, and Madelyn thought, *Go!* like she was telling them to run away. And they'd obeyed her; they'd fled her mother's swatting hand and dispersed over the yard.

The next day, Mother had pulled Madelyn out of bed and walked her down to the front door, pulling her roughly by the wrist.

Their yard was a cheerful riot of bright yellow petals. Not only the dandelions scattered through the grass, but the leaves on the oaks had opened, the orchard trees were dotted with pink and white, and the rhododendrons beneath the window had fat, curved flower buds, ready to open in a week. Madelyn had smiled in wonder before she caught sight of her mother's face. She looked like she'd come out to a yard full of vomit and feces.

"What did you do?" Mother had asked. Low voice, like a growling dog. A warning.

She hadn't done anything. She just loved the dandelions and told them to do what they already wanted.

Mother grabbed her arm. "You can't make things without taking something else. From someone else. And the only person here to take from is me."

"I didn't!" Madelyn said, and then cut herself off when Mother squeezed her arm. "I didn't know," she amended. "I didn't mean to."

"You need to learn to control yourself," Mother said. "You don't know what it means to practice magic, what kind of—" She cut herself off. "It starts with discipline. And sacrifice."

She took a pair of long, metal scissors from her pocket and handed them to Madelyn. "Cut them down," she said. And when Madelyn looked out into the yard, her mother answered the unspoken question: "All of them."

And she'd done it: cut down every dandelion, the fresh buds on the rhododendron, every cherry and apple blossom that she could reach. She had raw patches along her thumb and fingers where she'd held the scissors, where blisters had formed and then popped, the skin worn away. Mom had welcomed her back into the house with some cold lemonade. She'd barely drunk half a glass before Mom saw her hands and fussed over them.

That was the first night Mother took her down to the basement. She'd thought it was a nightmare, and Mom had told her that it was. But the next day, the garden had been different, more settled, no obvious cuts or bald spots. The blisters on her hand were gone, without even a single little callus to mark where they'd been. Instead, she had a thin white scar that cut between her fingers and across her palm. She'd shown it to her mother, who had given her a look. "How funny you are," she said. "That's from years ago. You've almost always had it."

"How did I get it?" she asked, and her mother shrugged, which was itself strange. She was constantly fussing over Madelyn's skin, face, body, clucking over any minor cut or bruise or blemish.

"Oh, it happened years ago. It's not surprising that you don't remember it."

She had wanted to ask if her mother meant when she was cutting down the dandelions, but she was suddenly afraid of the tension in her mother's shoulders, the tight angle of her cocked head. *No more questions,* something had whispered to Madelyn for the first time, and she let it drop.

The whispers were back now, and they wouldn't shut up. The pain was back under her skin too, and it wouldn't shut up either. Her scars ached miserably, burning under the thickened, raised flesh.

"Jane," she whispered. "Jane, Jane—"

She hadn't believed the invocation would work; the wellhouse was one thing, but this was inside her mother's house. The only magic allowed here was her mother's magic. Even Madelyn's was trapped underneath her scars.

But the air had turned cool and refreshing, and an impossible breeze rippled across the water. Madelyn pulled her legs close to her chest, suddenly aware of how exposed she was: so much of her skin bare, the ugly scars so livid that they seemed to shine. Stupid to be embarrassed in front of Jane, who was rising now from the bathwater.

"Sorry," Madelyn said. "I shouldn't have . . . it's stupid." *I'm stupid,* she meant.

Not stupid, said Jane.

"I didn't know you could come into the house."

I go where the water goes. She didn't say anything else, and Madelyn felt even stupider. Jane must have regretted ever talking to her.

"I don't think I can do this," she whispered. She was shaking. When had she started shaking?

She braced herself for Jane to tell her that she was weak. A disappointment.

So many stories start with a witch's daughter, Jane said instead. *Too beautiful to be seen by mortal eyes, or at least that's what the witch tells herself. Too soft and innocent for the sharp edges of the world. She has to protect her daughter, and so her love becomes a sword that cuts them both. A sharp pair of scissors, and the witch cuts pieces out of her daughter until she's the shape she wants. Small and containable. Safe from the world.*

Madelyn had spent so much of her life alone in her mother's walled and warded garden. Their house might as well have been a tower. Could she stop being a witch's daughter? If she stopped claiming the one who claimed her, what would be left? If she didn't want to be the daughter of a witch, what could she be instead?

"What happens to the witch's daughter?"

The world comes in anyway.

"Or she goes to meet it," Madelyn said softly.

Do you remember yet? Jane asked.

"Remember what?" At Jane's silence, she forced herself to smile a little. "I guess I don't."

She thinks she knows everything, said Jane. *But she doesn't.*

CHAPTER SIX

A rattling thump jolted Riley awake. She rubbed at her face and tried to place the sound. It sounded like it had come from her window. She sat up until she could press her face to the cold glass, looking out at the night.

A small bird, barely visible in the moonlight, sat dazed on the ground. It must have flown into the window.

"Shit," she whispered, then got out of bed and made her way outside to see if she could help it. There was a ring around the moon, which hung full and round, high over the mountains and trees. The bird was a sad, shivering lump on the frosted grass, and Riley bent down to pick it up. It was a robin, and it teetered in her hands, off-balance.

She heard the door open behind her, footsteps approaching. The warm scent of cigarettes and perfume. "A robin?" Mom asked, looking over Riley's shoulder.

Riley nodded. "It hit the window. Do you think it's okay?"

"Maybe. Let's make sure it's comfortable and warm," she told Riley.

Mom was supposed to tell her to find an empty box and grab some towels, so they could make a nest for it in the kitchen. But she didn't do that; she just waited.

"What?" Riley asked. She realized that she could smell

something underneath the perfume and clinging tobacco smoke, something rotten and meaty.

"Come on, Rye," said Mom. "There's a price to pay and a covenant to keep."

"Oh. Sorry," she said, realizing what Mom wanted her to do. She reached into the hole in her chest and tugged outward. Her ribs creaked open like a rusty cupboard, but this was the warmest place, wasn't it? This was where the bird would be safe, warm, and comfortable. She carefully placed the bird inside her and listened as it started to sing: an old song about two sisters walking along a river.

The world lurched suddenly, tilted on its axis, and sent Riley spinning over its edge. She snapped out of the dream as she hit her bedroom floor, clawing at the strangling sheets wrapped around her. What was that? A nightmare? A vision?

Riley heard the footsteps a second before her door swung open and Toby stumbled inside.

"Rye?" he asked. He was out of breath, like he'd run through the house at top speed. "Are you okay?"

He realized that she was on the floor and bent over, probably to help her up. She jerked away from him, pulling the blanket higher, nearly up to her chin.

"I'm fine!" she said. Her voice was . . . not fine, sounding panicked to her own ears. But it made Toby back away a little, hands up like she was a skittish animal, ready to bite. He was dressed in his normal dad-fit of jeans and an open flannel over an old, ironically named band shirt. This one said BAD HORSES on it, with a really bad drawing of a horse and cowboy. She'd stolen a handful of these shirts over the years, which he probably knew but never called her out on.

"Bad dream?" he asked.

I wish, Riley thought. The last twenty-four hours *felt* like a nightmare, even when she tried to recount it to herself. Men in golden masks and plant tendrils in her arms and *I hate it when girls scream—*

Toby was still waiting, fidgeting a little, so she nodded. "I guess."

She picked herself up from the floor, careful to keep the blanket over her chest. "Is it time for school?"

Toby cocked his head. "Not—I mean, yes, technically. But you know you can skip today, right?"

"No, it's fine. I want to go." She knew that *pretending* things were fine did not actually make them so, but it was an old habit from when her life was, at least in most ways, objectively worse: Mom cycling through rehabs and release programs and then breaking the conditions of her release and—it sucked, and moving through each day like nothing was wrong had given her brain a break from trying to fix something that she couldn't. Maybe not the world's healthiest coping mechanism, but it was familiar.

Besides, school was farther from the woods. Farther seemed better.

Toby left her to get dressed, and despite wanting to escape into her normal routine, she felt lethargy and dread weighing down her limbs. What was she supposed to do now? Would the wound heal on its own? Would she have to keep hiding it forever?

There was a mirror in her bedroom. She'd ignored it the night before, changed out of her muddy clothes in the dark, refusing to think about what she'd seen in the woods. She couldn't help the sudden thought that maybe, just maybe, she really had imagined it all. Accidentally inhaled some messed-up mushroom spores or knocked her brain out of sorts with some wild hallucinations. With the right drugs, therapy, yoga, and meditation—when her mom had been climbing toward sobriety, people had fallen all over themselves telling her how yoga and meditation would help—her brain would untwist itself into a reality that still made sense, one where the Wishing Tree was a myth, the Witch of the Woods was just an exhibit in her uncle's barn, and dead girls were for sure dead and not walking around Voynich Woods. But it had to start here: confronting the most impossible thing that she had seen and confirming that it wasn't real. Just spores or whatever.

Riley stood up, faced the mirror, and took a deep breath. "Spores," she said, and told herself she would do yoga every fucking day if that was what it took for this not to be real. She lifted up her shirt.

The wound had gotten worse.

She remembered a cleanly cut rectangle missing from her chest: bloodless, neat, impossible. The edges were now turning a bluish-black, rough and pebbled to the touch. She thought of a scab at first, but it looked more like bark, or the chitinous exoskeleton of a beetle. Spidery veins spread outwards from it, reaching up toward her neck. But in the center of the wound, it was opaque and dark, impossible to see into.

It didn't hurt. How could a thing like that be real and not have her screaming in pain? One way to be sure it wasn't spores, she thought. She shut her eyes, fighting off a wave of queasiness and cold sweat. She gingerly traced her fingers down her chest, hoping she'd feel smooth skin under her fingers and nothing else. But her fingertips slid into the hollow space where her ribs should have been, her lungs, the beat of her heart. The skin simply . . . stopped, and Riley's fingers dipped down into the hollow. She pressed further: one knuckle, two, until she touched *something*.

It twitched under her fingers.

She yanked her hand away, gasping for breath. She remembered exercises that counselors had taught her as a kid suffering anxiety: counting each of her fingers and each of her toes, bringing awareness back into her body.

But her body wasn't hers anymore. It had been made into something alien and awful, a ruined landscape. *The old covenant then,* something whispered from her memory. *A wish, a secret, and a boon.* She'd looked up the word *covenant* and found that it was some kind of contract, a deal. What kind of deal had she agreed to? And with who?

There was a knock at the door. "Riley? You coming down for breakfast?"

Riley flinched. "Yeah. I'll be right there."

After five years, their morning routine was almost set in stone, and Riley was feeling almost normal as they drove to the school. Roscoe's younger population had shrunk over the years—it wasn't like there was anything to stay for after graduation, and Toby regularly ranted about how everyone agreed housing was too expensive, but nobody wanted to build more of it—so now the high school had students from fifth grade through twelfth. The younger students had a separate entrance, and Toby dropped Sam off first. She'd been abnormally subdued that morning. It wasn't like Toby and Riley were particularly peppy either, but Riley was worried.

Riley reached out and snagged her sister's sleeve before

she could leave the truck. "Hey," she said. "Do you want to eat lunch together? I bet Mrs. Garza would let us eat in the library."

The library was shared between the middle and high school, and it was an escape from both of them. Mrs. Garza was old enough that she'd had Toby and Anna as students. She always asked after Toby and occasionally showed her age by asking after Mom. It was worth it, though, to have an escape.

Sam shrugged. "Maybe," she said, gathering her stuff. She slammed the door without saying goodbye.

"Why does it feel like she's mad at me?" she asked Toby.

Toby put the truck in drive to pull around to the high school entrance. "She's not, she's just . . . processing. She was in rough shape when she came back without you."

There was that feeling of something squatting in her throat again, making it hard to breathe. "What did she say happened?"

Toby looked at her from the corner of his eye, measuring how much to say. "I couldn't really get much out of her. Mostly that she thought it was her fault."

"It wasn't," Riley said.

"I know," Toby said. He sounded exhausted. "She will too. Just give her some time."

◆ ◆ ◆

Riley could feel eyes on her back, whispers trailing her down the halls and into classrooms. Roscoe was exceedingly boring. Every piece of news was discussed and chewed over, no matter how small, sometimes for years. No wonder all these stories about cryptids and ghosts existed, she sometimes thought; if you didn't have new gossip, you just transformed old gossip until it was weird enough to feel fresh.

The process was familiar to Riley from when her mother was in the messiest lows of addiction. This was worse, though, maybe because the truth was so much more terrible than anyone knew. The wound on her chest felt like a brand burning through her clothes.

"Is it true?" Hazel Morgan dared to ask her. Riley had elected to eat lunch in the library, which was small and usually abandoned. But nothing could stop Hazel when there was some kind of juicy gossip to be hoarded.

"Is *what* true?" Riley growled. She was never going to pass her stupid calc exam at this rate. On the other hand, she was having a hard time convincing herself that it mattered.

"That you were lost in the woods?" When Riley didn't answer, she blustered on. "Did you see . . . anything?"

"Trees," Riley answered. "Lots of trees."

She should have just shrugged the other girl off, or said something cutting and angry that would have Hazel stomp off in a huff. But Riley felt—not light-headed exactly, more like she'd become unmoored. She could still feel her body, feel the pen in her hand and the hard wood of the chair against her back and legs. But black lines were creeping across her peripheral vision, obscuring everything except Hazel. Who stared at her like Riley had something she needed.

"What would you give to know?" Riley whispered, or at least, the words came out of her mouth and throat.

Hazel had watery blue eyes, and they were staring hard at her, like they couldn't look away. It gave Riley a queasy thrill to be holding someone's attention like this. Not the kind of attention she was used to: pity from adults that curdled to hostility when she didn't act like a properly grateful little orphan, curious stares from classmates, like she was a PSA come to life.

This felt like Hazel was a marionette and Riley was holding the strings; she could control her with a twitch of her fingers.

"I—I don't have any cash on me—" Hazel stammered.

Riley thought of the coins hammered into the wolf tree in the woods. Did the actual value matter? Or did the coins stand in for something more? Something worth the exchange?

"What can you give?" she asked Hazel again. Inside her chest—inside the hole in her chest rather—something unfurled, reaching forward. Like a flower facing the sun.

Riley had never felt so physically aware of another person, like the air between them was alive, carrying the movement of Hazel's breath to her, the pulse under her skin, the heat of the blood in her veins. She could see the outlines of what Hazel wanted: for boys to notice her, to think about her and go to sleep with her name on their lips; for girls to like her, confide in her, be the most important person in their life, to be the center of attention.

This was so alien to Riley, who went through life hoping nobody perceived her. Attention was danger; attention was extra weight added to her life's precarious balance: keeping her mother's secrets, keeping her sister safe, keeping them all together.

It would be so easy to give Hazel what she wanted, Riley thought, or to give her something close enough so she'd never notice the difference.

Have you ever thought about what it means to give someone what they want? the voice, the one she'd heard last night and then again in the police station, whispered to her. *Or better yet, what they think they want? How much power you can capture from that exchange? How you can use that power for other things?*

That was a strange thought. Did Riley want power? She thought about how so much of her life was spent waiting for catastrophe, and still never being prepared for when it inevitably struck. What would she have done in the woods yesterday if she hadn't been immediately overpowered? Or at the station last night, when Ivy smugly pushed the drug test across the table?

Riley probed at what it was she felt, and realized that it was hunger. Not her own, but it could be, right?

"Riley?"

Riley lurched back from Hazel at the sound of Sam's voice. It felt like someone had shoved a handful of snow down the back of her shirt.

"Sam, what are you—" She cut herself off. She'd suggested they eat lunch together in the library.

Sam didn't answer. She raised her hand and pointed at Riley's chest. "What is that . . . ?"

Riley looked down; there was a growing stain on the front of her chest, wet and greasy, visible in the crosshatched pattern of her flannel. She remembered the dark tendrils pushing out of her skin, she remembered tearing them out, and the dark liquid that seeped out of the holes they left behind.

"Fuck," she hissed, slapping a hand over it. It should have been warm, right? Whatever it was, it was coming out of her skin and should have been warm, but it was cold to the touch.

"I'm actually not feeling that great?" she said in a rush. "I might just go home?"

Why was she saying everything as a question?

Hazel seemed slow to come out of whatever dreamlike state she was in, and she watched Riley throw her books into her bag with a detached interest. "But you said you'd tell me—"

"I didn't see anything," Riley said.

She threw her backpack over a shoulder, ignored Sam calling for her to wait, and fled.

◆ ◆ ◆

The high school had been built in the 1960s, and during a parent-teacher conference night, Toby had pointed out a bathroom by the old science wing and told Riley her mother had often snuck off there when cutting class. It was a narrow beige room, lit by gray sunlight filtering through a tall frosted window. The sill was covered in old graffiti and burn marks from previous generations of teenagers, who came in here to smoke. Riley had occasionally imagined peeling back the paint and finding something her mother had written, some message from the girl she'd been before.

Instead, she found someone's ballpoint graffiti: *Beware the Witch of the Woods.* Another person had crossed out *Beware* and written next to it *For a good time, call . . .*

don't even JOKE about that!!! someone else had added beneath.

One wish, one secret, one boon.

Wish this entire school would blow up and everyone with it.

She'll knock three times, someone else had written. *Drive her away with iron nails and walnut ash.*

y'all are EMBARASING lol

The argument continued, responses and counter-responses, arrows, a stick figure with a witch's hat, a crudely drawn middle finger. A whole different set of lore than what Toby collected from the old men outside Dunkin' Donuts.

She needed to hide, needed to get her head back together before she could deal with the rest of it. Riley closed her eyes, remembering the last moments before—before she'd died. Someone standing over her, saying *I hate it when girls scream*. The Dead Girl was real, so maybe the Witch was as well. *Guess what, Mom?* she imagined herself saying. *You were right—I was bad and the Witch of the Woods did get me. Turned me into . . .*

Into what? She'd seen the shape of what Hazel had desired, and wanted to reach out and take something in exchange. What did that make her? All the names of the monsters that had their own exhibits in Toby's museum scrolled through her mind, but none of them or their mythology matched what had happened to her.

More importantly, what had Sam seen?

Sam was the only one who ever saw Riley as *good*. Toby loved her, and she knew her mom did too, underneath the bullshit that came with addiction. But Riley could never shake the feeling that they'd both had to learn to love her after she'd been dropped into their lives by accident. How do you love something that arguably ruined your life? Sure, they'd never *say* that, but Riley sometimes thought her existence was an anchor, one that her mom and then Toby had been tied to, keeping them in Roscoe.

But Sam's love wasn't complicated by Riley's bullshit. To

Sam, she was brave, smart, funny, and strong, and had been since at least when Sam was in third grade and wrote an essay that described Riley in exactly those terms. Riley still had it in a folder somewhere in her desk.

Sam seeing those things in her allowed Riley to see them in herself. To *be* those things. And if Sam saw what had been done to her sister, then what would she think? Even leaving aside the impossibility of it, Riley had failed. That was what she felt beneath the fear, the disgust, and the rage: the shame of becoming a victim to something.

Of course, that was when Riley heard footsteps outside the bathroom door, just as she could feel her grip on herself starting to completely unravel. She ducked into one of the stalls, ready to wait out a gaggle of classmates on a collective gossip break, but it was only a single set of footsteps, moving quietly. The door whooshed shut, but the person didn't move to one of the stalls or sinks. They just stood. Waiting.

Fear prickled across her skin. There was no way out of here; the window was painted shut and the only door blocked. She was trapped.

"Riley?" a voice said. Familiar. Hushed and a little rusty.

"M-Madelyn?"

She pushed the stall door open enough to peek out. Madelyn stood by the sinks, hands sunk deep into her coat pockets. She looked shorter inside, swallowed by a Carhartt jacket that seemed too big for her. Scars livid in the blue-gray light. It was hard to gauge her age; she was about the same height as Riley, but there was a weathered scrawniness to her features that made her look older.

"I said I'd come find you."

"You didn't have to give me a fucking heart attack while doing it," Riley said, leaning against the stall. "How did you even find me?"

Madelyn seemed vaguely embarrassed. "Jane showed me how to get around the wards and watchers that Mom sets out. Once I was at the school, all the voices just kept singing at me until I found you."

That answer spawned about six more questions in Riley's mind. "The voices? Like, you asked for directions?"

Madelyn shook her head. A flush was deepening across her cheeks. "It's hard to explain."

"I'm seeing that."

She'd mostly avoided thinking about the girl who had found her in the woods—or girls, rather, because there was the Dead Girl to consider. Jane Doe.

"Where's your little dead friend?" asked Riley. "Is she about to pull a Samara and crawl out of the mirror?"

"A what?" asked Madelyn.

"It's from—you know what, never mind." Not everybody had a sister like Sam to keep them in creepy old horror movie references. "Where's Jane?"

"She can't come this far from the woods. She says the waters are too deep underground." Madelyn was watching her, her gaze skittering toward and then away from Riley like she was scared to get caught staring. "What happened?"

Riley stiffened, thinking she meant in the library, with Hazel, that weird moment. But no, she was gesturing at Riley's chest, the stain that had spread out across the top of her chest.

"Maybe . . . maybe you can tell me," said Riley. "Because I really don't know."

Riley came out of the stall and sat on the narrow window ledge. She liked to imagine her mother sitting here, whenever she came to hide out in this particular bathroom. Mom always looked older in her teenage pictures, gazing at the camera with this sardonic look, like nothing could faze her. In all the pictures after Riley was born, she looked impossibly young. Very fazed.

She'd only been a year older than Riley when she became a mother, which Riley tried not to think about very often. She had never been able to imagine going through something so huge that it altered your whole existence, all your plans for the future, even your physical body. Guess she didn't have to imagine it now.

She and Madelyn watched each other warily. Madelyn wore an earnest but haunted expression.

"What do you remember?" she asked Riley.

That was the question everyone wanted to know. It was already hard to remember; like whatever had happened to her shattered the memory, and she was trying to put the jagged pieces together, cutting herself on their sharp edges. Madelyn listened patiently, though, as she stumbled through the story.

"The last thing I remember is looking up at the wolf tree—"

"The what?" said Madelyn.

Riley blinked in surprise. She hadn't even meant to say it, really. "Sorry, I meant the Wishing Tree. Wolf trees are something I read about in one of my uncle's books—a term that loggers used to use for gnarly old trees like that."

Madelyn nodded. "It makes sense. There's something hungry in that tree. My—someone I know calls it Generous."

Warmth spread across Riley's chest as whatever was inside her settled. Like a purring cat. It seemed that she had a name for the thing she had made a deal with, the thing she'd unwittingly carried out of the woods inside her. Riley touched her chest, remembering the way the locket had come alive in her hand, the way it had burrowed inside her.

"Who calls it that?" asked Riley. "Who else knows about this?"

Madelyn winced. "I . . . I'm not sure." Before Riley could ask her to explain what she meant, how she knew the name of this thing but not who called it that, she continued. "You said the man was wearing a mask? With a sun on it?"

The change in topic was obvious, and Madelyn looked scared. Of Riley?

Riley had—or rather, *something* in Riley had wanted to kill the other girl last night. And sure, she'd been right to be suspicious, after what happened to her. But maybe Madelyn was right not to entirely trust Riley as well.

"A sun, yeah," she said. Madelyn's face smoothed out, relieved. "Or—I don't know. It looked like this."

She pulled a pen out of her backpack and drew the symbol on the window frame, alongside all the other graffiti. A circle with crossed lines in it, not a pentagram, but something more complex. It would make a good tattoo, Riley thought, if it didn't have horrible associations.

"That's not the sun. Or maybe not just the sun. It's a wheel," Madelyn said.

Riley had spent too much time looking up esoteric images, drawing them in her many notebooks, not to know the significance of the wheel of fortune. "Things moving in cycles," she said. She capped the pen, noticing that her fingers were shaking a little.

"I thought I could stop her," Madelyn said, and Riley looked back at her. "Stop the cycle. Interrupt it before . . . Something interrupted it, but I don't think it was me. Or not only me."

Riley asked, "Stop who?"

That wince again, and a deep breath. Maybe like she was controlling some ache, or maybe like she was just tired of Riley's shit. "I . . ." Her mouth moved, but nothing came out. "I can't tell you."

Her voice was shaking, and tremors ran across her limbs. Her hands had twisted themselves tightly together.

She was hiding something—Riley didn't need a creepy voice in her head to know that. When Riley started becoming unmoored again, she didn't fight it. She had been able to see what Hazel wanted—no, it wasn't seeing, it was more visceral than that. She'd tasted it, the sour edges of an emptiness she carried with her. Traced her fingers across the tangled knot of intertwining needs.

She needed to know what Madelyn wanted. Black veins crawled across her vision, and she turned to the other girl, stepping closer to her.

But when she looked at Madelyn, it was different. She was different. Like a smooth wall instead of a snarled ball like Hazel had been. She rose from the window ledge and took a step closer to Madelyn. She could see cracks in the smooth expanse that walled Madelyn off. *Fault lines*, Riley thought. *Weak places.*

Can you feel that? the reedy little voice asked her. Generous's voice if Madelyn was right. She could: how fragile that wall was, how easy it would be to tear open those fault lines. There was something in Madelyn that longed to unwind and spill everything out of her. "Tell me," she demanded.

Madelyn stumbled closer. The fault lines cracked; locked-down secrets and desires were buzzing under her skin. Not a tangled bramble like Hazel's, but more like when Riley had seen a group of boys shoot down a hornets' nest with a .22: a furious, staticky buzz, with overlapping voices that threatened to rise into a shriek. *I hate it when girls scream,* she thought again. That stunned bird feeling, bright red blooming out of her chest.

And then one of Madelyn's scars opened over her eyebrow. Blood cascaded down her cheek, shockingly red. The fault line sealed itself, and Madelyn shoved her, hard. Riley's hip slammed into the window ledge, and the throbbing pain pulled her the rest of the way back into her body, away from—from whatever that was.

"Oh shit," Riley said. She leaned forward, wincing. "Are you—"

Madelyn wiped her face, her hand coming away with a palmful of blood. Riley went to grab some paper towels, but the dispenser was empty. Of course the janitor never refilled anything in this part of the school.

"I said I can't tell you," Madelyn said. Blood was still sliding down her face, dripping off her chin and hitting the floor in big, fat drops. "She made sure that I couldn't."

Riley peeled off the flannel that she'd worn over a shirt. It already had the sooty, greasy stain over the chest, so what was a little blood? She wet one of the sleeves in the sink and gingerly approached Madelyn. "Here. I can—or if you want to?"

Madelyn let her approach; she looked like she wanted to flee, and Riley wouldn't blame her if she did. She felt sick as she carefully wiped at the blood on Madelyn's face. "Sorry," she said. "There's something *in* me. It—"

She willed the voice to speak again, confirm that it hadn't been Riley peeling open that crack in the unnervingly smooth front Madelyn put up. Hadn't been Riley who made her bleed.

It didn't speak. She could feel it watching her, though: a little curious, a little hungry.

"I'm sorry," she said again. She wiped again, looking to see if Madelyn was still bleeding, but the scar had sealed itself again.

"It's not your fault," Madelyn said. Her voice had gone even quieter, rougher. "But you can't do that."

"I won't. I don't even know what I did." She dropped the flannel shirt into the sink and turned on the faucet. The blood would probably wash out in the cold water, but she wasn't sure how she'd explain the oily stain on the front.

Riley could feel Madelyn's gaze. It was easy to guess what she was staring at; in the mirror, those blue-black lines were racing up toward her collarbones now, and the hole itself peeked over her tank top. The tank itself was sporting its own disgusting stain, spreading out like the rays of a sun. "It got bigger," she said.

She picked at one murky line above her collar bone until she got her fingernails under it. She hissed between her teeth and started pulling it from her skin. It came away slowly, and she winced the entire way. Eventually it snapped off in her fingers, part of it still embedded in the skin. It looked like the root of a plant at first, with tiny white threads branching off. But she peered closer, wiping it off with her fingers, and it looked like a thin metal chain, the kind that might hold a necklace or pendant—or a locket.

She dropped it in an empty sink and it landed with a faint clink. Madelyn was staring at her, and Riley felt acutely embarrassed, like she'd been caught picking a scab or popping a zit. But maybe Madelyn understood having a contentious relationship with your skin.

"Are your scars from . . . her?" Riley asked.

All she had was a pronoun. Riley glanced back at the graffiti by the window. The Witch of the Woods. *For a good time, call . . .*

Madelyn nodded. "They're like warnings. I used to be able to do things. I'd ask a flower to grow and it would bloom. But you can't make things happen without taking something else. From someone else."

It sounded like she was quoting someone.

"And she didn't like it, so," Madelyn finished.

"Why are you helping me if you're . . ." *Scared of her,* she thought, but that didn't do it justice. Riley understood what she had felt underneath those ley lines across Madelyn's body, filling the air around her like a poisonous gas: fear.

"This has happened before. We're all trapped in this cycle. And something bad happens at the end of it. But you—"

"The end of it?" Riley interrupted. "It started with this. How much worse can it get?" She gestured at her chest, the wound that was slowly cracking open wider.

Madelyn looked down at the blood from the flannel still swirling down the sink.

"If what almost happened to me is what happened to everyone else who's gone missing over the years, then why start caring now? Why risk more of that for me?" She pointed at Madelyn's hands, where thick scars cut across the skin.

"Because nobody comes back from the woods," Madelyn said. "Until you did. I thought I could disrupt it, but I didn't need to. You brought yourself back, so I thought, maybe we could help each other?"

Riley looked up in the mirror and saw a flickering presence behind her: Anna Walcott, younger than Riley had ever seen her. Short brown hair in a pixie cut, bootcut jeans and a lowcut tank top, treating the dress code like a war of attrition that she might never win but wanted to keep fighting forever. In the mirror, Anna sat on the window ledge, slouched beneath the drawing Riley had made, the sun that was a wheel that was a cycle.

Riley turned her head, just to confirm that the windowsill was empty.

If it's help you want, Anna's reflection said, *I still owe you a boon. And a secret. All you have to do is ask.*

That same voice. Not her mother's, but close enough to hurt. This was the second time Generous had pretended to be her.

Riley reared back and punched the mirror. It splintered under her fist. Pressure bloomed across her hand, but no pain. Darkness was pooling across her knuckles, turning them a slick, iridescent black. It was cool and heavy against her skin, like armor. An exoskeleton.

Coming to school had been such a stupid idea.

"Um?" said Madelyn. "Are you okay?"

"The ranger," she said, because there was no way to answer

Madelyn's question. "Mr. Bancroft. I saw him. He told me to go up the path to the Obelisk. But he told the police he never saw me. We should start with him."

"Start with him how?"

He had to know something, Riley thought. He had to be involved. Why would he lie to the police about seeing her? "Sneak into his house. See if we can find something. Evidence."

Evidence for what, Riley didn't know. But aside from Madelyn herself, it was the only lead that she had.

CHAPTER SEVEN

Madelyn followed Riley through a series of abandoned hall-ways. She had always imagined that a high school would be . . . busier? That there would be people hanging out at lockers, gossiping, betraying each other, breaking up with each other. Kissing each other?

But the only person who saw them leaving was a lunch-room worker in a hairnet and apron, leaning against the wall outside and scrolling listlessly on her phone. Madelyn went to turn back, but Riley stood in the doorway. "Most of the lunch workers are here on community service," she whispered. "They don't care enough to tell on us."

Riley walked casually past the woman, nodding respectfully.

"Don't suppose you have a cigarette," the woman said as they passed.

"Don't smoke," Riley said.

The woman looked back down at her phone. "Kids these days," she said wryly. "Enjoy your freedom while you can."

The storm that had boiled over last night had left the air crisp and clean, sweeping out the last of the late-summer dust. Instead of the roads, Riley took Madelyn down a set of train tracks that cut through the town. "More direct," she said.

Riley filled her in about Bancroft once the train tracks spilled them out onto a yellowing field on the outskirts of town: He was a ranger tasked with patrolling the Voynich Woods recreational area, checking people in and out during daylight hours and charging them for parking in the lot. He was (and apparently always had been) a bit of a jerk. He had been the last person Riley saw before she found the Wishing Tree—or the wolf tree, as Riley called it. That sent an illicit thrill up Madelyn's spine, because she knew instinctively that her mother would hate the name. She didn't like it when you called things what they really were, instead of something that sounded nicer.

"So we're breaking into his house while he's working and hoping to find what, exactly?" she asked.

"Evidence," said Riley, then pursed her lips. "Or maybe just answers. Maybe a connection to . . . her?"

Pain throbbed under Madelyn's scars. It had been hard to convince herself to meet Riley this morning, after her mother's pre-dawn visit. But she told herself that she'd be punished either way; why not earn her mother's rage for once?

"Maybe," she said cautiously. No blood, but the pain felt like a constant reminder that even away from her mother's watchers, she was still watched.

"And if we find that connection, then maybe—maybe helping me will help you?" Riley made a face. "That sounded less stupid in my head."

Madelyn felt her lips quirk in a smile, and the conversation trailed off into silence. Usually, other people's quiet made her nervous. Her mother's quiet could be dangerous. Jane's tended to be heavy, as if weighed down by everything Jane could say but chose not to.

Riley's quiet was companionable. Maybe it was just the afternoon around them, this small taste of freedom: walking down railroad tracks past backyards where women in knit scarves and housecoats hung laundry to dry in the sun, or kneeled bent over in gardens, pulling up the carrots that grew in orderly rows. A couple of preschool-aged kids played on a rickety backyard jungle gym that swung and leaned noticeably with their weight. One of the children saw them and waved, and Riley waved back. Madelyn, after a moment, copied the motion.

This was the world that Mom wanted to protect her from. Laundry lines and gardens and walking on railroad tracks with someone who, if they could trust each other, might be a friend.

"Are you okay?" Riley asked, interrupting her thoughts.

"I'm fine," Madelyn told her.

"You looked . . . I don't know. Sad?"

Madelyn, as a rule, didn't like to look at her feelings too closely. She liked it even less when other people saw them, noticed them, commented on them. But of course, it wasn't other people, just her mother.

Her mother, whose attention was forever inescapable.

Or was it? Jane could slip through it. Madelyn had hurt herself plenty of times trying to break her mother's rules; maybe she should try slipping around them instead.

"I'm—I'm thinking about a story that Jane told me. About a witch's daughter." She waited, but there was no tightness in her throat, no blood in her mouth. "How the witch locked her in a tower to keep her away from the world, but the world got in anyway."

"And?" Riley asked.

"And what?"

"What happens then?" Riley had, while Madelyn was lost in her thoughts, started walking along the narrow metal rail. She seemed at ease with it, her shortened steps practiced and precise. "Is it a prince who gets in? Is it a metaphor for losing your virginity, like most of those old fairy tales? You would not believe how many dick jokes and sex euphemisms are in the old versions of those stories, by the way."

Madelyn felt like she'd been dropped into an entirely different conversation. "I don't think it was a metaphor for that?"

Riley looked over, her balance wavering for the first time. She wheeled her arms out and caught herself, just barely, from falling. "Oh. *Oh*, you mean—witch's daughter. A story. Right."

"Right?" Madelyn asked.

Riley was blushing. "So what happens to the witch's daughter when the world comes in?"

Madelyn thought of the drawing Riley had made in the bathroom: the world, the wheel. "It's the end of everything," she said.

Riley stepped down off the railroad track and stopped walking. "You said that like it's a good thing."

"If everything's bad, it would be. Right?"

Riley's eyebrows drew together, and she started walking again. After a moment, she said, "I don't think endings are ever that simple. Fairy tales and folk stories always make them sound neat and clean, but . . ." She trailed off and didn't speak again for long enough that Madelyn had resigned herself to more silence, though not as amiable.

"I don't think any endings are painless," Riley finally said. "Even when everything is really bad, you never feel like you're going to survive the ending of it."

◆ ◆ ◆

Bancroft's house looked no different from the houses they had passed in Roscoe's downtown: a run-down two-story farmhouse, maybe a century old. It looked oddly unlived-in, to Madelyn's eye. The grass was overgrown, crowded with leaves and fallen branches. All the curtains inside were drawn closed. Paint was peeling off the outer walls; curls of it littered the grass, and long strips were gone from the siding. They went around to the side of the house. Madelyn was definitely new to crime, but even she knew breaking into someone's front door wasn't very smart.

"Guess we could break the window," Riley said. "I don't have enough of a signal to find a lock-picking video on YouTube—"

"It's open," Madelyn said. She nudged the side door open with her foot, and it swung open a little.

"Cool," Riley said, though her voice made it sound the opposite of that. "I mean, cool for us not having to break a window. But that's weird."

"Is it?" asked Madelyn. "This is my first burglary."

"Mine too," said Riley. She held up her hand, and after a second, Madelyn did the same, and Riley high-fived her. *Oh, that's what that is,* she thought. "But yeah, people don't leave their doors unlocked around here anymore."

Her house had locks, Madelyn thought, but they were all on the inside. Her bedroom. The basement. It was strange to think about people locking things out, rather than each other in.

She went inside first, slipping through the narrowly open door and into the dark kitchen beyond it. Riley followed her.

She'd never been in a stranger's house. She wasn't sure what to expect, but the house itself looked neat, and weirdly empty. Parts of her house were empty, but much of it was taken over by her mother's many projects. She was used to living in eccentric clutter.

"People usually have furniture, right?" she asked Riley. There was no couch or TV in the living room adjoining the kitchen. There was a table and chair in the kitchen, but that seemed to be it.

"Yes, furniture is definitely a thing people have. Also, food? Plates?" Riley opened the cabinets, which were empty. So was the drawer Madelyn opened. "And no silverware."

Riley ran her finger along the kitchen counter. A layer of gray dust covered the surface. It was like nobody had even breathed in here for months.

"Is this the kind of evidence you were hoping to find?" whispered Madelyn.

"There's nobody here," Riley told her. "His truck's gone, and he never married. You can talk normally."

Madelyn shrugged noncommittally. "Feels strange to talk normally when we're breaking the law."

She stopped, turning around in the kitchen. There was something off in the air, a sour taste that made her wrinkle her nose. She wrapped her arms tightly around her torso. "Do you feel that?" Madelyn asked. "There's something wrong here."

"Wrong how?" Riley asked.

"Like the Wishing Tree," said Madelyn. "The wolf tree. That feeling, like when your ears ring so bad you can't sleep."

Riley, she saw, couldn't feel it. "Rancid vibes never killed anyone," she said, moving to the doorway. "I was hoping for like, a confession? Journal entries? I don't know. Clarity, at least. So far, all of this is making it weirder."

"Why is it so important to . . ." Madelyn knew it was a stupid question, even as she opened her mouth. But Riley was staring at her expectantly. "Never mind," she said quietly.

"No, finish your question," Riley said.

"Why is it important to know what happened to you?" she asked.

Madelyn had a bad memory, piecemeal and moth-eaten, full of holes. Sometimes, things she clearly remembered contradicted what her mother told her was true. And other times, when she asked about things she didn't remember, her mother would get quiet in a dangerous way, and Madelyn would shy away from the question. At a certain point, she had realized that there was more peace in not knowing what happened to her than in trying to find out. At the end of the day, anything she knew about herself would get subsumed by what her mother wanted her to believe.

But Riley looked at her like she'd grown a second head. "It's my body. It's me, and I don't know what they did, or why, or how to make it go back to normal. What if I'm dangerous? What if I hurt someone?" She gently took Madelyn's wrist in her hand and pulled it up, so that the scars disappearing under her sleeve were visible. "Don't you want to know what these are from and why you have them? I saw you bleed fire, but then in the bathroom—"

Madelyn took her hand back. Her skin seemed to buzz where Riley had touched it. In the bathroom, it had felt like Riley was prying her apart with her gaze. Madelyn had almost welcomed it. Wanted it. It had felt nothing like her mother's scrutiny, or Jane's cold judgment, but something wilder, thrilling. Right until her scar burst open like a warning shot.

That was the other thing: Her body wasn't always on her side. Sometimes it was an enemy. "I don't know if my body is mine," she said. "Not all the time."

Riley shook her head. "How can it not be yours?"

Madelyn opened her mouth, then winced as a sharp pain spread across the hand Riley had held. Just a tiny line of blood had opened up, a warning.

"Never mind," Riley said. "Just—it is yours. You belong to yourself." Then she backed up a couple of steps and muttered, "I sound like a fucking after-school puppet show."

In the hallway beyond was a door that looked like it led to a basement, and stairs leading to the second floor. Riley made for the basement door, but Madelyn's hand on her arm stopped her.

"Not the basement," she said through a clenched jaw. "I don't like basements."

That was, to put it generously, a vast understatement. She hated basements. Just imagining the feeling of clammy air on her face made her want to claw her skin off.

Something must have come across, though, in her tone or her face. "All right," Riley said. "We can look upstairs first."

Madelyn wished she could channel some of the energy of Circe from *HMS Broomstick*; there'd been a recurring gag about her love for mystery novels and whodunits, and when there'd been a real death during a Murder Mystery Dinner Theater show on the ship, she'd been the one leading the hunt for the killer. (It had been the cook, who had served up toxic puffer fish on the victim's plate after he'd complained about every single thing he'd been served.)

What would Circe do in this case? Start gathering information.

"What do you know about Bancroft?" Madelyn asked.

"I never really got to know him," Riley admitted. "Not as anything but the old grumpy guy who's worked at the gatehouse for as long as anyone remembers. He chews tobacco, and it's gross. And he was the last person I saw before . . . you know. Except for Sam."

There were two rooms upstairs, plus a bathroom, all of them just as dusty as the kitchen had been. "No bed," Riley observed. "Where the hell does this guy sleep?"

She was right; these rooms were as minimally furnished as the ones downstairs. But in one of the rooms was a pile of blankets, a shelf with a few books and trinkets, and cups on the floor filled with a dark liquid that smelled bitter and rotten. "Ugh, that's foul," Riley said. "Fucking chewing tobacco."

The smell wasn't coming just from the cups. There were streaks of the same liquid on the blankets and up the walls, smeared across the carpet.

Madelyn took a closer look; one of the cups had only a little liquid in the bottom, but there was something else in there. She nudged the cup with her foot, and it tipped over. The liquid spread out across the stained carpet, and a rusted nail rolled out.

"What the *fuck*," Riley whispered.

Madelyn remembered, in a flash, her mother taking her to the wolf tree to gather its treasures. Coins, of course, ribbons, bits of jewelry, locks of hair . . . and iron nails, wrenched out of the bark.

"Hey," Riley said. "What is it? Do you know what that means?"

She had felt it downstairs, that cold, electric unsettledness to the air. Generous's magic, which was also her mother's magic. But her mother wove those objects into charms: wardings, watchers, hexes when she needed. Why was this one loose and rattling in a cup?

"No," she said. "Not exactly."

Riley wrinkled her nose when Madelyn slipped the nail into her pocket, but said nothing. They did a circuit of the rest of the room. Madelyn went to a shelf and looked through the books piled up there, which all looked old and well-read. She froze at the sight of a red leather-bound copy, a familiar title in faded gold lettering: *Frankenstein: or, The Modern Prometheus*, by Mary Shelley.

She pulled the book off the shelf and examined it. It too was wrinkled and stained with the same gray-brown liquid she'd spilled on the floor. She flipped through the pages and saw one that was dog-eared, with a shaky box drawn around a paragraph.

For a few moments I gazed with delight on her dark eyes, fringed by deep lashes, and her lovely lips; but presently my rage returned; I remembered that I was forever deprived of the delights that such beautiful creatures could bestow.

"Is there something in the book?" Riley asked.

Madelyn showed her, and Riley frowned. "Incel vibes," she said. Madelyn had no idea what that meant.

"I think it's my book," said Madelyn. She could ask what "incel vibes" were later. "Not that part, but—" She flipped to the front of the book, knowing what would be there already. A bookplate depicting a black cat looking up toward a full moon, above the words EX LIBRIS. Someone had written their name below it, but it had been furiously scribbled out. "I remember this," she said. "My—she said I'd never—how did it get here?"

Her head was starting to hurt. The chorus of voices, which had been so quiet on the walk here, was getting louder and more cacophonous.

"Let's look at the basement," Riley said after a moment.

Madelyn could feel her muscles tensing. Like they were going to run her out of here if Madelyn didn't get with the program.

But she was very used to controlling inconvenient impulses to run away, so she gritted her teeth and followed Riley.

But Riley stopped her, frowning. "Is it something to do with your scars?"

Your scars. Madelyn wasn't sure why that phrasing stopped her, but it did. Maybe because her mother never even called them *scars*, never mind referring to them as something that belonged to Madelyn. They were always *them*: *stop picking at them, or they'll never heal; you'd be so pretty if it weren't for them.*

"Yeah," Madelyn said, but her throat closed around any other explanation she might add. She waited for Riley to press, demand to know more. She almost wanted it.

But Riley didn't ask. Just looked at Madelyn, looked away, and then solemnly held out a hand. Madelyn stared at it, unsure what she was supposed to do. Was this another high five? It seemed like the wrong position. Riley flushed and started to turn away. Then, like Madelyn's hand knew what it wanted even while the rest of her was confused and acting stupid, she grabbed Riley's hand.

It was cold and dry, and her fingers curled over Madelyn's like comforting little icicles.

In the basement, gray autumnal light filtered through the squat, dirty windows that sat at the tops of the cement walls. Boxes and old furniture stood in neat piles. There was a workbench of sorts, with old, rusted tools lined up neatly along the wall, though it looked as disused as everything else.

No furnace like the one at home, which Madelyn was fervently thankful for.

The chorus of whispers that dogged her had gone entirely when she was at the school. She'd felt more alone than she had in years. Here in Bancroft's house, they were hushed but present. A respectful audience, like they were touring a church or a famous library.

The voices stirred, suddenly. Madelyn unconsciously tightened her hand around Riley's.

"What is it?"

The whispers rarely sharpened into words she could understand. She thought, but wasn't sure, that they used to speak more clearly to her. But now there were too many of them talking over each other, like static in her head. She shook her head slowly, trying to understand something, *anything*, of what they were trying to tell her.

The whispers got louder. Almost as loud as when she'd been on Riley's trail, when they sounded like a tornado from inside her skull.

"Shut up," she muttered.

"What?"

She dropped Riley's hand and pressed her fingers against her temples as if she could smother the whispers. "Someone's down here," she said.

Riley stiffened, her fists clenching at her sides as she looked around the room, posture changing from slumped in disappointment to rigid with fear. Madelyn marveled for a moment that it was so easy to see what Riley was feeling, how her emotions moved across her body so obviously. She'd always pushed her own feelings so far down, hidden and dissembled and distracted herself from them.

Riley shifted her weight in her boots, turning around in a slow circle. Something pulsed beneath her skin, and Madelyn remembered Riley after she'd come back to life beneath the wolf tree, the anger and the barely contained violence. It was strangely thrilling to see that turned on something else.

Until "something else" stumbled out from behind the old boiler in the corner and turned out to be a child. One with the same dark curls and freckles as Riley.

Riley stumbled back, almost losing her balance on the concrete. "Sam," she said, and Madelyn remembered the night before, how she'd said the same name. This must be her sister.

"Sorry, sorry, I didn't mean—I just wanted to—"

"Sam, what the hell are you doing here?" Riley growled. "*You* should be in school."

"So should you," Sam countered. "You were acting all weird in the library, so—"

"So you followed me?"

"You're not supposed to go off alone," Sam said, her voice shrill and breaking. "You're not supposed to leave me—"

Riley reached out and pulled Sam into a hug. Something electric and bitter spread over Madelyn's tongue, the way it did sometimes when she watched her favorite episodes of *HMS Broomstick*; the ones where the coven all came together to protect Peggy, the three witches' niece, who wasn't yet a member of the coven. Scenes like that always made her feel younger, hungrier, angry that other people seemed to eat so well when she had to starve. What would her life have been like if she'd had aunts? Siblings? Anyone else besides her mother, a dead friend, and a chorus of whispers haunting her house? She turned away but couldn't stop biting into that bitterness.

Madelyn could hear a car engine, the crunch of gravel under wheels. She ran to one of the windows and stood up on tiptoes to stare out of it. "We have a problem," she said. At the sisters' confused looks, she pointed outside. "Someone pulled into the driveway."

Riley, after a second of shock, leapt up the stairs and pulled the basement door shut.

"See if any of the windows open," she hissed. Madelyn hurried from window to window, but they were all painted shut. She looked back to Riley, but the other girl shook her head. No luck either. The engine outside cut out, and a door opened and closed.

Riley looked terrified; her fingers twitched, her eyes

were bulging out of her face. Madelyn had seen Riley in full cornered-animal mode, having been on the bad end of it only the night before. How long before her pores started leaking black goo or growing spidery, strangling tendrils out of her skin? And why shouldn't she be afraid? This man might have killed her, or helped whoever had.

They hadn't found evidence one way or the other. So maybe it was time to try a different approach.

A very different, probably very stupid approach.

She huddled in close to Riley, trying to gently usher her back without setting her off. "Riley," she said. "I'm going upstairs. I'll get him to leave the house."

Riley, if anything, only looked more afraid. "Are you kidding me?"

"He won't hurt me," she said.

"How do you know that? You can't know that."

Because only my mother is allowed to hurt me, Madelyn thought.

Riley was looking for evidence that he'd been the one to kill her. Madelyn wanted to know how—if at all—he knew her mother. What he knew about her mother's plans. And they wouldn't find that lying around his house.

The voices in her head had gotten quieter. Madelyn wanted to think that after years of bitter disappointment, they were pleasantly surprised by her now.

I can be brave, she thought. *I can be clever, like in all the stories.* All the stories that her mother had let her read as a child, then taken away the second she'd tried to be like them. The only thing she was allowed to be was her mother's daughter, and only her mother was allowed to say what that meant.

"I don't have time to get into it," she said. "But he won't hurt me."

Riley had her hand around Madelyn's wrist again—she thought of last night, when it had tightened enough to make the bones creak, and how different that had been from when she'd touched it again upstairs. This touch was somewhere in between; Madelyn hadn't realized you could make a catalog of the different ways a person could touch you, the different ways it could make you feel. She wished she had time to explore that revelation, but if she fixed this now—gave Riley the answers that she so desperately wanted—there might be time later. Madelyn tamped down the nervous tremor in her fingers and gently extricated herself.

She waited, listening as the heavy footfalls traveled across the linoleum floor, then toward the stairs to the second floor. She'd have to be quick. She shot a glance back at Riley, who was still looking at her like she'd offered to throw herself to the wolves.

She doesn't know I'm a wolf too, Madelyn thought. *Or a wolf's daughter, at least.*

It was hard to hold on to that sense of confidence once she was actually upstairs. She shut the door to the basement silently, panicked for a moment, then shouted, "Hello?"

She could practically feel Riley's disapproval from the floor below, but it was too late to come up with a real plan. "Hello!" she called again. "Mr. Bancroft?"

There was a pause on the stairs, then footsteps coming back down. She hadn't been sure what to expect from Riley's scant description of the man. He was tall, rangy, still wearing a forest-green jacket and his boots, which tracked dirt and leaf litter across the linoleum floor. He filled the doorway between the kitchen and the hallway, like he was too tall for his own house. He said nothing, only looked at her. "The . . . the door was open," she said. It seemed like a safe place to start. It had the benefit of being true.

He glanced toward the door, then fixed his stare back at her. "Yeah?"

"Yeah," Madelyn said. He continued to stare at her. "In case you were wondering why I didn't knock."

She had expected hostility, been prepared for menace. She wasn't sure how to deal with overwhelming awkwardness.

"Do you know who I am?" she asked. At his nod, she took a deep breath. "My mom said to find you if I needed help."

Bancroft raised a hand, and Madelyn tensed. But he just used it to scratch his throat underneath his jacket. Had he blinked? Madelyn was pretty sure he hadn't blinked.

"Help," he echoed.

"Yeah. I, um . . . Got lost?" *Wait, no.* "I mean, I lost something, in the woods, and was looking for it, and then I accidentally came out on this side of the woods—"

"I should take you back to your mother," Bancroft said, cutting off whatever the heck that had been.

Which she wanted to be thankful for. She needed to get him out of his house so Riley could escape without him realizing. Problem was, Madelyn did not want to go back to her mother. She didn't want her mother knowing she had left the house at all. But maybe she could convince her mother that the watchers had broken. Maybe in the storm? And she'd innocently wandered off. Would she believe it?

It didn't really matter. Madelyn had made herself this trap and now had to step into it. "Yeah," she said. "I need you to take me home."

Home, home, home, the whispers echoed in her head, a rare moment of them being in chorus, in a tone that sounded a little like a warning and a little like despair.

Bancroft looked behind his shoulder, at the stairs. "Now," Madelyn said, trying to keep him from going to the basement. "I don't want her to worry about me."

And that, at least, was true. Bad things happened when her mother worried about her. Bancroft slowly turned away from the stairs and faced her. He scratched again at his throat, digging his nails into the tender skin hidden under his coat's collar. "Let's go, then."

INTERLUDE: THE WITCH

Excerpt from *Bury the Echo: A Local Historian's Perspective on Folklore, Forests, and Other Important Stuff, or So I'm Telling Myself (Working Title)*, by Toby Walcott

The Witch of the Woods is somewhere between a local boogeyman, used to scare children into behaving, and a cryptid, on whom all manner of strange occurrences are blamed. The missing of Voynich Woods are often blamed on her, naturally, but so is everything from potholes (numerous, considering Roscoe is about 60 percent dirt roads) to the coyote population and, according to at least one neighbor, the number of ticks carrying Lyme disease. The temporary spates of warm weather in February and March are called "Witch Thaws" by locals, and they're said to be caused by her bad dreams waking her out of an ursine hibernation. (We'll see how that legend fares with climate change, I guess.) Every child growing up in Roscoe is threatened with the Witch for disobedience. Talking back, coming home late, lying, stealing your parents' cigarettes or booze: Any sign of badness could put the Witch's eye on you as a future victim.

But if she's the conduit for the strange and unlucky, the Witch of the Woods is also sometimes the one offering impossible solutions to impossible situations. One of my favorite Witch stories was recorded in the *Roscoe North Star* in 1850. It was said that the Witch met someone who had escaped slavery and was making her way toward Canada and freedom. The Witch gave her a canvas sack and told her that if enslavers got close, she should tear open the bottom of the bag and spill its contents on the ground. When the woman heard hounds baying on her trail at the edge of the woods, she did as the Witch instructed. The devil jumped out of the bag and called down such a storm that all the men and all their dogs were swept away in an ensuing flood. (Hilariously, both abolitionists and enslavers cited that story as "proof" that their side was right.)

This is stupid, but I had this thought right after Anna disappeared: that she had taken up the mantle of being the Witch of the Woods. Maybe she'd fought the devil to a draw to take up the title, or won it while hustling the pool tables at the Purple Pig. Better than imagining the alternative, right? I still always look for her during a thaw. Riley and Sam, if you ever read this (god, please don't read this unless it's a real book), you should know: Your mother would have made a good Witch.

Lillian left Roscoe as soon as she could without looking unforgivably coldhearted. She had enjoyed, for a while, being the center of attention after news of Camille's disappearance broke. But the reporters' focus on her was, in the end, only as a proxy for her sister. They hardly asked Lillian about what she'd seen; instead they asked a thousand questions about her sister, discarding her story for the ones they created. In their hands, Camille became clay, and they shaped her into something like their mother's treasured Dresden figurines: a little lost lamb, a gauzy princess. Something sweeter and softer than Lillian's sister had actually been. *You've got it wrong,* she wanted to shout at them sometimes. *She liked bloody ghost tales but cried whenever the cat got a bird. She named every tree in the orchard and insisted that the ones she talked to gave better apples and pears. Her sense of humor was terrible, even for a child. She could sulk for days and, when she was angry, would pinch me so viciously it bruised. She was beautiful, and she was silly, and she was real.*

Her parents' grief was even worse. Her mother was particularly overwrought in her hysterics, while Lillian's stepfather had all the vitality of an empty burlap sack. Lillian had always feuded with the both of them, and arguments with her mother had long since established a rhythm, a pattern by which a simple disagreement would escalate into a screaming match, accusations stacked atop counter-accusations. Her mother believed that Lillian was constantly undermining her, sabotaging her every chance at happiness. Of course, this was ridiculous; if anyone was being sabotaged, it was Lillian.

Since Camille's disappearance, however, the tenor of their fights had changed. Her mother called her cruel names and spoke a constant litany of accusations. Her stepfather had given up on attempting to keep the peace between his wife and stepdaughter, and Camille, of course, could no longer step in to distract them or soothe their tempers.

One night, Lillian made a poorer attempt than usual at pretending to be meek, penitent, and guilty, and her mother had confronted her. She followed Lillian upstairs, shouting wild and drunken accusations—some of them ironically close to the truth—and Lillian was, abruptly, done with pretending. She had tired of the script and no longer saw any use in playing along. Things had changed.

She looked at her mother and, maybe for the first time, saw her as she really was: not the towering figure she'd always been in Lillian's mind, a fierce dragon keeping her locked away like in a fairy tale, but a small, miserable woman, so greedy for love that she'd made her own daughter into her competitor. She stood swaying, one hand braced for balance against the oak door frame, her face blotchy and red from anger and the wine she'd sucked down at dinner. Her feet were bare, knobbly toes pale with the cold.

Lillian stopped shouting back at her, and started laughing.

Mother stared at her, shocked and . . . was she scared? For so long, Lillian had wanted nothing more than her mother's love and adoration; she wished she had known that her mother's fear would taste so much sweeter. "You are afraid of me, aren't you? You've called me a devil a hundred times, but now you think it might really be true." Lillian stepped forward, and Mother stumbled back, her bare feet slipping on the tiles.

"Look at me," Lillian demanded, thrilled by her mother's terror. "Look at me. See what I've become."

See how powerful she was; see how little her mother's cruelties mattered in the end, because Lillian had found that her own cruelty was more than a match for it.

What was the line in *Hamlet*? "Sorrows came not in single spies, but in battalions." Everyone was shocked, of course, that Mr. and Mrs. Voynich would perish so soon after their youngest daughter: Isabel Voynich first, from what the doctors declared apoplexy, and Phillip Voynich only a few weeks after his wife's funeral, from a terrible car accident. The town of Roscoe was shocked, but nobody was exactly surprised.

Just like nobody was surprised when Lillian Voynich, last of her name, announced that she could not stay in a house that reminded her of the family she had lost, and so would leave Roscoe and spend time abroad. She wanted to sell the house and the surrounding forest, but she was wary of letting the woods fall into someone else's hands when they contained so many of her secrets. She also had the idea that in five years' time, when Generous's wish came true for her, she might overwrite her own bad memories in that house with new ones of her daughter.

Lillian's intended world tour did not last long. As soon as she left Roscoe, a strange thing started happening to the skin of her hands: Dirt found its way into her nails, the lines of her palms, and covered her skin in a thin layer of grime. It didn't seem to matter how often or how carefully she cleaned herself, but she couldn't resist scrubbing at her skin until it was red. A few weeks after she left, the grime developed into a rash covering her hands. A few weeks after that, her cuticles started peeling away from her nail beds, and her fingers became pruned and soft, hideously numb, and the skin started to fall away at the gentlest touch. She soon wore gloves all the time, and long sleeves as well, to hide bruises that never healed, but turned black and seeped fluid that smelled like the bottom of a pond. No magic she could work made a difference, and the doctors she consulted could determine no cause.

Lillian found herself thinking compulsively of the springs in the forest around the house, cold as the heart of the mountain. One morning, she woke up from dreaming of dipping her ruined hands in the frigid water, as if that might settle the maddening itch under her skin. One didn't need to be a witch to realize this was no idle dream.

She returned to Roscoe, expecting it to seem smaller and more provincial than ever, but still somehow surprised by how much it had shrunk from her memory. There were fewer people on the streets in downtown Roscoe, fewer open shops; the outskirts revealed a lot of fallow fields, empty of grazing dairy cows or sheep.

The woods seemed darker than in her sun-dappled memories. Her driver passed the gatehouse, the only remnant of her parents' dreamed-of resort. She tugged off one of her gloves; the rot and infection had retreated from her nail beds. But a sense of *wrongness* still persisted, and it only became worse when she ventured into the woods themselves. Her skin prickled with the feeling of being watched, unwelcome. She made her way back to the Wishing Tree, though the oppressive atmosphere amid the trees threatened to make her knees buckle.

The Wishing Tree had died. Perhaps that was to be expected, considering the poisonous resentment that soaked the ground around it, like marsh gas erupting from underground. The bindweed that she had planted was sickly, leaves blackening in patches, white flowers giving off a corpsy perfume. She sent her senses into the ground; she had mixed in the objects from Generous's tree, little remnants that carried the power of all those foolish wishes and secret hopes. She'd doubted that such things could be used to work magic, but they had glowed in her sight with power, little magics on their own that could be repurposed. Their power had dimmed.

The trap she'd made had been beautiful: life and death, blood and iron, need and desire joined together. Lillian had sacrificed the thing she loved most in the world; Camille's pain and suffering had formed the bars of Generous's cage, and Lillian's grief was the lock and key.

Speaking of the devil—*and he shall come,* she thought, with a hysterical little laugh—the creature that had given its name as Generous paced balefully in the trap she had constructed. It had taken so many different forms since she had first met it in the woods: sometimes an animal, sometimes a man, and sometimes some chimeric creature that Generous might have taken from Lillian's nightmares. She could feel it trying to shift its shape now, but the trap held, Generous's shape held inside the vessel she had formed out of—well, out of Camille.

She stepped around the trap she had made, circling it, examining it. She leaned in close, nearly over the border she'd made, and then a force made her stumble back. She could feel the delicate web of magic stretch and buckle under the force of Generous's rage.

Not just Generous. The anger tasted so familiar, it could only come from Camille.

"No," she said, and for the first time felt regret sink its cold fingers into her.

She had been convinced that Camille, if called upon, would sacrifice herself for Lillian's happiness. She had said it often enough, hadn't she? That she could not be happy when Lillian was not, even though she had no idea how desperately unhappy Lillian was, how her future had closed in all around her until she knew it would take a miracle to save her.

"What would you do for me?" she had asked Camille one night. "If it meant I could be happy?"

"Anything," Camille had said. Hadn't she? But if she had, why could Lillian see Camille staring out from Generous's eyes? And why was she looking at Lillian with so much hate?

One of the first magics Lillian had taught herself was divination. She'd made her casting set from the tree's treasures: a couple of coins, one with a scarred face; bones from an unlucky fox that had wandered too close; the ribbon from Camille's nightgown. When she cast them, they were blunt in their instructions: Return home. Her power was tied to Voynich Woods, to the tree whose roots grew around her sister's. The longer she was away, the weaker her power would become.

What about the trap? She posed the question to the bones. She had broken Camille, bound her to Generous, and in doing so, had created something hungry enough that it would eat through itself. If left alone, it would dissolve itself, free Generous, and come after Lillian directly. She would have to sate Camille's rage and renew the binding that tied Generous to her.

Sate it how? she asked the bones. *Let Camille's rage fall on another person*, they told her. *Let it consume them, and she might sleep for a time.* But Lillian could not leave her unwatched.

She could not leave at all.

Lillian scratched absently at the raw, itching spots that dotted her hands and arms.

She asked in desperation if there was anything else she could do. This time, the bones gave a rather confused answer, hinting that she could unbind Camille and Generous herself. The configuration of the objects—the coins in opposing corners, the ribbon stretched between them, fox teeth scattered in a rough line—promised healing and harm both, a new deal for freedom that yet condemned her. She was tempted to throw the little divination set across the clearing, but she gathered it up instead, tucking it away in her bag.

"Little sister," Lillian called from the edge of the clearing. She didn't dare step closer. She thought of the locket she'd hung around Camille's neck, unforgivably unsentimental, she could see now. She could feel both Camille and Generous inside that clearing, testing the trap that she had made. "I'm sorry," she told Camille. "I shouldn't have left you alone with it. I—"

Camille's rage and resentment writhed and seethed, not even acknowledging her words. The thing in the clearing, she reminded herself, was not her little sister, just broken scraps and remnants attached to Generous. This was just its revenge: to turn her trap back on herself, to keep her in a house where she'd spent some of the most miserable years of her life.

She stood up, dusting the leaf litter off her knees. The clearing looked empty, but she could still feel Generous's attention on her, quieter but no less present than Camille's rage. Lillian gave it a little ironic curtsy. She still had the better of this deal, after all. She was the Witch of the Woods. She had her power, her magic, and in five years, she would have a child. No, a daughter. She didn't need to consult the divination bones again—she was sure that her wish-child would be a perfect little girl. Lillian made her way back to the house, already starting to think of names.

CHAPTER EIGHT

Riley stood with both hands covering her mouth, cowering against the rough cement wall in a corner of an old man's basement. She had pulled Sam close to her; her sister was shaking as well.

What are you doing? she thought. *Why are you letting her do this?*

She couldn't make out the conversation happening above her head, only the soft, controlled tones of Madelyn and Mr. Bancroft. Mr. Bancroft's heavy footfalls shaking dust down from the floorboards, and a softer creaking that she supposed belonged to Madelyn.

"Riley—" Sam whispered, but Riley held a finger up to her mouth, shushing her.

The front door opened, then shut. Riley darted over to the window and stood on tiptoes to watch Madelyn follow Mr. Bancroft to his truck. *Last chance,* she thought, though she wasn't sure what she could do. Break the window? Try to save Madelyn from saving her? The truck started and backed down the driveway while Riley was still trying to come up with a single shred of a plan.

"What do we do?" Sam whispered. "We can't let her go with him."

"*We* can't anything," she said, rounding on her sister. She was angry, even though Sam was thinking the same thing she had been. "What are you doing here? Did you follow me?"

"No!" Sam said, then must have realized what a ridiculous lie that was: She just happened to show up in the same place at the same time as Riley? She shifted into a counterattack instead. "What are *you* doing here? Who was that girl?"

Before Riley could think of a halfway decent lie, Sam added, "Is she your girlfriend?"

Complete static filled Riley's brain for a second. She looked Sam in the eyes and spoke slowly. "Do you think that breaking into someone's house is . . . a good first date?"

Sam shrugged. "No? Wait, does that mean she *is* your girlfriend? Because you were like, super into talking to her on the way over. You didn't even notice when I accidentally kicked a rock on the railroad tracks and it hit the rail and made this really loud—"

"She's not my girlfriend," Riley said. She could feel her face getting hot and tried to remember what she and Madelyn had even talked about on the long walk over. The questions Madelyn had asked ("You go to school every day?" "Your uncle just lets you leave the house?") gave Riley a pretty depressing idea of what her life was like, but they'd found things to talk about. Mostly the weird TV show that Madelyn was obsessed with. It had been an oddly pleasant walk, and Riley had thought to herself that she was glad for the distraction.

"Then why did you take her on a date to break into this house? Who lives here, anyway?"

"Mr. Bancroft," Riley said, trying to usher Sam to the stairs. She had no idea when the ranger would come back, and they needed to be far away from here when he did. She tugged on Sam's arm, but Sam had planted her feet on the cement floor and refused to move.

"The ranger in the woods?" Sam asked. "Why?"

See, here was the thing: Riley knew how to lie. She didn't do it often, as a rule, but when it was necessary—to get a teacher off her back, to stop Sam from wheedling her, to avoid a question that got too personal—she could press down the guilt and let out the lie. But her body had turned strange; there was a hole in her chest and a voice in her head, darkness oozing beneath her skin. Her little sister had followed her to a strange man's stranger house, and even if she hadn't seen everything Riley had, it didn't matter.

"Something did happen, didn't it," said Sam, when she didn't answer. "In the woods. I just turned around and you were gone, and I whistled for you but I didn't—there was—"

Riley knew how to lie, but Sam knew how to look for the truth, to hunt it down again and again. And Riley was no longer sure that keeping the truth from Sam would protect her from it.

"Something happened," she said. "I found the Wishing Tree."

Sam was looking at her carefully. Riley didn't want to tell her all of it—couldn't stomach the idea of doing that here, in this strange, unnerving house—so she settled on saying, "And something else found me there."

"Mr. Bancroft?"

"I don't *know*," Riley said. "I thought if I could find something that tied him to the woods or the disappearances, I could figure out what to do. Figure out what happened to me."

If you wanted to know, you could have asked, her mother's voice whispered. *I still owe you a secret.*

Like there wasn't a price attached to that. She was definitely going to keep that from Sam.

"It doesn't matter," she told Sam. "There wasn't anything upstairs. We need to get out of here before he—Sam!"

Sam had run back to the spot by the boiler where she'd been hiding and knelt down. "I saw something when I was hiding," she said. She wriggled her hand down into the narrow space behind the tank and slowly pulled something out. An old cigar box, with a fading picture of an old man in a cloak, carrying a lantern.

Sam shook the box. Things rattled inside it.

"Let me open it," Riley said, reaching for it.

"I found it," Sam protested.

Riley grabbed it out of her hands before she could argue more. What if it was booby-trapped? Or full of bones or teeth or mummified mice or something? Honestly, Sam would probably be more excited about mummified mice than anything, but that wasn't the point.

Riley was mildly disappointed to see that it just seemed to be a little keepsake box. There were some photos, a couple of folded pieces of paper, a single glove, an old house key, a couple of necklaces or something—

One of the chains looked familiar.

"Let me see," Sam said, pulling the box down so she could look inside. She spotted the chain quicker than Riley had, touching the matching one around her neck.

"Is that . . ."

Riley carefully pinched the chain between her fingers and

pulled it out. There was a long silver whistle on the end. The same one she had worn, and lost, in Voynich Woods.

• • •

"We should tell the police," Sam said for the third time.

They'd left Mr. Bancroft's house behind and were now walking home. Bancroft wasn't their neighbor by normal town standards—he lived more than a mile and a half from Toby's house—but they were in the same tangle of roads in the borderlands between the woods and the town. They took a shortcut through a farmer's field, mostly empty but for some distant, staring sheep, and then climbed up the hill to walk on the path beyond the tree line. She didn't want to be on the roads in case Mr. Bancroft drove past, and in the trees, she didn't have Voynich Woods in her peripheral vision.

"You want to tell the police that we both skipped school to go break into some old man's house, in case he was . . ."

She still didn't even know. She'd found evidence, sure. Of what, though?

"But he has something to do with the disappearances," Sam insisted.

The box they'd taken from his basement was in Riley's backpack. Sam hadn't fought her for its possession. Even if it wasn't a bloody knife or the mask with the sun/wheel, just touching the box felt bad.

"We don't know that," she said.

"That's your whistle!" They'd found other things. Shoelaces. A pair of cheap earbuds. A key ring with a picture of a cat encased in plastic. Riley had stared hard at a brass key with a faded orange sticker on it, trying so hard to remember if she'd seen it in her mother's hand, if it would fit into the doorknob of that old apartment on Route 18, just past the McDonald's. But nothing *conclusive*. They'd look through the other stuff at home, but Riley didn't know any more than when she'd woken up this morning.

"Toby ordered that whistle off Amazon," she said. "And they're sold in like, every camping store everywhere."

"They're trophies. He's probably a serial killer," hissed Sam, with the conviction of someone who had watched hundreds of hours of true-crime documentaries. "Maybe they can finger-print the box?"

"And whose fingerprints would be all over it?" Riley asked, waving her hand. She was trying not to think about Sam's easy accusation of Bancroft being a serial killer. "I don't want to talk to the police. They already believed Bancroft over me. And—"

And if they did believe her, someone like Lieutenant Harvey would have a lot of follow-up questions. He'd want to know what happened to her, and he'd want to see proof, and it would be a battle to convince him, and Riley already felt like she was fighting for her life.

She realized that she was walking alone; Sam had stopped a few feet behind. Her head was ducked down, and she seemed to be looking everywhere except at Riley.

"If we don't tell anybody, what happens if he comes back for you?"

That bass note kicked in Riley's chest. Sam's distress was etched in obvious lines on her face, the downward curve of her mouth, the tight furrow between her eyebrows. Riley thought of her sister's insistence that it was her fault. She'd confessed it like a crime.

"It'll be fine," she said.

"Stop saying that!" Sam said, loud enough that she scared up a couple of crows from the trees. They swooped into the air, scolding the girls for the disturbance. "This is just like when Mom disappeared. No, it's worse. Because I believed you back then. And now I know you only say that when things are really bad."

It felt like the ink in Riley's veins was pooling in the hollow of her throat, thick and sticky, hard to swallow around. She walked back until she stood in front of Sam: close enough to touch, to grab her sister's shoulders, but not sure if it would be welcome.

"Nothing that happened was your fault," Riley said quietly.

Sam's arms, which had lain limply at her sides, twitched, then grabbed hold of Riley. Her small fingers bit into Riley's sides. She still didn't speak, and that worried Riley. Was it stupid to want to make her sister feel better when awful, paranormal shit was going down? Probably, but Riley never claimed not to be a complete dumbass when it came to Sam.

Sam opened her mouth, hesitated, then said, "What if it was the Witch of the Woods?"

It was a quick leap from trophy-keeping serial killers to the Witch of the Woods. Riley wanted to dismiss it, because the Witch had always just been a boogeyman, the local scare tactic to get children to go to bed on time. Something for the old men to discuss over giant cups of Dunkin' coffee.

"Everyone says that she's still there."

"Everyone saying something doesn't mean—"

"I know it doesn't mean it's true," Sam said, exasperated. "But there was something in the woods that day."

They were standing on a narrow dirt path that wandered through the trees behind the houses on Hillcrest Road. Dog walkers used it, mountain bikers, the odd person on horseback. She'd never really considered before how thinly the veneer of Roscoe lay over this part of the mountain.

She couldn't believe she'd never asked Sam what she'd seen. She'd been lost too, hadn't she? And she had come home as well.

"What did you see, Sam?" Riley asked.

"It was weird in the trees," she said.

"Weird how?"

"I don't know how to say it," she said. "Like . . . warm where it should have been cold. Summer in some spots, even though it was fall. When we got to the Obelisk, I kept thinking I heard someone singing, but I knew I wasn't hearing it? Like, it was in my head, but my ears kept confusing it for something that was in the air. And then I turned around, and you were gone. I used my whistle, but I didn't hear anything back. I tried to find you, and—it started raining. And . . . then I was home."

"And then you were home?" Riley repeated. "You mean, you found your way home?"

"I guess," Sam said. "I just remember being soaked and coming out of the trees, and Toby was there. And I told him you were . . ."

Riley thought of what Jane Doe had said. *She got home safe. I made sure of it.* At least there was one entity in Voynich Woods that wasn't horrible. She hugged Sam again. "Come on," she said. "Let's go home."

◆ ◆ ◆

Riley wouldn't normally look twice at a strange car in front of Toby's museum—it was always open for self-guided tours, and it was still tourist season, after all. But next to the white SUV sat one of Roscoe's police cruisers.

She had a moment of panic, thinking that Bancroft had come there, ready to have them arrested for breaking into his house. But no, this was a new SUV, bright white where it wasn't splattered with mud from back roads, and not his old truck.

Riley and Sam snuck quietly up to the barn, where they could hear voices, and peered through the doors. Toby stood there with Sergeant Bajrovic and the woman from DCFS, Ivy.

"Shit," she whispered. She pulled Sam around to the side of the barn, then pushed the cigar box from Mr. Bancroft's into her hands. "Take this, go up to your room, and don't come down until they're gone."

"Who is it?" she whispered back.

"Family services," Riley said, grimacing. "They were at the police station last night too."

Sam's eyes grew round. The middle school wouldn't let out for another thirty minutes or so. It was conceivable for Riley to come home early, but Sam skipping school would definitely count against them in any kind of investigation Ivy opened.

Sam was too little to remember as much about the constant carousel of DCFS agents coming through Mom's and then Toby's house, but she knew enough not to argue. She took the box and went around the back of the barn, crouching below the windows. The barn was a couple hundred feet from the house, tucked farther back away from the road. If Sam stuck to the far edge of the fields, where honeysuckle was overgrowing the old fence, she could stay out of sight while sneaking into the house. As long as someone distracted Ivy, anyway.

Riley took a couple of grounding breaths. She was tempted to run to her room alongside Sam, but she worried that would just give Ivy an excuse to come into the house. She stood up straighter, then remembered who she was and slouched a little.

The three of them were standing in front of the exhibit about lampmouths, the little floating lights that led travelers astray, like will-o'-the-wisps. If you got close to them, they looked like hanging filaments, but they had teeth and an appetite for human flesh.

"We try to make it a little scary," Toby was saying. He was wearing the same strained smile he gave neighbors who said something casually homophobic, or teachers at school who complimented Riley's or Sam's grades despite their "difficult upbringing."

"Gotta give them something they can write about on Tripadvisor. But we keep it as focused on the history and facts as we can."

"Of course!" Ivy laughed. She was standing a little too close to Toby; Riley could see it in the way he shifted back and forth, hands stuffed into his coat pockets. "And the history is *so* fascinating, isn't it?"

Sergeant Bajrovic stood impassively to one side, looking

deeply uncomfortable, and she was the one who spotted Riley first. "Hi, Riley. Looking better today."

Riley felt herself mirroring Toby's strained smile. "Hi, Sergeant Bajrovic. Hi, Ivy. This is a surprise."

"I did say that I'd check in on you," Ivy said. Her warm smile morphed into something more serious. "Your uncle was nice enough to give me the grand tour. So informative! You really do your research, huh?"

Toby made some awkward jazz hands. "Historian. I dropped out of grad school when, uh . . . my sister needed help. But I was always a little obsessed with the local stories."

Sergeant Bajrovic nodded. "It's true, he was."

"That's right," Ivy said. "You went to high school together. I should have just asked you for the lowdown instead of trying to get through the case notes. Trying to sort through all the shorthand was so annoying."

Toby was practically sweating, even though it was a cool day. He'd never had much of a game face for DCFS encounters. Anna hadn't either, but she always defaulted to a resting bitch face that looked like she was just waiting for a chance to eat the caseworker alive. Toby had a resting "please leave me alone" face, which usually resulted in the opposite.

"Was that everything you needed, Ivy?" Toby said.

"Oh, yes," she said. "Thank you."

Ivy was looking at Riley with a canny expression, and Riley couldn't help but glance with that inner sight into what Ivy wanted.

Hazel's wants had been a diffuse cloud around her, half-formed and yearning. Madelyn's had been sewn up inside her.

Ivy's were neat, contained, like a portal in her chest that

matched the hole in Riley's. But it was like looking through a window into the dark, with strange things moving out beyond. Riley felt herself drawn into that darkness. Looking at the ocean had made her feel like this: insignificant, small, infinitely weak in comparison. Like she was lucky that nothing had decided to bother with her.

But she'd never been lucky in her life.

Something had seen her looking. Something was looking back, and she couldn't seem to drag her gaze away from it.

"All right, I'll walk you to your car," Toby was saying to Ivy. "It was great meeting you, Ivy. Let me know if you ever want to come on a real tour, okay? Right, Riley?"

"Sorry, I zoned out for a second." It was Riley speaking, thankfully, not her body steering itself without her. "Nice seeing you again, Ivy."

Ivy smiled and said, "Really, please reach out if—"

Riley was already walking away, anxious to get away from Ivy's gaze. She made her way to the front porch and collapsed in one of the old wicker chairs, not glancing back until she heard Ivy's car start up. Toby was talking quietly with Sergeant Bajrovic. They both looked back at Riley, in a way that made her want to sink into a hole; both of them were obviously worried. Obviously seeing Anna when they looked at her. If they only knew where she'd come from.

Toby shook Sergeant Bajrovic's hand and then came back to the porch and sat on the chair next to Riley. Once the two cars were gone, she asked him, "What did Ivy want this time?"

"Nice invasive home inspection," he said. It had been a while since DCFS had demanded one of those. "Apparently, having you pee in a cup wasn't enough. She tested me, then dug through everyone's bedrooms and commented on how I hadn't taken the trash out in a couple days. Like I might not have anything else on my mind?"

"Sorry," she said. She felt like she was just made of apologies when it came to Toby. Was this what her mom had felt like? she wondered. Like bad luck just followed her, infected everyone around her? If it wasn't stupid supernatural fuckery, it was the mundane garbage of authorities flexing their power, all of them just waiting for her to follow in her mother's footsteps and screw everything up.

Toby nodded. "You don't owe me an apology, not for that." He scratched at the raspy stubble on his chin. "An explanation might be nice, though."

Riley froze. "For what?"

"For why you and your sister are both home instead of in school."

Shit.

"Yeah, good thing Ivy didn't notice Sam's light on," said Toby. Riley cringed. Sam's room was in the back of the house, facing the barn. Her sister was incredibly smart about so many things and still remained a complete dumbass about others.

"I didn't feel good at school," Riley said. "And told her that I was cutting out during lunch. She . . . followed me home."

It had the benefit of being sort of true, even if it ignored a huge swath of the afternoon.

Toby nodded, but his shoulders were still tense. "And it didn't occur to you to call me for a ride? Or tell your teachers?"

"I'm sorry—" she said again, but he steamrolled right over her.

"Or that maybe you disappearing *again*, now with your

sister, might give me a heart attack? Christ, Rye," he said explosively. He leaned back in the chair, digging his fists into his eyes. "The school called me five minutes before Ivy showed up and started demanding to know how often I clean the goddamn bathroom. I had to make small talk with her while feeling like I was going to puke."

"You said I didn't have to go," she tried, even though she knew, as she said it, that it was the flimsiest excuse.

"I don't care that you weren't in school," he shouted. Riley flinched back; it took a lot to make Toby raise his voice. "I care that you think I'm so stupid or uncaring that I wouldn't notice that you had disappeared! Again!"

He stood up and leaned out over the porch railing, staring hard at the fields. "I hate this. I hate this so much, because it's exactly what your mom did. Something would happen and she would just disappear into it. Shut me out, shut your grandparents out. Her friends. Everyone."

Riley sometimes forgot that her mother's disappearance had happened not just to her and Sam, but to Toby as well. His older sister. Even after Anna had pushed all those other people away, Toby had stayed. Had dropped out of school, had come back to a hostile hometown, just in case she deigned to let him help her. Stayed here when she finally did disappear, because someone needed to clean up her mess.

"I'm trying not to be mad about this. But it's easier to be mad than scared, and Riley, honey, you're scaring the shit out of me," said Toby. "I messed up with your mom, and I promised that I wouldn't let this happen to you too."

Riley couldn't move. She was frozen by Toby's words—

worse, by the grief in his voice. Then she thought again about what he'd said.

"How did you mess up? With Mom?"

The tension went out of Toby's frame, and he sagged against the railing a little. "I shouldn't have said that."

"Why?"

"Rye, it's not—I don't really want to get into it, and it's not relevant. We can talk about it later."

That floating feeling was coming back into Riley's body. The same she'd felt with Hazel in the library, untethered from her body, but plugged into something else.

One wish, her mother's voice whispered to her. *One secret, and one boon. I can tell you if you want to know. Tell you more than he would even be able to.*

Riley could see her again, a faded, flickering outline: Anna with her short, choppy hair and black eyeliner, sitting next to her brother on the porch railing. One foot propped up, the other swinging restlessly.

Do you want to know what he's seen in the woods? Generous asked, her mother's lips shaping the question. It was no longer content to be a voice in Riley's head, it seemed. *Why he's so obsessed with the strange things in the Voynich Woods that he built a museum about them?*

"No," Riley said. The piece of Generous inside her dug its roots into her. She could feel the prickly sensation as it crawled up her throat, spread out around her.

"No what?" Toby said warily. He didn't turn around, thank god.

The porch tilted slightly sideways. Riley could hear birdsong,

loud and piercing. It took her a moment to realize it was coming from inside her chest, another to remember her dream
that morning: pulling open her ribs and placing the dead bird
inside. But if it was dead, what was singing?

"No, we can't talk about it later," Riley said, but it wasn't
her voice, or at least, her idea to speak. It was like the birdsong
flowing through her, sharp and forceful.

Toby turned to her then. His eyes grew wide at whatever
he was seeing, and she raised her arms up, shielding—herself?
Toby? She didn't want him to see her; she didn't want to see
him reacting to whatever he saw. "Don't look at me," she said.
"Just tell me."

Toby jerked his head down. "She was using again," he said
in a rush, like the words were being jerked out of him. "All the
signs were there, but she'd been doing so well that I didn't want
to call her on it. I thought—it's a rough patch, she needed to
get through a few weeks and then . . ."

Riley leaned back. The words sat in the space between them.

"She promised me," she said. "After she . . . After I found
her . . ."

Toby knew what she meant and didn't make her say it. "She
promised me too," he said.

"She almost *died*," said Riley, suddenly spitting mad. "I
believed her."

"I did too. I wouldn't have let you and Sam live with her
again if I hadn't. But she called me that day, told me her asshole
boss had accused her of stealing from the till, and she . . ."

"She what?" Riley said. She could see it, just like she'd seen
Madelyn and the girl in the library: secrets and desires and
fears, the tangle of them. Instead of Madelyn's cracked wall or

Hazel's vague outlines, Toby's were wrapped tightly around him, almost strangling him. "Tell me," she demanded.

"She was going to give up her parental rights," Toby said.

The words didn't even make sense at first. Her mom? Giving up Riley and Sam, after fighting tooth and nail for years to keep them? Her mother had told her *countless* times that Riley and Sam were the most important things in her life—the only reason she hadn't fallen farther into drug use, the only reason she kept trying to get clean. All so they could stay together, be a family.

Riley stared at him. "What?"

"She—" Toby's hands curled into fists on the porch railing. "She thought that it was only a matter of time before DCFS took you and Sam, that she'd never be able to get clean if she stayed in Roscoe, and . . . Rye, please—"

"Tell me." There was a terrible weight in the words, a terrible compulsion behind them.

"She couldn't get clean if she stayed in Roscoe," he said again. "And she could never afford to leave Roscoe with the two of you. And I told her she was probably right."

Toby looked like he was going to throw up, pale even in the golden afternoon light.

Riley looked over at the . . . it wasn't her mother's ghost. Echo, maybe? "She was going to leave us?" she asked. "And you told her she should."

Anna, or the thing that looked like her, didn't meet Riley's eyes. Toby still seemed frozen, either from finally having told her this secret, or from the thick, heavy magic she could still feel radiating out of her. There were no more answers either of them could give.

Riley stood up jerkily and ran inside, up the stairs. She ignored Toby calling her name, ignored Sam's curious, wary look from her doorway. She went into her room and shut the door, locked it.

When she looked in her mirror, she could see the barest discoloration staining her skin above her shirt collar, faint enough to be a smudge of dirt, maybe. But when she unbuttoned the flannel, she could see that the edges of the wound were peeling up and out, hard as bark. It was reaching up past the neckline of her tank top now, nearly at her collarbones. The dark lines branching off it looked like thorny brambles, tangling around each other. The skin surrounding it was a bruised, rotting purple.

She could see her mother in the reflection, the same as she'd seen her on the porch, in the bathroom of the high school. Anna sat on her daughter's bed, staring at her.

"Why do you always look like her?" Riley asked.

If Generous was going to haunt her like this, she wanted to know why. But she already did, didn't she?

"It's because she did disappear into the woods, right?" Riley asked. "She's not lying in an anonymous grave somewhere, and she's not a fugitive. You took her and . . . what? Ate her? Consumed her? Cracked her open like you're doing to me? What happens to the people who disappear?"

Generous looked down at her mother's hands; Riley hadn't seen them in years, but they were instantly recognizable: the hooked scar across her thumb, the faint freckles, the torn cuticles. "Everybody who hears that call and follows it to the clearing? They want to disappear, at least a little bit."

"So she'd given up."

Generous turned its gaze back to her. "She didn't give up. The song can be many things; it's made to exploit. You heard your sister calling your name, didn't you?"

"What did she hear?" Riley said. "Her dealer?" It was so stupid that she could still be hurt by all this, but she couldn't help it. Every time she thought that she had settled her feelings about her mom, something happened and it was a fresh wound all over again.

"She heard your voice," said Generous. In her mother's voice, and with her mother's face.

Riley whirled around, fist raised, ready to strike out. But of course, the room was empty; it was just her head that was crowded with ghosts.

CHAPTER NINE

Bancroft wouldn't stop staring at her, eyes drifting over to her even while he was driving. His jaw worked as they drove, and Madelyn remembered what Riley had said about chewing tobacco. The smell of it filled the car: bitter, metallic almost, and sweetly rotten. Every so often, he leaned out the window and spat a stream of it out.

"So you know my mother?" Madelyn said. Circe, while pursuing one of her mysteries on the HMS *Broomstick*, never came right out and accused someone of something. She always asked sideways questions, moving around the accused in circles. Madelyn could do that, she thought. It sounded better than falling into a panic that her mother might discover she'd found ways to get around her wards and watchers.

"Known her for longer than you have," said Bancroft. There was a teasing lilt to his voice, and a lazy smile that didn't seem to sit right on his face. It made her uneasy, this hint that he knew more than she did.

"Is that why you have my copy of *Frankenstein*?" she asked.

"I have more than that," he said. He smiled again, like he had a secret, then spat another stream of grayish-brown liquid out the window. "Your mother told me to get rid of it, before it corrupted you."

"Why would a book—"

Bancroft cleared his throat with a rough, phlegmy sound. "'I will avenge my injuries; if I cannot inspire love—'"

"'I will cause fear,'" she said. Like the words were waiting in her mouth, needing only a prompt.

He raised his eyebrows and grinned again, his teeth gray and his gums stained dark. "You have no idea, do you? No wonder Mother keeps you so close."

She didn't like the way he smiled at her. She was starting to regret her plan—what plan? more like impulse—but tried to pull Circe and her persona back around her. Tall and severe, but with a disarming smile that she could switch on to charm people, switch off to intimidate them.

"Do you know what happened to the girl who got lost in the woods yesterday?"

He looked at her for a moment, considering. "I might," he said. He leaned out the window to spit again, and she noticed something: a scar, high up on his neck, that looked a lot like hers. As he leaned out, the scar stretched, and she realized—it wasn't flesh that had knitted itself together.

It was a seam. She could see stitches, neat and tied off with white string.

"I might know that she was chosen. Sent up to the Wishing Tree. Chest cut through and heart offered up. Only she came back, didn't she?" He turned his smile back on her. "Should we keep comparing what we know and don't know?"

The bottom dropped out of Madelyn's stomach. The chorus in her head shrieked.

His chuckle was wet and amused. "You don't have to worry, Maddie. I'll fix it. Mother made me a mask for these situations."

"Let me help you," Madelyn said, switching tactics in desperation. "Let me go and I'll help you. I can free you from her control. I'm—I'm a witch too."

"There's only one witch in these woods," he said. "And you'll never be it."

"I have magic too," she insisted, but her voice shook, and she wasn't sure she believed it.

"Maybe, but she's bound you tighter than a book," Bancroft said softly. "I bring you back to her, she'll be happy with me. Maybe finally give me my reward."

"What reward?" Madelyn demanded, desperately hoping that she could still bargain with him. Then he looked at her, and she remembered the paragraph someone had marked in the book. *I remembered that I was forever deprived of the delights that such beautiful creatures could bestow.*

Madelyn realized that they were approaching the long, winding road that led to her house—far closer than Bancroft or anyone should have been able to reach, with all the wards Mom kept in place. "Y-you can't be here," she said. "The wards—"

"I have a pass," he said. He opened his mouth, stretching his jaws open unnaturally wide, and in the back of his throat, Madelyn could see a dull shine. Tarnished coins from the Wishing Tree lined his throat. He reached his dirty fingers into his mouth and plucked one out, glistening with more of that foul brown fluid. He laughed as Madelyn recoiled in disgust and flicked the coin toward the ward: a deer skull with honeysuckle growing over it, the empty, caved-in skull stuffed with a rotted lace handkerchief. The coin landed a little short, and Madelyn realized that there were other coins in the dirt around it. Had Bancroft left them all? How long had he been coming to her house? She'd thought she'd known every danger that her house contained; it wasn't safe by any stretch, but it was *known*. What else was it hiding from her?

I may have made a mistake, she thought, feeling her stomach cramp in fear.

Bancroft wiped his damp fingers on his shirt. "I showed you mine. You gonna show me how *you* got past the watchers?"

She had definitely made a mistake.

Circe, in the murder mystery episode, had made a quick escape over the side of the ship when the cook realized she was onto him for murdering the picky passenger. Madelyn could do the same. She grabbed the door handle and yanked. Bancroft was driving slowly over the narrow and rutted dirt road, and it might hurt to jump out, but it wouldn't kill her. She'd take a twisted ankle or broken wrist over whatever his rancid smile promised.

He laughed at her when the handle clicked uselessly, the door stuck fast. She shoved herself against the window, not understanding the door's refusal to move. Bancroft's laughter rang in the car.

"You could try breaking the window next, if you want?" he offered. "But this is what I do. It's what Mother made me for."

Bancroft's truck finally came to a stop in front of the house. He got out and took his time coming around the car, and when he unlocked her door, she heaved it open and lurched from her seat. But he was too quick. He grabbed her by the collar of her jacket, and when she tried to wriggle out, he shook her like she was a recalcitrant kitten. He was strong, arms like tree limbs, and he hauled her up the splintered steps of the house as easily as he might have carried a bag of groceries.

She twisted out of her jacket and bolted down the steps, but Bancroft caught her first by the wrist and then by the hair, dirty fingers digging right into the scalp. At some point, Madelyn had taught herself not to scream; nobody was around to hear it, and it only ever made her mother angrier. But one tore itself out of her at this.

"Why are you fighting?" Bancroft said, dragging her inside. "Don't you love our Mother?"

Here in her mother's house, she'd never been able to work any magic. Not since the dandelions, since that first dream of waking up in the basement. All her scars stayed stubbornly shut, as if too scared to disobey her.

But the house was filled with her mother's clutter, and she grabbed desperately at the piles of random, half-finished projects. Papers fell to the floor, paintbrushes and crochet hooks went flying, and then a pair of sewing shears were in her hand.

Madelyn drove them into what she could reach. She felt the shears catch in the soft part of his neck, and something cool and wet spilled out over her knuckles, something that smelled like sweet rot and dead wood, the peppery smell of crushed insects. Nails and sodden bits of cloth and moss cascaded down to the floor. But Bancroft didn't stop, yanking her down the creaking wooden stairs into the basement. Coins tumbled on the steps as he went.

He shoved her into a room under the stairs. It was the size of a closet, wide enough to sit but not to lie down. There were no lights, and the ceiling sloped down steeply enough that Madelyn hit her face on it. She'd never been able to shake the feeling that she was locked in a coffin while she was in it.

An hour or two ago, she'd been in the sunlight, walking with Riley. She'd done the brave thing, the stupid thing, thinking she'd be able to turn the situation around. When had anything ever gone her way, though?

It took her a long moment to realize that there was light leaking through the keyhole in the door. She pushed her face against the cold metal of the door plate, trying to see through the narrow hole. Bancroft was leaning against the wall. That dark liquid had spilled down over his jacket and soaked into his shirt. He looked at it in confusion. Bancroft's skin had taken on a greenish tinge, and he pressed his fingers clumsily to his neck. He turned briefly, and Madelyn could see that there was a long, neat slit open beneath his jaw. Not ragged like Madelyn had clawed it open, but—

Like she'd torn the seam holding him together.

He pawed at his throat again, and Madelyn winced, thinking that he was trying to—literally—pull himself back together. But he instead simply ran his fingers along the opening in his skin, like he was curious, exploring.

His hand shook and fell away from his neck. Something rolled out from his fingers: a tarnished coin, which fell onto the floor with a dull clink. Twisted, rusted nails followed it, rattling onto the cement. They'd been inside him.

"Mr. Bancroft?" Madelyn asked urgently. "I can help. I can—Mr. Bancroft? If you let me out, I can—"

She racked her brain, trying to think of what she could offer him.

"That girl," he said. Whatever power had kept him going was fading fast. His skin looked like moldering old paper, misshapen and wavering.

"What girl?" she asked. "Riley? What did you do to her? What did Mother do?"

No answer. She slammed her hand against the door, over and over. "Mr. Bancroft? Fuck!" she said.

Had she ever said that word aloud in this house? She couldn't remember. Mother didn't like it. Especially didn't like to hear it from Madelyn, who should be clean and purehearted in everything she did.

If you only knew, Mother, Madelyn thought. But that was the problem, wasn't it? Mother did know. She knew what Madelyn really was, and that was why she brought her down to the basement. She wasn't purehearted, she wasn't good, she had disobeyed and she deserved—

She hammered against the door again, until her hand was hot and throbbed with pain. "Please!" she screamed. "I'm sorry. I'll be good! I'll—"

The strength ran out of her legs. "Jane," she said. "Jane, Jane, Jane, please, I—"

There was no water here. There was nobody to help her. She didn't remember what was coming for her, only that it was bad, only that it would destroy the small pieces of herself that she'd managed to make her own. Her mother would come home and find her, and then—

What? What was going to happen to her?

Something was moving under Madelyn's skin, aching to burst out of her. But it took so much effort to force her sluggish magic past the scars that she'd stopped trying. Until she had heard Jane singing down in the well. Until Riley had needed her help.

Madelyn gradually became aware of her body again, the cold of the cement seeping into her skin. She wasn't sure how much time had passed. She was tempted, for a second, to stay where she was. Wait for what was coming, whatever it would be. What did it matter, after all? Whatever Riley thought, Madelyn's body didn't belong to her. It was and always would be at her mother's beck and call.

Madelyn had absent-mindedly started running her fingers across the walls of the closet when she felt a scratch in the wood. She looked closer, shifting next to it. Tiny words had been scratched into the plaster, a whole column of them. At the top, the words looked the most faded. Each line looked newer, the scratches fresher and their lines sharper.

Madelyn was here.

Madelyn was here.

Madelyn was here.

Madelyn was here.

Madelyn was here again.

The voices were kicking up a ruckus, so loud that it was hard to think around their noise. "Is this you?" she asked. She'd always known the house was haunted. She just had assumed it was haunted by other dead people. Not dead versions of herself. Was that what happened in the basement that she couldn't remember? She thought of Mr. Bancroft, the seam that she'd seen across his neck. Was that what her scars were? If they opened up, would coins and nails come spilling out of her?

This is a dream, some dead version of herself had written.

But I keep having it.

There was a spot on the door where it was splintered, filled with narrow gouges, as if someone had—over and over again—scratched at it until they could pull a splinter free.

She dug her nails in until she could yank out a piece, then paused, with the point of it hovering over the soft, damp plaster. She thought about that word "again," and how resigned it looked. She wondered how many had just sat in the darkness, never seeing the notes.

Never again, she scrawled. A promise to all the parts of herself that she couldn't remember, that she'd lost along the way. Madelyn shut her eyes, trying to recapture some of the feeling she'd had while walking with Riley through town, the ordinary things that they'd talked about in between conversations about life and death and the "stupid paranormal shit" that Riley now found herself mired in. She tried to lose herself in the memory of sunshine on her face, the wideness of the sky when there weren't trees all around her.

She had almost lulled herself into calm when she heard the front door open and shut, then her mother's measured footsteps coming down the stairs. Madelyn quietly moved back to the keyhole.

"Oh," Mom said, spotting the corpse. "Mr. Bancroft. I wasn't expecting you to stop by." Her mother stepped gingerly over the pool of liquid that had collected around him. She squatted down next to Bancroft, pushing his head until it swiveled away from her, exposing the long tear in his throat. "Well, that's not great," she muttered, then sighed. "I really need you up and about tonight. But I've got time for a field repair."

She moved out of Madelyn's sight and rummaged around on the other side of the room before coming back and crouching down next to him. There was a long, curved needle in one hand, threaded with rough white thread.

Madelyn thought at first that her mother hadn't realized she was there—or maybe she wished for it, even if it meant she'd be left locked in this coffinlike room. But Mom looked over her shoulder, right at the door's keyhole where Madelyn had crouched. She sighed again, a familiar tone of disappointment.

"You know, Maddie, my mother," she said, then scoffed a little. As if just the memory of Madelyn's grandmother was a disappointment. Madelyn had never met the woman. She'd asked about her grandparents once, and Mom got a dangerous look in her eyes and asked Madelyn, *Aren't I enough family for you? Why do you need anyone else?* Madelyn recognized a warning in her mom's voice when she heard it, and she had never asked again.

"My mother hated that I had a spark of creativity in me. That I could make beautiful things and breathe life into them. Transform what was ugly and useless and make it useful and wonderful. She thought there was something rotten in me."

As she spoke, she slid the curved needle through Bancroft's opened skin, first one flap and then the other, and pulled them back together with quick, graceful tugs.

"And all I ever wanted to do was create. Make beautiful things and breathe life into them. Transform what was ugly and useless and make it wonderful."

It was almost hypnotizing to watch, calming, her mother's clever hands working their magic. She didn't flinch as the needle went through Bancroft's flesh, and neither did he, obviously. He was dead.

"Or," her mother said, "take dead things and give them a new purpose." She tied off the string, took her long, sharp scissors in her other hand, and cut cleanly through the thread. Then she picked up the coin that Bancroft had torn out of his throat, pinched open his mouth, and pushed it deep back into his mouth. His limbs twitched weakly.

"Guess we'll need more than that," Mom said, sighing. She walked off again, and Riley heard her open a drawer with a loud, metallic rattle. She came back cupping a handful of something she couldn't see. More coins, Madelyn thought, until some of them fell out onto the floor. Twisted iron nails, dark with age.

"I don't think he really needs to talk anymore. Right, Maddie?" Mom had her fingers deep in his mouth. "I suspect he might have said more than I wanted."

She sent a sly look over her shoulder, and Madelyn had to fight the urge to pull away from the keyhole in the door. But then her mother turned back to her work, thankfully blocking Madelyn's view of Bancroft's face.

There was a short, cut-off groan, and Madelyn forced herself to look again. Bancroft was getting jerkily to his feet, her mother helping to keep him from overbalancing. He was making these short, panting groans.

"Up we go, Mr. Bancroft. There we are. Feeling a little

steadier on your feet?" Her mother moved back a few steps, and Madelyn caught a glimpse of dark metal spikes protruding from Bancroft's mouth. Like he'd eaten a spider, and its legs were stuck in his lips. She looked away before her brain could come up with more things that were even more awful than reality.

"I think that it's time for you to bring me the girl," Mother said. "She's been resistant so far, and time is running out. The net's getting weaker."

Bancroft nodded miserably and made a garbled sound. *Yes, Mother.* Mother patted his cheek.

He went unsteadily up the stairs, and then it was Madelyn and her mother, the thick wooden door separating them.

Why was it that the voices in her head always fell silent whenever Mother came so close? Were they as afraid of her as Madelyn was?

There was a snap of metal as her mother unlatched the door, a creak as she opened it. Her mother looked so beautiful standing with the basement light haloing her hair, beautiful and stranger than anything Madelyn would find in the woods. Her mother had always been an artist, capturing and crafting beauty, and if Madelyn had inherited any of her talent, she would have tried to capture this moment, freeze it. Just the two of them: her mother in the light, and Madelyn forever in her shadow.

She took a step forward, and Madelyn scrambled back until her head hit the slanting wall behind her. Her mother kept coming forward, reaching her spidery fingers out until they caressed Madelyn's cheek. She might as well have pinned her in place.

"Maddie, sweetheart," her mother said, and Madelyn tensed up as she was pulled into a firm hug.

It wasn't that her mother was never affectionate with her, but her mother's hugs had always been a little hungry. Madelyn's participation was unnecessary; her mother was hugging her, trying to impart affection to Madelyn, and it was her role to accept it. She always felt like some small animal being toyed with by a big predator, and as unpleasant as it was, trying to fight it or run away would be worse.

"You're the most beautiful thing I ever made," Mom whispered. "The biggest miracle. And the biggest mistake. I guess it's time to start over again."

And with that, she started to drag Madelyn out to the dark recesses of the basement.

CHAPTER TEN

Riley's room had a window in it that was tilted at a forty-five-degree angle, built below the eaves of the steep roof. She'd always thought it was strange, but Toby had told her that a lot of the older farmhouses had them. They were called witch windows. Witches supposedly couldn't fly into them, so any children sleeping inside were protected.

He'd also told her that this was, in all likelihood, complete bullshit. This area had plenty of hang-ups about witches, but the windows were just an architectural quirk. But it made for a good story, and good stories were what he dealt in.

She'd crawled out her witch window when, after she'd been holed up in her room for a couple hours, Toby started trying to talk to her through the locked door. There was a gable beneath the window where she could sit, as long as she didn't mind dangling her feet off the ledge. From here, she faced the tree line, the path that led up to Voynich Woods. She watched the sun retreat behind the mountain.

She hoped Toby thought she was just being dramatic. Like, whatever had happened on the porch was just teenage hormones or something, instead of wondering how she'd forced him to spill a secret.

"Do you think walnut ash means the ashes of walnut wood, or like, actual burnt-up walnuts?"

Of course, there was a matching window in Sam's room, a few feet over from Riley's. Sam had snuck up at some point while Riley was wallowing, and had her face pressed to the glass.

"What?"

Sam opened her window and leaned out. "Are you still sulking, or can I come out too?"

Riley had literally never been able to stop Sam from doing anything, ever, so she shrugged her assent. Sam clambered out next to her, sitting a careful few feet away.

"The lore says that the Witch can be stopped by fire, or nettles, or walnut ash."

"You have to stop calling the old guys at Dunkin'—"

"Shut up, this was in one of Toby's notebooks." Sam held it up to demonstrate. "Someone wrote in to the *Roscoe Independent* in 1903 to say that walnut ash over a doorway will keep witches away, but that if one hexed you, to hit yourself with stinging nettles until the curse was broken. Also that you could keep from getting tricked off the path by lampmouths by wearing . . ." She squinted at Toby's notes. "Pig fat mixed with mint extract. Gross."

"You still think this is the Witch of the Woods?" Riley asked.

"It's not the lampmouths," said Sam, looking up from the notebook. "What were you and Toby fighting about?"

About Mom. About me. About how I'm turning into something that scares him, which is true, but not the way that he thinks it is. "We weren't really fighting," she said, instead of any of that.

Sam scoffed at the obvious lie. "He was yelling. Toby never yells."

"Not at you," said Riley, but Sam had a point. Toby got frazzled and occasionally quiet with anger, but he wasn't a yeller. Mom had always been, and Riley could remember occasions where he'd stood there while she screamed out frustrations, not just with him, but with everyone and everything: the local cops giving her the hairy eyeball, other parents at the school being snobby assholes. She'd had so much anger at the world, constantly exploding outward. Riley wanted that feeling instead of this one, like she kept getting up only to get kicked back down.

"Here," said Sam. She was holding something out. It was the whistle from Mr. Bancroft's box: the one Toby had given her and that she'd worn so dutifully right up until it no longer mattered.

Riley didn't take it. "I thought you wanted to fingerprint everything. Send it to the FBI."

Sam gave her a dirty look, extremely visible even in the fading light. "You were right, okay? They wouldn't be able to do anything. All the things in there are super common, and our prints are probably all over it now. So . . ." She trailed off, still holding the whistle out to Riley.

She took it, though with an odd reluctance. She stared at it, thinking about how she'd believed so firmly for so long that it would keep her safe. Three whistle blasts, and someone would come and find her. She'd never used it, and something else had found her instead.

Definitely not worthy of becoming a tattoo. If Riley was still here for her eighteenth birthday. If she was still *herself*. She shoved it into her pocket and looked back over at Sam.

"Was there anything else in the box?"

"It's mostly junk, like you said," Sam replied. "Some of it probably belongs to the people who disappeared. Like, the earring is in Amy Macready's missing poster, and something that definitely looks like a Boy Scout's scarf that could have been from Lyndon Roach. But . . ."

"But?"

"It's for a lot more than ten people." Sam picked at her nails for a second. "And if there's anything of Mom's, I don't recognize it."

Riley thought back to her conversation with Generous: the confirmation that her mom was *gone*, realizing that Toby had kept something from her for so long, had felt—it felt a little like dying all over again. But the hardest part was the relief in knowing. It made her feel like the worst of daughters, like she was somehow breaking a promise she couldn't remember making. She didn't want Sam to feel like that; her first instinct was to protect Sam, always.

Sam still dreamed of Mom coming home, but this—the not knowing, the suspension between wondering if she was gone because she couldn't come home to them, or didn't *want* to—felt cruel.

"That key in the box," said Riley. "From Mr. Bancroft's house. Can you get it?"

Sam looked at her carefully, then nodded. They both went back into their respective bedrooms. Riley went to her dresser; in the back of the top drawer was the ugly little box that Sam had made in kindergarten, where Riley had once hidden a small wad of cash. Now it contained . . . honestly, the same kind of junk that had been in Bancroft's cigar box. Mementos.

One of them was an old brass key with a hexagonal head. She'd never thrown out the key to their old apartment on the outskirts of Roscoe. She wasn't sure why. Or maybe it was more accurate to say that she'd decided not to examine why, just stuck it in the box where her mother had once stolen her emergency money.

Riley realized now that she would never know if it was for drugs or their electric bill or something else entirely.

She grabbed the key and took it to Sam's room. Sam was there, holding the other key, the one from Bancroft's box. She stood amid the usual whirlwind of chaos that was her room: clothes all over the floor, books and papers and empty snack bags in haphazard piles. Riley recognized the particular brand of mess that Sam fell into when she found something new to devote hours of her life to researching. Her bed was half-covered in books: collections of ghost stories and paranormal encounters, the *Weird Roscoe County* book that Toby frequently complained about for its bad research, and old photo books of Roscoe and the surrounding area.

"Can I see the key?" asked Riley, and when Sam gave it to her, she put the two keys next to each other, lining up the jagged teeth so they looked like two tiny mountain ranges, side by side.

"They match," said Sam. "Is that . . ."

"It's our old apartment key," Riley confirmed. She handed the one they'd found in the basement back to Sam.

She could see Sam wrestling with what that meant, the implications of it. Testing out possibilities and other explanations. It took her a moment to force the next words out of her mouth; this was maybe the hardest thing she'd ever had to say, and she felt a twinge of sympathy for Toby. "Mom's not coming back."

She knew it would hurt Sam to hear the words. She hadn't counted on it hurting herself to say them as well, even if she'd known, even though she'd suspected for much longer than that. Was that why Toby hadn't told her?

She waited for Sam to start crying, or to start yelling. Instead, she just looked at the keys for another moment. Then she turned, shoved everything off her bed, and curled up on it. Riley, after a moment's indecision, lay down next to her. The silence between them felt too fraught to risk speaking. She felt a wave of anger at her mother, old and familiar; once more, Riley was left to clean up the mess she'd left behind. Left to maintain the lie until she couldn't anymore, left to bear the bad news, left to wrestle with the empty space where Anna should have been. The anger had been eating away at her forever. She'd read once about a coal mine that caught fire decades ago and had been burning ever since. It felt like that: All the resentment was stuck inside her with nowhere to go, so it slowly hollowed her out. Made her poisonous to be around.

Sam sat up suddenly, jostling Riley. She wrestled her own whistle, which she was still wearing—she even slept in it, always a believer in its talismanic power to keep her safe—off her neck and undid the clasp. As Riley watched, she slipped the thin chain through one of the holes in the key and let it slide down until it clinked against the metal whistle. Then she looked at Riley, waiting.

She looked down at the key she'd held onto for five years. Part of her was tempted to throw it away, like she'd wanted to dump the whistle. It reminded her of what she didn't have, what hadn't saved her. She felt scraped raw still, even though she'd mostly tamped down on her feelings because Sam needed her.

But she'd always been crap at refusing Sam anything, even a request to wear matching trauma accessories. So she pulled the whistle back out of her pocket and slipped the key onto the chain as well.

Generous chose that moment to speak. *Wait,* it said. She wasn't sure if it could hear her when she cussed it out in her head, but she'd give it a try anyway. But then it said, *Someone's coming.*

It seemed to pull her attention to Sam's open window— the witch window, she thought to herself, and felt a trickle of unease run down her spine.

She looked out toward Voynich Woods. All the normal evening sounds—crickets and cicadas, the occasional owl or distant coyote—had gone quiet. The darkness clarified, dissipated like fog. A figure stood out in the night, way up by the tree line.

"Someone's out there," she said. Maybe it was Madelyn, having gotten through her mother's—what had she called them? Wards, watchers.

"Is it your friend?" Sam asked. "Did she come back?"

If it was Madelyn, why was Riley feeling like this? Taut and pulled tight, thrumming with tension, nerves all screaming at her. The last time she'd felt like this, things had started crawling out of her skin. Jane had had to get between her and Madelyn. The idea of Sam seeing her like that—

"Go downstairs," she told Sam, trying to stomp down on the fear roiling beneath her skin. "Get Toby."

She went to maneuver herself through the angled window, remembered the whistle and key still in her hand, and quickly put the chain over her head.

"Riley, no!" Sam said. "You can't. When you left before, you—"

"I came back," Riley said, with a calm assurance that she absolutely did not feel. "And I will this time."

The figure tugged something out of its pocket and pulled it over its face, and she could barely make out the cheery gold outline of the sun.

"Get Toby, lock the doors, and don't—don't look, okay?" she said to Sam, and her voice wasn't hers anymore. It scared her a little, but the feelings were distant, outside of her. Or maybe she was outside of them? She didn't mind either way. She'd had enough of feeling like a victim, an anchor, an underground fire poisoning the world around her.

"Riley? Riley!"

It wasn't a huge height, exactly, but something in her brain told her to jump, so she did. Blue-black veins were growing over her forearms, up her neck, and into her hair. The limbs that she'd seen come out of her chest when attacking Madelyn unfolded again, stretching out and touching the ground a half second before her feet did.

The man in the mask stood, watching. Waiting for her.

Riley took a step forward, then another, then she was running.

She remembered, suddenly, Generous's voice speaking from behind her. *What do you want?* it had asked. The locket in her hand. If she'd opened it, would she have seen this? Herself transformed into something too horrible and dangerous to try and harm? Something that could never be hurt or abandoned? There was birdsong in her chest again, and power flowing through her veins.

A dark sheen was descending over her vision, fracturing a single image into a hundred overlapping frames. In every one, that golden wheel watched her die; oversaw her rib cage getting pulled open, something else put in, grafted onto her. Pain chasing her down into darkness.

She thought of all the things that made her, Riley Walcott, the anchor that dragged other people down. Something had given her the chance to become something else. Maybe something more? Something bigger, at least. She could use it. She could be the thing in the woods that everyone was afraid of.

The man in the mask didn't seem afraid, yet, but she could be patient.

CHAPTER ELEVEN

The basement again. The overhead lights again. The hissing rumble of the old coal furnace again. Mother had lit it while Madelyn watched, because the basement got too cold otherwise. For her, she meant. She didn't seem to worry about Madelyn's comfort.

"Why?" Madelyn whispered.

"Why what?" Mother asked.

She thought of all the Madelyns who'd come before her: failed experiments, every one of them. "Why did you make me," she asked, "if you don't even like me?"

Mother didn't meet Madelyn's eyes. She was scanning Madelyn's exposed body, strapped down onto her table. Looking at where she should cut, alter, rearrange. "I thought it would be different," she said quietly. "Every time. I thought *I* would be different. A good mother for a good daughter. But you never come out right."

She pressed her cold hands down on Madelyn's scar, the one that ran between her collarbones and down the soft swell of her belly. Pain flared under her touch, rippling out in waves beneath Madelyn's skin.

When Madelyn sucked in a breath to scream, Mother

slapped a hand over her mouth. "Don't. I don't like it when girls scream. I never have."

She shuddered, and then looked down at Madelyn's scar again. It parted easily under her concentration, blood spilling out of the sides and rolling down Madelyn's stomach. Her body betraying her again, another reminder that it wasn't hers. It stung like a paper cut, a hot and unexpected pain. But Mother was watching her, and she couldn't scream, she wouldn't scream.

Madelyn squeezed her eyes shut. She was trying so hard to control her voice, but the words slipped out in a sob: "I hate being your daughter."

Mother said, "My mother once told me that it was a pity I'd never have children, because only then would I understand how much pain I really caused her." There was a smile on her mother's face. "Joke's on her," she said, and a moment later, added, "Actually, I guess it's on both of us."

Her mother had her open like a book, and Madelyn could feel her fingers digging inside her. She imagined what her mother saw: every small secret she had kept from her; everything she was ashamed of or disgusted by; every time she'd wished her mother was dead; every time she'd cried because she didn't know how to make her mother love her.

Madelyn tugged at the restraints wrapped around her wrists and ankles. She wasn't even thinking about getting away but about covering herself up, protecting all the most vulnerable bits of her that weren't supposed to see the light.

The air was thick with iron and salt, the meat-smell of her insides. "Why didn't you just drown me this morning? Why can't you just kill me now?"

It must be easy, she thought. One cut seam on Mr. Bancroft, and he'd spilled out all over the floor.

Her mother leaned down, close to her face. "Why would you say such terrible things to me? I love you, Maddie. I'll do it right this time. You'll be the daughter I wanted, and I'll be the mother you deserve."

Riley, she suddenly thought, would have some pretty cutting words to say about how terrible that was. She imagined Jane lifting her hand in a swift slicing motion across her throat, grinning until her decayed lips stretched wide over her jagged teeth. *Heh, cutting.*

Madelyn felt a little stronger, thinking of them. Strong enough to crane her neck and look down, to see what her mother was doing to her.

She'd seen her mother's charms and felt the power spinning out of them. Generous's wild energy corralled and focused, balanced by pieces of life—brambles, bird's eggs, seeds—and death or inert matter—bones, of course; teeth; chunks of limestone with fossils embedded in them. What she saw inside herself was similar, but far more complex. She'd imagined a loose collection of objects under her skin, like Mr. Bancroft. Instead, it was like seeing a universe in miniature, washed in blood. Magic was literally threaded through her veins, the same as she felt in the presence of the wolf tree. All around it, her mother's work trapped it, trammeled its wildness. She traced the lines of the scars, saw how they connected to hexes that would pry open her skin and make her bleed as a warning. It was all there, in her mother's hand.

The whispers in her mind were no longer whispering, but shouting, screaming. They had no words; it had always been like trying to listen to someone speaking in a room above or below you.

How many times had her mother unmade and remade her? What was left of those previous versions of herself? How many of her memories were hers; how many had belonged to other Madelyns?

It felt awful to be pulled apart like this, shameful, to have her inner workings exposed. But her scars were open. The pain that lived under her skin was gone. *You belong to yourself,* Riley had told her, and right now at least, it was true.

She shut her eyes and clamped her mouth shut. *Help me,* she thought to the voices, all those dead Madelyns. *Stop fucking yelling and help me.*

She always thought magic required intense focus. Her mother would talk about sacrifice and skill and concentration, but for Madelyn, it was the opposite. She was always working so hard on keeping herself together, toeing the line, obeying the letter if not the spirit of what her mother said. Not thinking too much, not remembering what shouldn't be in her mind, stepping around every crack in the facade while pretending she didn't see it. She realized she had been doing her mother's work for her, keeping herself small and unnoticed, living in a fantasy world.

The voices said, *Let go,* and Madelyn did. Heat flooded her, hot and dry as August's sun-drenched days, dusty and waiting for a spark to light up.

The voices said, *Burn,* and Madelyn did.

Her mother gasped, pulling back from the table. "Maddie, what—"

Madelyn had gotten used to the warmth of her own blood sliding down her skin, but now it was *hot.* There was a roar building up inside her head, one that sounded like the coal-burning furnace in the corner.

Did you throw scrap parts of the other Madelyns in there, Mother? she thought, looking at the furnace now. *Mix their ashes in with the mud you made me from? Is that why there's fire burning permanently under my skin?*

More blood, and then her mother was flinching back, shading her eyes. Another of Madelyn's scars burst open and more fire came spilling out.

Her mother was screaming. It sounded like music, and all the whispers sang along. Fire crawled from her body, up the walls, to search for something to devour. It found her mother's workbench, and the stairs, the space beneath them where Madelyn had been locked up, over and over.

And then it found her mother, the apron she was wearing, the wool sweater and twill pants. It found her eyebrows and eyelashes, then the tumble of auburn hair.

Madelyn sighed. She couldn't remember ever feeling so warm, relaxed, drunk on all the pain finally being let out of her skin. She considered, for a moment, staying here. The fire didn't burn her, just danced along her skin joyfully. Even now, something inside her was reluctant to leave the contained world her mother had created for her. She considered, for a moment, sitting here as the rafters burned and the house eventually toppled in on her.

Then she thought of how much her mother would, in a way, love that: Madelyn dying when she did.

Madelyn yanked her wrists free, snapping the restraints like they were made of cobwebs, and did the same with her ankles.

Her mother was flailing, haloed in flames. Her eyelashes

were gone, her skin was blackening, but her eyes still found Madelyn's for a moment. Her mouth hung open. Was she speaking? Was she crying?

Did it matter?

The whispers told her to leave, and she did. Madelyn let fire drip off her as she walked up the stairs, letting them burn behind her. She left charred footprints on the wooden floors, trails of smoke and blistering paint. She ran her fingers over the table where she'd sat—too afraid to move, even though she'd been alone—until the varnish bubbled and smoked, the curtain smoldered, and flames reached up toward the second floor.

When the fire inside her finally exhausted itself, she picked up some clothes from the laundry room and grabbed a roll of duct tape. She taped herself together before getting dressed, then went outside just as flames started licking up the walls.

The heat from her burning house was a comforting hand on her back, urging her forward to the garden, then the orchard beyond it. She walked through the garden and into the old orchard, rotten apples crunching under her bare feet. She found the well and fell against it.

The voices had finally gone quiet. She wondered, for a moment, if that was what had been burning inside her: all those previous Madelyns that were put together and then pulled apart. She wanted to think that she had freed them. Freed herself. She should be happy, shouldn't she? But she just felt exhausted, empty, and alone—like part of her was still down in that little room under the stairs.

Madelyn's skin was so hot and filthy, and she looked down into the dark water for a long moment. *Drowning is supposed to be nice,* Jane had said once. It had the vague shape of a joke, but Jane's jokes were all obvious, and usually kind of stupid. Drowning sounded better than what she was feeling right now, so she slipped her legs over the side, then let herself drop like a stone down the hole. The water was shockingly cold, numbing, exactly what she wanted. She thought—with equal parts hope and shame—that the water would take her back to the gray non-place that lived between her memories.

But Jane was suddenly there, next to Madelyn in the water. She put her hands out to Madelyn, pulling her toward the surface. Madelyn struggled for a moment; she didn't want to be in the world anymore. She didn't want to be *this.* She thought again of *HMS Broomstick* and the coven's opposites. She wanted to go through the Bermuda Triangle, whatever that was, and switch places with some unscarred boy who was always whole, who had never been her mother's creation, didn't have Mother's mark carved onto every piece of her.

But Jane was, had probably always been, stronger than her, and Madelyn eventually went limp and let herself be carried back up the well, into the orchard. Night had fallen, but it was full of flame and the charcoal smell of her mother's house, still burning.

Jane dropped down next to her. *It's not finished,* she told Madelyn.

"Why can't it be?" Madelyn asked, but she remembered Bancroft suddenly, her mother's instructions to him. She groaned.

You have to finish it, Jane said. *You're closer than you've ever been.*

"Why does it matter?" Madelyn asked. She looked closely

at Jane, but her face betrayed nothing. It never did. "Why do you care what happens to me?"

I'm in this cycle with you, she said.

"But—"

That's enough, Jane said quietly. *We don't need to . . . keep spilling our guts out.*

"Oh god, please shut up," she said, wiping her eyes. It made her eyes sting worse, and she realized she'd probably smeared blood into them. "Stop . . ." She shut her eyes and forced herself to say it. "Stop adding insult to injury."

She got unsteadily to her feet. "We need to help Riley. Can you take me to her?"

To the edge of the woods. I can't go farther than that. Jane nodded to Madelyn's torso. *What about . . .*

Madelyn lifted her shirt up and made a face, pressing at her skin where it hung open, despite the tape. Her scars had always zipped themselves together afterward, but these seemed content to gape open. Hopefully, Riley would have a needle and thread.

CHAPTER TWELVE

As Riley ran, she felt her body shift, go liquid, transform. The roots that kept emerging from her skin were back, pushing out and tangling over her body, fitting together like plate armor or slamming to the ground as extra legs. It took Riley seconds to cross the hundred yards between her house and the man, and then she was crashing onto him like a wave.

Cold fury fueled her, though it sat next to a simmering resentment that didn't feel like it belonged to her. She wanted to hurt him. She would make him afraid like she'd been, make him hurt like she had. She would destroy him and then she would—it didn't matter what she'd do after that, did it? Riley could feel the rest of her life receding from her, becoming small and distant; all that mattered now was the man in front of her, and making him suffer and hurt and scream for mercy. She'd consume every bit of his pain.

Riley had never been in a fight, at least not a physical one, and while her rage made her stronger, it didn't suddenly teach her how to land a hit. The man easily dodged away from her. He moved fast, not entirely human. He bent and twisted at strange angles to dart around her blows, and Riley felt a frustrated growl building in her chest, a bass rumble that built up to a razor-edged shriek. Why didn't he fight her? He'd had no qualms about knocking her out when she was alive, scared—still human. But he'd drawn her out here, and if not for a fight, then for what?

She wasn't fast enough, and a sharp stinging fire arced over her arm. He moved in quickly, his arms reaching up toward her head, and Riley managed to jerk away from him, falling back a few steps.

Riley saw differently through the dark sheen that covered her eyes. Her vision was fractured, shattering a single image into a hundred overlapping frames. Colors were muted, and movement was magnified.

She saw it from dozens of different angles: the moment when he saw the whistle dangling around her neck, the brass key banging against it. His gaze followed it like it was a hypnotist's pendulum. It made him sloppy, and he reached forward to grab it, no longer mindful of Riley's wild swings.

She snapped her hand forward, grabbing at the mask and yanking it off.

It was Mr. Bancroft. He had changed since she'd seen him in the woods, and not for the better. The skin of his face was sunken and ghoulish. His mouth was studded with rusted nails that someone had pushed through his lips and tongue. But it wasn't blood running down his chin, just more of that same gray-brown liquid she'd always mistaken for tobacco juice. His normally neat uniform was stained and ripped, and thick, twisting thorns had torn through some of it, bursting out of his skin. He smelled rank, like the slime at the bottom of a compost barrel.

He tried to speak through the nails, but no words came out. Just a pained mumble. He reached up and fumbled at his face, but he didn't seem to be coordinated enough to pull any of the nails out.

Riley thought distantly that she'd see this in her nightmares, if she didn't die here.

Bancroft fixated again on the whistle and key that were swinging from the chain around her neck. He had taken the whistle from her, taken the key from her mother, or maybe her mother's body.

He was fast, possessed by whatever magic made him move. He reached for her, crowded up close. He grabbed at the chain around her neck, and she grabbed his wrists before he could break it off. The spines and thorns growing out of his arms pressed through her shining black armor like it was nothing, and Riley snarled as she felt them puncture her skin.

The darkness that covered her limbs suddenly choked her. She couldn't move; she could barely breathe. Her vision was doubling. She was outside Toby's house; she was in Voynich Woods, the Wishing Tree looming up before her.

The dead girl she'd seen in her dream, with the iron rods through her hands and chest, was there now, not at a distance, but close enough that Riley could have reached out and hugged her. The fury that had filled Riley, lit that fire inside her—it was coming from the girl. It filled the entire clearing, towered up into the branches of the tree.

Then the vision was gone, so quickly that Riley wasn't sure she'd seen it. But the anger now was no longer fueling her. It threatened to consume her, swallow her whole. The dark ichor that covered her, with its wild smell that was like blood and sap, pressed against every inch of her, suffocating and strong.

A tiny, remote voice spoke to Riley. *I should have warned you*, it said. *I thought I could control her. But she—*

Then the voice was drowned out in that waspy buzz of anger and rage, and Riley was drowning along with it.

CHAPTER THIRTEEN

Jane had brought her to the edge of the forest, to one of the creeks still swollen from the storm the night Riley died, and Madelyn had started running. Just like that afternoon, the whispers urged her on. She hadn't lied, exactly, when Riley asked how Madelyn had found her. The voices always whispering in the back of Madelyn's head had helped. But Riley's presence was like a thread constantly tugging at Madelyn; she'd followed it into that out-of-the-way bathroom at the school, and she followed it now.

She expected something to stop her as she sprinted. Her mother would suddenly appear in a flash of lightning, grab Madelyn by the throat, and tear her open. The trees themselves would turn against her and catch her in their branches. A hole would open up and close around her ankles, or every monster that lived in the forest would line up against her.

She realized that this was the same way she used to imagine the catastrophic consequences if she ever left her mother.

Your mother is dead, she told herself. She looked up and saw a haze of smoke over the trees, from where her house was burning. *Your mother is ashes by now.*

The thought should have been more comforting. But Madelyn only felt empty.

That was when she saw Riley. At least, she thought it was Riley. She didn't even look human anymore. Those rootlets that she'd seen come out of Riley now covered her in a mass of squirming, jagged shapes: armor that writhed and snapped at the air. Fat drops of pitch-black ichor dripped off her, soaking into the ground around them. Bancroft stood there, watching, dancing back whenever Riley got too close to him.

Something was wrong. She could feel it in the deepest part of her guts. Bancroft must have done something to Riley, turned her into this.

Madelyn didn't know how much magic she had in her after burning her mother and the house. But if it helped Riley?

As she ran, the scars on her hand opened up again with a familiar sting, and fire spread over her left hand. She thought about how the darkness that lived under Riley's skin could be shaped. She concentrated on the warmth in her hand, the blood in her palm, until she felt it harden into a long, glossy blade. She kept moving toward them. All of Bancroft's concentration was on Riley, on slashing away at her, and he didn't see Madelyn until she had plunged the knife into his back.

Bancroft gave an inarticulate scream and whirled around, hands grasping for her.

That momentary distraction was all Riley needed. She tackled Bancroft, knocking him down and rolling over. Two of the limbs pierced through his arms, stapling him to the ground. Riley seemed beyond hearing, beyond sensing. Still, as she raised two of the limbs over her head, Madelyn felt like she should stop her somehow. This didn't feel like Riley's rage; it felt older and colder. But she was frozen in place.

Riley's arms fell on Bancroft with the finality of guillotines.

Impact, a wet crunch, and then nothing. Not even a gasp, not a whisper. Just the harsh grate of Riley's breath.

"Riley?" she said. "Are you—"

Riley raised her fists again and slammed them back into his chest cavity, then again. She was growling, low at first and then rising higher to a scream.

This wasn't Riley, Madelyn thought to herself. She remembered those first few minutes with Riley at the wolf tree, the instinctive rage that had clouded over her when she'd been pulled out of the ground. The Riley who had flung herself at Madelyn, ready to kill, only more monstrous. Riley had still been visible underneath the substance seeping out of her skin then. Now she'd been completely subsumed by it.

Madelyn could feel Riley's attention turn back toward her. Riley's body was bent into a totally different shape, extra limbs snaking out and thudding into the ground, tearing up sod when they retracted. Two long, ovoid compound eyes came down over a triangular head, regarding her.

"Riley? I'm trying to help you," she said, but Riley crawled toward her again, intent on finishing what had been interrupted the night before.

Madelyn took a step back, then another, trying to remember what Jane had done to snap Riley out of this state.

Before she could, her foot snagged on an uneven bit of ground, and she fell backward onto the grass. Riley darted toward her, and Madelyn opened up the scars across her arms, letting the fire blast out of her. Riley ducked back, circling Madelyn, like she was trying to find a good angle of attack.

Madelyn, scrambling to her feet, couldn't help but wonder: Was she just stupid? Had the Riley who'd first awoken, rage-filled and violent, been the real Riley? Had everything that happened in the interim been her just biding her time until this happened again?

"Is this you?" she asked. Her scars were still open, but the flames were guttering, and black spots were dotting her vision.

There was no sign Riley had heard her. She stalked forward, still shy of the flames, but full of predatory intent.

"Riley, please," she said. She felt so stupid; it felt like her mother had won somehow, that the dangers she'd cited to Madelyn as reasons to keep her locked away from the world, warded and watched and wretchedly lonely, were now proving themselves real. Was this better or worse than if she'd been unmade in her mother's workshop?

At least here, nobody would bring her back and make her experience this all again.

Madelyn was so intent on her messy impending death that she didn't notice they weren't alone in the field anymore, not until Riley turned her gaze back toward the house. Two people were running toward them. The smaller of the two figures reached them first, carrying long, leafy sticks in one of her hands.

It was the girl from Bancroft's basement—Riley's sister, Sam. The girl looked ridiculous, short and slight, charging in with a stick as a weapon against whatever Riley had become.

But then she whipped the branch over Riley's shoulder, and Riley staggered from the blow. She groaned, a terrible noise, and shifted to face her sister.

Sam didn't hesitate but whipped the branch right across Riley's transformed face. The leaves whistled through the air, and she hit Riley again and again. Not hard, not bone-crushing hits, but Riley lurched each time the leaves touched her. The second skin that had encased her sloughed off.

"Give her back!" Sam screamed. She thrashed viciously with the branch until the armor was gone from Riley's skin, and she held up a hand in surrender to the girl.

"Sam," she panted. "Sam, stop. It's okay."

Sam threw the stick down, and then squeezed the hand that had held it, like it hurt. "Stinging nettles," she said. "The lore *was* right."

CHAPTER FOURTEEN

Physical sensations were filtering into Riley's awareness now that she had shed that other skin: The air was damp and cold, her knees were wet where she knelt in the grass, and her skin throbbed where Sam had gotten her with the stinging nettles. She could hear the distant footfalls of Toby coming after them. She wished that she didn't remember the past few minutes, that she had been booted out of the driver's seat of her body, been a passenger as something else took over.

It wasn't true. The anger had been her anger first, until it seemed to consume her. Anger and a hunger to hurt people. She could still remember the way Mr. Bancroft's ribs had cracked under her fists, how she had turned to Madelyn with the full intention of doing the same thing to her.

Mr. Bancroft was staring blankly up toward the tree canopy, where the stars wavered between the branches. There were blue-black lines etched onto his skin, like she'd infected him. She made the mistake of looking down at his chest. The inside of Mr. Bancroft resembled the kind of slurry you'd find at the bottom of a dirty pond, dotted here and there with grimy coins, nails, a single child's shoe. Riley wanted to throw up.

Oh god. Mr. Bancroft. She couldn't let Sam see—

Madelyn must have realized it at the same time, because she stood up, interposing herself between Sam and what was left of the ranger.

"Riley?" Toby's voice called. She'd never heard him sound like this, edged with panic. "Sam, answer me!"

"We're okay," Madelyn called back.

They weren't. Riley wanted to run right into the woods and let them swallow her. But her legs were rubber, half-numb and senseless. Maybe this *was* a nightmare. Maybe she could wake herself up. Maybe she could still take everything back, get a do-over.

Toby skidded to a stop next to them. He was carrying the rifle that normally lived locked away in the hall closet; Riley couldn't remember the last time she'd seen it in someone's arms. His hands went slack on its stock as he took in the scene.

"Is that Mr. Bancroft?" he said quietly.

Riley nodded. Sam gasped and tried to peek around Madelyn again.

"Don't, Sam," Riley growled. "Don't look. I *told* you not to look."

"Okay. All right. Okay," Toby muttered. He pulled himself out of some kind of spiral and looked at Madelyn. "Who are you?"

"Um. My name is Madelyn. I'm . . . a friend?"

They both looked at Riley, for some kind of confirmation, and she nodded. Like, *Yes, you're a friend*, to Madelyn. Like, *Yes, you can trust her*, to Toby.

Toby swallowed, and when he spoke, his voice shook. "Okay. Can you take Sam back to the house, Madelyn?"

"Toby," Sam said, a soft whine in her voice.

"Super not the time to argue, Sam," he said, voice taut and brittle. "Go back to the house. We'll be right behind you."

"It'll be okay, Sam," Riley said, making an effort to sound like she believed it. She watched her and Madelyn walk away, as Toby took a few steps closer to Mr. Bancroft's body.

"He's really . . . wow. I couldn't really see from back there. Sam told me to get the rifle and nettles. But when we were running, it looked like—I don't know, like—"

"I killed him," she said. Because that was what he was asking, wasn't it? She had bits of Bancroft's putrefying flesh clinging to her arms, still. Her knees weren't just wet from the grass. A puddle had spread out around him and soaked her pants.

"All right," Toby said. "I am going to puke. Give me a second."

Toby stumbled a foot or two away and loudly threw up. Riley tried to wipe her hands off on the grass as Toby spat a couple of times, then wiped his mouth.

"Did he hurt you?" Toby asked. "Are you okay?"

She laughed hollowly. "Never been better?"

She meant it to sound like a hollow joke, sarcastic. But it came out strangled, harsh—like the sap under her skin had taken over her voice. It sounded monstrous.

"Okay, this is—I'm—Jesus." Hysteria was edging into Toby's voice, and he seemed to be fighting it off by pure willpower. "Rye, let's get you cleaned up. No, not in the house. Backyard first. We're gonna hose you off."

Riley peeled herself up from the ground, Toby's arms steady around her.

"You're gonna get gross too," she said.

"Yep," he agreed. "Honestly not that worried about it right now, though."

She'd killed someone. Shouldn't he be horrified by her? Disgusted? She was a monster. But he didn't falter as he led her to the spot in the backyard where the hose was messily coiled up.

She remembered doing this on hot, high summer days: she and Sam using the sprinkler to turn the entire backyard into a mud pit, Toby using the hose to clean off all the mud sticking to them and their clothes. Then they'd lie out on the deck to dry off in the sun, music playing through the tinny speakers of her phone.

It was cold now, and Sam watched with large eyes from the back door, Madelyn lurking behind her.

"The water's gonna be cold, okay?" Toby said gently. "I'm sorry, but it'll be better if we keep all of this outside. Then you can have a real shower."

The water that poured over her was icy, like the river at winter's end. Riley thought about the deep underground spring Roscoe's water came from. She wished she could somehow be there right now, that the earth would open up and swallow her. If she was going to get the world's ugliest, most awful superpowers, that should have been one of them.

"Close your eyes," Toby said. "I'm gonna get your hair and face."

Riley closed her eyes and concentrated on the icy water tracking down over her scalp, face, and neck. "Okay," he said, turning it off. "I'll be right back. Gonna get—"

"Here," Madelyn said. Riley opened her eyes. She was

standing a few feet from them. "Towel, some new clothes, and a trash bag for the old ones. I asked Sam to get them."

She sounded apologetic, and Riley wondered why. Madelyn stood there awkwardly, until Riley said, "My bedroom's upstairs. Sam can show you where the shower is if you want."

"Sure," said Madelyn uncertainly, setting everything down on the porch railing. She looked between Riley and her uncle, then headed back inside.

"Can you not look?" she asked Toby. Not that it mattered. He'd already seen more than she'd ever wanted him to.

Toby turned his back. Riley stripped, then quickly toweled off. She slid on the fresh clothes while Toby, face pale and mouth set into a grim line, stuffed what she'd been wearing into the bag. God, she was tired. But Toby was standing there looking at her like he was trying to reconcile this drowned-cat version of her with whatever she'd been out there.

"I guess we should talk," she said.

◆ ◆ ◆

Toby, a few months after Riley and Sam came to live with him and on the advice of their pediatrician, attempted to give Riley the sex and puberty talk. He had fumbled it so badly, stuttering and turning red and fidgeting with the notes he had actually printed out, that she was left more confused than before. Riley had waited a week and then told him she would take care of it when it was Sam's turn, as long as she could have his notes and never talk about it again.

All this was to say that they weren't strangers to hard conversations, but this was maybe the hardest.

They sat in silence for a long while, out on the front porch, until he eventually asked, "You want some water? I could use something to drink."

Riley nodded, and after a long, lingering look, he went inside. She heard him rummaging through the kitchen.

When he came back out, he handed her a cup of water. He had poured himself a generous glass of wine. "In case this actually makes the conversation easier," he said, taking a big gulp. He waited a moment.

"Did it?" Riley asked.

"Nope," he replied, and set the glass down on the railing.

She'd remarked once that it was odd that there were only two chairs on the porch when all three of them liked to sit out there, and Toby told her he liked to sit on the rail, facing them, so he could see his favorite girls' faces. The two of them now were sitting side by side, staring out at the yellowing fields. She could feel the woods at her back, as if they were listening in.

"So," Toby started. "Just to make sure I have everything straight. You turned into . . . something not human. Killed the forest ranger, who on closer inspection, also didn't seem very human. Then you maybe tried to kill your friend? And according to Sam, it has something to do with the Witch of the Woods."

Riley set her glass down. "I don't know about the last part."

Toby nodded and finished off his wine in a second gulp. He didn't seem to know what to say.

"Something happened in the woods," Riley said, fumbling

at the buttons of her pajama top. "I don't know exactly what, and everything I do know makes me hope I never remember the rest of it, but I . . ."

It had been a while since she'd really looked down at everything that lay beneath the collar of her shirt. She wished she'd shown it to him when it was still small enough to be called a wound. Now it was a crack that spread sternum to belly button. Still, no turning back now.

She lifted her head, spread the two halves of the shirt, and let Toby see.

"I woke up in the woods with this."

Toby froze for a long moment. "Holy fuck," he said, immediately starting to hyperventilate.

"You said you'd believe me," Riley said.

"I do. I mean, Rye, if I thought I was hallucinating, it would have been—" He waved a hand toward the yard, the tree line where Mr. Bancroft's body still lay. "But like, just to be sure. You're showing me a massive open wound on your chest with black shit running through it and not, like, another ugly tattoo, right?"

"It's definitely not a tattoo." She buttoned her shirt back up. "When I was lost, I found the old Wishing Tree. And it was like . . . something trapped me. There was a man, and he was wearing a mask, and he—"

She didn't know how to finish. She didn't want to either, didn't want to remember the pain or the darkness that had rushed in around it.

"I had this . . . dream, that I made a deal with someone. Something. I could go home, but they would come with me. And when Mr. Bancroft appeared again, I was so angry that he was here, that he did this to me and then came to my home, and the other thing just—took over." But that wasn't quite right. "Or, it didn't take over, it just gave my feelings a shape."

She was afraid to look at him. Toby was in the business of believing stupid stories, but there was a world of difference between a tall tale and what was happening to her.

"We'll talk about the deal stuff in a second," Toby said. There was a strange look contorting his face. "But first, can I hug you again? Because Jesus Christ, I'm so glad you're still here."

Riley let herself be hugged. When they parted, she asked, "Am I a monster?"

"No," he answered immediately. "Not even a little."

"But I'm . . ." She gestured at herself. "You saw me. I changed. I killed someone."

"The person who hurt you," Toby pointed out. He leaned back in his chair. "And if he did that to you, I wouldn't care if he was the fucking pope. Let someone else turn the other cheek. I'm glad he's dead, and I'm going to make damn sure nobody finds him. I just wish I could have done it for you, honestly."

Riley stared at him. Most of the boys from Roscoe—hell, most of the people, period—treated violence casually, like a natural by-product of growing up country. You got used to butchering your own deer, watching your father kill a dying pet because the vet charged for that, throwing punches outside of school with someone who'd been your best friend last week and probably would be again next week. Toby had never been like that. Her mother had said that Toby got in fights in high school, but he never started them, and had never been able to shrug them off like other people. To hear about him wanting to kill someone shocked her.

Riley swallowed. "I'm sorry," she said.

Toby looked over. "What? You don't—there's nothing for you to be sorry about."

"This wouldn't have happened if—if I—"

"If you hadn't what?" Toby said. "Gone after Sam? Like anything in the world could have stopped you?"

Riley tried to summon up the energy to smile at that, but his tone was so gentle that it broke past all the walls that she had built, all the defenses she'd constructed, everything that was keeping her upright. Riley couldn't remember ever crying this hard, like pieces of her guts were being yanked out her throat.

She had a moment of terror when she thought the tears coursing down her face would be black as well, her eyes infected with the same tarry substance that had spread to the rest of her body. She was almost too terrified to look and confirm it, but forced herself to, wiping at her eyes with her hand.

But the tears were clear, like they'd always been. Somehow, that made her cry harder.

She couldn't help but feel that this *was* her fault, though, that it had to be. There must have been a point where she made the wrong choice, stepped left when she should have stepped right.

She had to find a way out of this. This had happened to her, but she could feel the cracks it was creating in her family. There had to be a way, right?

"What did you see in the woods?" Riley asked, remembering

Generous's hints that afternoon: Toby had seen something in the woods, something that led to his obsession with Voynich Woods and its many stories. "When you were younger?"

"How did you . . . ," Toby started to ask, then sighed and leaned back in his chair. "When I was your age, your mom took me to a party in the woods with her. Not far in the woods, because even as drunk and horny teenagers, there were always too many stories, you know? It was just by the gatehouse. And Anna wasn't popular, exactly. But she was cool, you know? She was tough and she never cared what people thought of her, and that was unimaginable to most of us. Meanwhile, I was her nerdy little shadow with braces and acne, who could recite dialogue from *Star Trek*. And I was drinking, and there was this guy who was actually, I thought, flirting with me. But it was—it turned out not so much, or maybe he was and went full gay panic." At her confused look, he added, "Not that kind of gay panic. The kind that people used as a defense for hate crimes."

She wanted to reach back in time and squash that guy like a bug.

"Anyway, it got ugly," he said. "I ran, and instead of running back to the party, I ran to the woods."

Riley could feel a different kind of magic taking place; it was like what she'd done that afternoon, pressing Toby to get the truth, but that had been blunt and forceful. This was subtle, something woven between the telling of the story and the hearing of it. "Why?" she asked.

"Maybe I thought facing a monster would be easier than facing everything else. Maybe because I felt like a monster too."

She couldn't imagine anyone thinking that way about Toby,

and wanted to fight anyone who did. But that wasn't what this story was for. "What did you see?"

"Lampmouths," he said. "It looked like someone was shining a penlight maybe thirty or forty yards off. Just swaying in the air. Then a couple more blinked on, like they were little eyes. And I thought, Why not follow them? Can they do anything worse to me than what that boy had been prepared to do? Getting lost forever in the woods sounded pretty nice right about then."

Toby drummed his fingers against the arm of the chair. Riley thought of the woods at their back. They sat in silence for a while.

"But you didn't."

"I didn't. I just stood and watched the lights in the trees, so grateful that I got to see them. I spent a lot of time in the woods after that, chasing down ghosts and monsters and everything else I could think of. Kind of gave up on people for a while, to be honest."

"Did Mom know?" she asked Toby. "About the boy?"

"I never told her. At first it was out of denial, and then later it seemed too late. Like, why bring up something that happened three weeks ago? Then it was six weeks, six months. Then we had other things to worry about." He cleared his throat. "I never thought I would tell anyone—about the boy or the lampmouths. I'd have to carry them both, but at least they balanced each other out."

Riley launched herself at Toby, grabbing him in a tight hug. It felt more like a collision, but he caught her anyway. She wanted to bury the image of his wounded self under the reality of him, here and now. But they existed side by side, refusing to be subsumed.

Maybe the same could be true for her, someday.

"We're going to figure this out," said Toby, letting her go. He gestured to the back, to where Bancroft still lay in the trees. "I'm going to deal with that. You find your friend and try to get some sleep."

CHAPTER FIFTEEN

Madelyn had retreated to the barn during Riley and Toby's talk. She wasn't sure what she'd been picturing when Riley said her uncle ran a museum about Voynich, its monsters and missing people. She definitely hadn't imagined exhibits about monsters in former horse stalls, with hand-painted signs and murals painted on particleboard. Her favorite was the lampmouths—little hanging lights that led travelers astray.

She drifted over to the corner where GIFT SHOP was painted on a wooden sign next to an old cash register. There were T-shirts and cards, prints and postcards of the monsters, the barn, and the gatehouse, which she'd only ever seen from a distance. Then there were more esoteric gifts: crystals and bundles of herbs, and a collection of bracelets made from hemp twine and plastic beads with a sign that said PROTECTION CHARMS $1.

"Do you feel like you need protection?" Riley said. She'd entered quietly from the same door that Madelyn had. "Because Sam and I made those one time our power went out, and it was craft or kill each other. So I can't promise that they'll protect shit."

Madelyn didn't really know Riley that well, but she could see that something had changed. She looked a little lighter, less desperate. Maybe it was putting Bancroft in the ground—figuratively at least, though she'd seen Toby carrying a shovel toward where they'd left him.

Madelyn looked down at the charms, picking one of them up. It felt good in her hand, comforting somehow, to trace the cheap plastic with her thumb. There was a lot of power that you could put into objects; her mother had taught her as much. Bancroft had spilled the same coins that her mother had sent her to gather from the tree. When her mother had cut her open, Madelyn could feel her rearranging something inside her.

Which reminded her . . .

"I need to ask you a favor," she said. "You know how Bancroft, he wasn't, like, a real person? With guts and stuff?"

"Yeah?" Riley said. "Which honestly makes sense, given how weird his house was."

"My mother made him. The nails in his mouth—they're tokens from the Wishing Tree. She uses them to make things like the wards around the house and—"

"And the ranger protecting the woods?" Riley said. "That's so messed up."

As messed up as making a daughter? Madelyn wanted to ask, but couldn't force the words out. She wanted to be cool and blithe, like it was no big deal that she wasn't real.

"Wait," said Riley. "She's . . . the Witch?" At Madelyn's nod, she added, "You're not bleeding. Or are you?"

Most of the blood had washed off on her impulsive trip down the well. "No. The hex is gone."

There were two chairs behind the desk with its old cash register. Riley gestured to them, and they sat together, knee to knee. "What happened?" Riley asked.

"I killed her."

Riley stared at her for a moment, then gave a sudden hacking gasp. It took Madelyn a moment to realize she was laughing, a deep and ugly sort of laughter.

"Sorry," she said. "I just remembered this douchebag Toby used to date who would always say 'synchronicity' in this stupid voice, and then I imagined him just"—she was struggling to speak through her laughter—"just popping up and going, 'Synchronicity, man!'"

"Because we both killed people?" Madelyn asked.

"It's stupid. I'm sorry. Too many things happened, and I don't know how to deal with any of it." Riley took a deep breath, shaking the fit of laughter off. "Start from the beginning? Tell me what happened."

"Bancroft took me back to my mother. And she was angry. And when she's angry at me, she doesn't think, 'I need to punish Madelyn.' She thinks that she needs to fix me."

Riley was staring at her, all traces of humor gone from her face.

"Which means unmaking me." Madelyn thought about the writing in the closet under the stairs. "She's done it before. A lot."

"When you say unmaking you, do you mean—"

"It's probably easier to show you," said Madelyn. She unzipped the jacket and lifted up her shirt. The duct tape hadn't held up as well as she'd hoped, given her race through the woods and subsequent fight. The strips she'd used were barely hanging on, and Madelyn yanked one off impatiently.

Riley went pale at the sight. "Oh god," she said. "Oh, what the fuck."

She shut her eyes, slammed a hand over them. For someone with a hole in her chest, Riley was being pretty dramatic about this.

"Sorry," Madelyn said. She turned away to hide the worst of the carnage for now, pulling the rest of the duct tape off. It hurt, but not as bad as having your mother rummage around your insides did.

"Okay," Riley said faintly. "Is the favor to sew you back together? Because like, I don't know. I really don't know if I can do that."

"Oh," said Madelyn. Maybe she should have left the duct tape alone? "I'm not sure if there's anyone else I can ask, though. Would your uncle or sister—"

"Definitely not. They found out I'm a weird undead monster tonight, and I think that's probably enough for them. What about Jane?"

"Her fine motor skills aren't great, because of the whole . . ." Madelyn wiggled her fingers.

Riley was quiet for a long moment. "Are you sure? We didn't even have home ec because of budget cuts. I can't sew for shit."

Madelyn smiled. "I'm sure. And you can probably use staples." She'd seen a staple gun in a corner of the barn. Her mother never used anything so crude on her—at least not that she could remember—but she had on furniture upholstery. It didn't seem that different from what she needed Riley to do.

Besides, she wasn't sure she could stay still with someone standing over her with a needle and thread. She kept running her fingers over the beads in the protection charm that Riley and her sister had made, rubbing the plastic until she could hear herself think again. *It's not Mom,* she told the whispering voices—or maybe she was really telling herself, *it's Riley.*

But that thought made her stomach swoop dangerously as well. If she'd hated the idea of her mother's fingers pulling her apart, seeing everything hidden from view, the idea of being bare and exposed in front of Riley was difficult in an entirely different way.

"Are you sure you want to do this in the barn?" Riley asked. "And . . . staples?"

Madelyn nodded and lay down on the floor. "You said you can't sew."

Riley peeled off her sweatshirt—it was actually Madelyn's, the one she'd given her—and folded it, then slid it under Madelyn's head.

"Thanks," she said, a little overwhelmed. All this fuss for her.

Riley went to fetch the staple gun, saying, "You're asking me to staple you shut on the very unhygienic floor of my uncle's barn. That feels like literally the smallest thing I can do to make this less horrible."

"You'd be surprised," Madelyn said.

Riley pursed her lips. She separated the open halves of Madelyn's jacket, and the brush of her cold fingers against Madelyn's skin made her shudder. But not in a bad way? Or at least not the way her mother's touch had.

"Okay," Riley said. "I'm going to start at the top."

Madelyn knew the layout of her body, the topography of the scars that crossed them. She tilted her head back a little as Riley pinched her skin together, trying to give her better access.

"You didn't ask," Madelyn said.

"Ask what?"

"What I am."

Riley glanced at her face, then away. "Can you hold here?"

Madelyn put her fingers where Riley's were, holding herself shut. Riley picked up the staple gun, took a breath to try and steady her hands, then placed the cold metal down against Madelyn's skin. Squeezed it.

Madelyn felt the sharp pinch of metal at the same time as she heard the *ka-thunk* of the stapler. She kept her face still, not wanting to flinch and startle Riley.

Riley lifted the gun away and swallowed hard. "Are you okay?"

"Fine. It doesn't hurt that bad. Like a paper cut."

Riley nodded. "Okay, well, it's gonna probably take another fifteen paper cuts. Are you sure you're—"

"This is better," Madelyn said. And it was. She wasn't held down, the voices were a small murmur instead of a maelstrom, and her mother was dead.

"'I'm not going to ask what you are," Riley said. "It sounds rude when it's put that way. And besides, I already know. You're Madelyn. You're whoever you say you are." Riley pressed her fingers back down, about half an inch farther down Madelyn's sternum. "Hold here?"

Madelyn did, and Riley pressed the staple gun down. *Ka-thunk*, and she was a little more together. A little more herself.

She had always felt like her mother's creature. Or creation, and a disappointing one at that. "She made me. And she always made it seem like . . . like I owed her for that," she said.

"Typical shitty parent move," Riley decided. "Always thinking you should be grateful for the most basic-ass stuff."

"I found out that I'm not even the first. She keeps making and unmaking me, because I'm not perfect."

Riley's hands, the pinch of skin, the cold metal. *Ka-thunk.* They were falling into a rhythm. "Maybe not a *typical* shitty parent, then," she said. "Still sucks."

She had a strange look on her face, skin a little flushed. Her eyebrows were pushed together in what could be frustration. Madelyn winced when she felt the next staple dig down into bone. It felt like she'd made a mistake talking about herself, or talking about parents, maybe. But the silence made her nervous, made it too much like being on her mother's table again. So she started talking again. "There's this one episode of *HMS Broomstick* that used to scare me so much when I was a kid." Madelyn paused, realizing she had no idea what "when I was a kid" meant. It felt like a long time, and if she'd been forced to guess, she'd have said ten years ago. But had it been ten years ago? Or twenty, or thirty-five?

She dragged her mind back to the episode before she could get too lost in the weeds pondering that. "And it's the one where two of the witches make this construct, right? Because the housecleaning staff keep finding, like, toads and things in their rooms, so they've stopped cleaning there. So they steal a stevedore's uniform and stuff it full of pillows and fluff from a life jacket, and they perform a spell to give it life, so it can keep their rooms clean. But then Peggy—she's Sibyl's niece, she's not a witch yet but she has magic, but she doesn't know it—she finds Steve—"

"Steve?"

"Steve the Stevedore. He's the construct. And she treats him like he's a normal person, and she teaches him how to play

Ping-Pong and shuffleboard. But then her aunts find out, and they warn her not to keep treating him like a person, or he's going to start becoming one."

Pinch. Cold metal. *Ka-thunk*. Pinch. Cold metal. *Ka-thunk*. "Okay," Riley said. "What's bad about becoming real? It worked out for Pinocchio."

"Who's Pinocchio?" asked Madelyn.

"It's super weird that your mom let you watch this weird old sitcom that I've never heard of, but Pinocchio wasn't allowed."

"She didn't like shows or movies where witches were evil. Or ones with bad mothers. Or dead mothers. Or . . . actually, there were a lot of things she didn't like."

"Well, you said she's dead, so we can watch whatever you want. I cannot wait to introduce you to the wonders of YouTube."

Madelyn shifted a little, as the voices picked up the phrase and began to echo it in her head. *She's dead. She's dead.*

"So what happens to Steve the Stevedore? Why is it bad that he's becoming real?"

"Because the rest of the world will never accept that he's real. They'll look at him and see a monster. The only person who'll look at him and think he's a person is Peggy. And she tries to get her aunts to make him real-real, but they can't agree because they want him to keep cleaning their rooms but can't afford to pay him."

Riley's face darkened at that. "Maybe they should clean their own fucking rooms then."

Madelyn smiled. "That's what Peggy says. But without the 'fucking.'"

Riley had to duck her face into her sleeve as she spat out

a string of giggles. It took a minute for her to resume the rhythm of stapling Madelyn back together, and when she did, she was still smiling a little. Madelyn reminded herself not to stare.

"So do they make Steve a real stevedore?" Riley asked.

Madelyn shook her head. "There's a fire on the shuffleboard court, and he sacrifices himself to save Peggy. But then they all agree only a real person would have done something like that. So it's . . . happy, I guess."

But they never mentioned Steve the Stevedore again, and that was what had given Madelyn nightmares. If he was real, why didn't they remember him? Talk about him? Miss him? His life—or creation—had no impact on any of the main characters, and his destruction—or death—hadn't either. So how could he have been real?

"We have got to get you some new TV to watch," Riley said. She had stapled her way down Madelyn's sternum and was now poised over the swell of her stomach. "No offense, but this show sounds stupid as hell."

"Some critics think it was really ahead of its time," Madelyn said, dimly remembering the forums she had visited, back whenever they still had a computer. However many years ago that had been.

"Last one, I think," Riley said. "Hold it here?"

Madelyn closed her eyes, trying to take in this feeling. *Frankenstein* had assured her that the world would never treat her with kindness or touch her without disgust. She was a monster, after all, but here she was.

Ka-thunk. The last staple went in, and then Madelyn felt the shivery sensation of the long seam down her front knitting itself closed. How many times had she felt this? she wondered. Would she ever know?

"I can't believe that worked," Riley said softly. "I mean, I believed you, I just didn't believe—never mind."

She tossed the staple gun away and stood up, groaning and shaking out her legs. "Did you want to keep that?"

Madelyn looked at her hand, only now realizing that she was still holding the charm bracelet from the little gift shop, one that Riley and Sam had made. She stammered out, "I can pay for it," and started digging in her pockets.

"What? No, it's literal trash. Everything in the gift shop is. Here." She put her hand out, and Madelyn, confused, put the bracelet in it. Riley fastened it around Madelyn's wrist, tying it snugly against the skin.

"Come on," she said. "I'm going to sneak you up to my room before anyone asks you awkward questions about where you came from."

CHAPTER SIXTEEN

Riley couldn't remember the last time she'd felt this exhausted, like there was a timer in her brain counting down the seconds to a full shutdown, and if she didn't lie down soon, she'd face-plant onto the floor. She let Madelyn have the first shower, then took a long one herself.

Madelyn had been sitting on the bed and stood up when Riley opened the door. She was wearing a pair of sweatpants and one of Toby's many ironically named band T-shirts that Riley liked to steal. This one was for a band called Bisun Bisun, with a flock of winged buffalo flying into the sun. It was probably older than Riley.

Riley collapsed on the bed. "This day was really . . ." She trailed off, unable to think of a descriptor. It was just a lot. "A big day," she settled on, with a tired, punch-drunk laugh.

Madelyn didn't join in, and Riley thought at first she'd forgotten what she'd said the night before. But she had the base of her palms pressing into her eyes instead, not listening.

"It doesn't feel real," she said finally. "I hurt my mom. I ran and got away from her. But I don't feel bad about hurting her, or happy about getting away. I don't feel anything."

Riley wished that someone, at some point, had taught her how to effectively comfort someone. Like, they should have taught that instead of precalc. TV made it look easy, like you would instinctively know whether to hug someone or put a hand on their shoulder or like, say something. She felt frozen, though, awkward as always in her body, so she said nothing.

"Why didn't I do this before?" Madelyn said. "I let her keep doing this to me. I don't know how many times it happened. She kept making me into her creature, and I never stopped her."

"Maybe you tried. You might not remember," Riley pointed out. "You said your memory's kind of jumbled. Maybe when she remade you, she messed with your memory."

Madelyn shrugged. She seemed skeptical.

Riley shifted onto her side, facing Madelyn. She thought briefly of sleepovers she'd gone to as a little kid, the narrow gap between two bodies that could hold all kinds of secrets: who were you crushing on, what had hurt you, what you hoped your future would hold.

Madelyn's voice was a hoarse whisper. "I thought getting rid of . . . of the Witch would help. That things would make sense after, and whatever she did to me—did to *us* would stop. Get better."

The witch is dead, Riley thought. *Long live the witch.* What she said was, "Maybe it takes a while. It'll stop getting worse and start getting better."

She could hear the doubt in her voice. Even if her life had lent itself to believing things would get better, Riley was pretty sure she was just constitutionally not built for optimism. But the wound on her chest had, if anything, only gotten worse, with indigo veins spreading up her neck and down her belly.

"Are you worried that you're like me?" Madelyn said. "Like, not a real person anymore?"

Riley stared at Madelyn, but her features were smoothed and sanded by the lack of light: only impressions of skin and scars. She hadn't been worried about that, but it was obviously still on Madelyn's mind. "You don't think you're real?"

Madelyn was silent, and Riley let herself move a little closer to her, trying to see her face. "I'm not a person, I'm—an experiment. One that failed over and over."

"Failed according to who?" said Riley. "Your mom? She doesn't get a vote. She sucks." She gestured between them, their scars, their wounds, and whatever horrible shit they still had going on beneath it all.

Madelyn cracked a small smile, then dropped it. "But you saw what I am. That's not real. She wanted a real girl, a real daughter, and I never could be that, so she . . ."

Riley scraped up the last of her energy, because this wasn't a conversation you could have in the morning light. "She can't blame you for being what you are."

"Who can she blame, then?" Madelyn asked.

"Herself? For being an evil bitch?" Riley said.

Madelyn snorted softly, which Riley took as a win. Madelyn's hand was next to hers, skin hot against Riley's fingers and their perpetually poor circulation.

"Hey," Riley said softly, because she just did not want to talk about mothers anymore, maybe ever again. "After this, what do you want to do?"

Madelyn looked at her. "What do you mean?"

"You're free from your mother. I'm pretty sure Toby would

let you stay for a while, at least. So what do you want to do?" Madelyn looked a little lost, so she added, "You could go to school, or at least get a GED. You could leave town. Or maybe we could find some long-lost relatives that you could stay with?"

Madelyn, if anything, looked even more overwhelmed. "I don't know. I never really thought that far ahead."

"Okay," Riley said. "Smaller stuff then, not long in the future. What's something you want to do? Or try, or see?"

Madelyn thought about it for a moment, then said, "I want to see the ocean."

Riley grinned. "*HMS Broomstick* inspired you?"

Madelyn shrugged, but she was smiling a little. "They always made it look really pretty."

"A cruise is probably beyond us financially, but maybe we can take a road trip."

The memory of her last road trip snagged in her chest, like she'd swallowed a fishhook. Mermaid Day with her mother and Sam. She pushed the memory away. Today had been long and awful enough already without going back to that.

"What's a road trip?"

Riley settled back against the bed. "It's traveling by car, but instead of getting somewhere as quickly as you can, you take back roads and detours to see creepy statues and weird little museums."

"Like your uncle's museum?" Madelyn asked. She sounded half-asleep already.

"He and Sam probably know every haunted hotel and ghost tour between here and the coast."

She could feel the darkness gathering around her, pulling

her down toward sleep. She was thinking of Mermaid Day, and wondering if you could write over bad memories with good ones, like a tattoo covering scars.

◆ ◆ ◆

Toby didn't wake them for school the next morning, and when they ventured downstairs, books and printouts were spread out across the living room, all of Toby's old history research. Sam was flipping through one of his many notebooks full of bullshit stories from the old guys down at Dunkin'. There was a map of Voynich Woods, with certain areas shaded in or marked with Xs. Toby himself looked like he hadn't slept. His pallor and the bags under his eyes rivaled Riley's. He was clutching an oversized mug that said WORLD'S OKAYEST GHOST HUNTER that was half-full of coffee, and writing furiously in one of his notebooks.

Riley should never have worried about either member of her family not believing her.

"I'll kill you if you incorporate me into your ghost tour," she warned Toby.

Toby shrugged and said, "You sure? We can probably charge double for a tour with an actually undead guide."

They stared at each other, stone-faced, until Riley's lips quivered and cracked into a smile, and they both broke into laughter.

Madelyn's confusion and concern was all over her face, and Riley shrugged apologetically to her. "Sorry, in this family we turn horrible trauma into stupid jokes."

◆ 223 ◆

Madelyn smiled uncertainly. "It's okay," she said. "What else are we going to joke about?"

"I already called the school and said you and Sam weren't feeling good," Toby said. His voice had that nervy edge of over-caffeination. "Let's hope they don't ask for a doctor's note. We need to figure out what happened to you, Rye, and how to reverse it. We're going to go through this logically, try to pin-point the cause, and then brainstorm some possible solutions. Starting with what the three of you saw that day."

Unlike at the police station, when she'd felt defensive, angry, and resentful of the constant reminders of her mother's mistakes, talking through what had happened made it, if not sensible—none of this shit made sense—then at least some-thing she could wrap her head around. It felt like an unbur-dening, like Toby and Sam were taking some of the weight of carrying this from her.

She noticed that Madelyn didn't mention Jane Doe. She wasn't sure why—Sam would have been thrilled to know she was one degree away from *the* Dead Girl—but didn't force it. Madelyn probably had her reasons, and Jane seemed to be her friend.

Toby was taking notes—you can drop out of grad school, he liked to say, but you can't give up compulsive note-taking. "Okay, go back a bit. What do you mean when you say *really* dead?"

"Her throat was cut, and there are spikes in her hands and through her heart."

Toby was leaning back into his chair, tapping his pen against his knee. "It sounds a little similar to some of the legends about the threefold death, though that usually involves drowning. There are also some bog bodies that were recovered with—"

"It's a binding," Madelyn said. Riley and Toby both looked over at her in surprise.

"How do you know that?" asked Riley.

"I just . . . do?" Madelyn said. "I don't have a very good memory, but I remember that. Hands, heart, and throat. Remove someone's will and voice and ability to free themselves."

"So someone made a deal with something that lived in that tree," said Toby. "Then bound it to the dead girl you kept seeing. Did you get a look at her face?"

Riley nodded. "Long dark hair, white girl. Maybe a little younger than Sam?"

"Camille Voynich," Sam said immediately. Riley gaped for a second, then put her face in her hands. God, how many times had she looked at the picture of the Voynich family in the barn?

Toby sorted through the piles of papers until he handed one to Riley: a photocopy from Roscoe's long-defunct newspaper about Camille's disappearance. Her face was splashed across the page, bigger than the text. There were two pictures, one a portrait with her family and the other of her alone, obviously cropped from some other image.

"So Camille goes missing," Riley said. "And then lots of other people go missing, over the next ninety years."

"Until one person comes back," Sam said.

"Technically two," Riley said. "You and I got lost at the same time."

Riley's musing was interrupted by the soft growl of a car engine. The four of them looked at each other; it sounded like it was pulling into the driveway. Toby got up and peeked through one of the windows.

"Christ, it looks like it's Ivy again. Riley, why don't you take

Madelyn upstairs?" Toby said. "I'll see what she wants this time. Sam, you go too."

Riley nodded, standing quickly and helping Sam up from the couch, then following her and Madelyn upstairs. They gathered in Riley's room, mostly because Sam's chaotic mess wouldn't have accommodated all three of them.

Sam was staring at her sister's chest, and Riley realized that she'd had a fist pressed over the wound.

"Does it hurt?" she asked.

Riley didn't look at her, wondering how much of the truth to tell her. "No," she said. She kind of wished that it did. "It doesn't feel like anything. Doesn't feel like it's me anymore."

Sam nodded but didn't look mollified. She sat in the old armchair that Toby had found and reupholstered with Riley as a birthday project a few years ago. Madelyn, on the other hand, was taking a slow circle around the room, looking at the books, the photos and sketches Riley'd taped up on the wall, everything she'd been too tired to notice the night before, probably. Riley wondered what Madelyn's room in her mother's house looked like. She pictured it being totally empty, like a room in an asylum or prison, or overdone with all kinds of weird decorations, a mash-up of witchy aesthetic and LIVE LAUGH LOVE. Either way, she was pretty sure Madelyn wouldn't have had much input on it.

She looked back at Sam then, still sitting in her chair. She'd pulled out a piece of paper and was folding it and unfolding it. Unfolded, Riley could see that it looked like a circle of girls holding hands. Folded, it was just a single girl, standing alone.

"What's that?" she asked. Sam's many interests didn't extend to origami.

Before she could answer, Sam suddenly flinched and let out a hiss.

"What's wrong?" Riley said.

"Paper cut," she replied. She held out her hand, where a line of blood was welling up on one of her fingers.

"I'll get a Band-Aid," Riley said.

As she left, she saw Madelyn bending down to pick up the paper girls that Sam had dropped. "Where did you get these?" she asked. Something in Madelyn's tone sounded off, but Riley could ask about it after getting Sam bandaged up.

She was sorting through the bathroom cabinet looking for the box of Band-Aids when she realized she could hear someone singing. The voice was high and thin, not particularly pleasant.

There was the first aid box. She pulled it out of the cabinet and dug through it until she found the nearly empty box of Band-Aids. The song was getting louder though, distracting. It must have been whoever had been at the door. Had Toby gotten waylaid by some random off-season carolers? She thought she recognized the song—something about two sisters walking by a river, one that Toby used to play on his guitar. "Don't get any ideas," he'd say, and that was right; the song ended badly for one of the sisters, didn't it? There never seemed to be happy endings for sisters in old songs.

"Riley?" Toby called upstairs. "Do you mind coming down for a minute? Ivy just has a question for you."

Riley groaned and didn't even try to disguise it. She could pass it off as just being a moody teenager. She set the Band-Aids down—Sam would survive a minute without them—checked in the mirror that nothing supernatural was showing on her face or neck, and went downstairs.

Toby was sitting at the kitchen table, staring out the window. There was something odd about the way he was staring, something that immediately made Riley's hackles stand on edge. Was something out there? For fuck's sake, had Mr. Bancroft revived himself *again*?

"Toby?" she asked, but he didn't even acknowledge her. Didn't even look.

When Riley turned around, Ivy had snuck up behind her. She smiled brightly and said, "Hi, Riley. Do you mind holding this for me?"

Before Riley could tell her, as politely as possible, to fuck off, she slipped something over Riley's head. It felt a little like a necklace, but the second it touched her skin, everything went black, and Riley was falling, falling, falling.

CHAPTER SEVENTEEN

Madelyn had a memory of sitting with her mother on the parlor floor, a pile of paper and two pairs of scissors between them. Her mother was showing her how to fold and cut the paper to transform it from a rectangle of paper into a circle of paper girls, holding hands. Madelyn was frustrated that her girls were wrong: lopsided and crooked, unlike her mother's perfect figures. She kept cutting too much, and their joined hands would break apart. It was one of the rare memories she had of her mother being happy with her, patiently tracing out over and over where she needed to cut, guiding the scissors around the little wedge of folded paper. "We can keep going until they're perfect," she had said.

"Where did you get this?" Madelyn asked Sam again. Sam was staring at the line of blood on her finger, which had started to drip down toward her fingernail. "Sam?"

Sam blinked slowly but didn't respond. The blood beaded up on her finger, then dripped to the floor.

"Riley?" Madelyn called, because this was wrong. Something was wrong. She dropped the circle of paper girls and ran to the bathroom. It was empty, and she looked down the hall. She couldn't hear anyone speaking. Had Toby gotten rid of the person at the door already? She crept downstairs, feeling relieved when she caught sight of Riley sitting in a chair in the kitchen.

"Riley, there's something—" she started to say, turning the corner. The words died in her throat when she saw her mother sitting between Riley and Toby at the kitchen table, looking through some of the papers that Toby had gathered.

Her skin was clear, glowing and healthy instead of blackened and blistered. Her auburn hair flowed over one shoulder in a windswept braid. Madelyn had a vertiginous moment, wondering if she'd hallucinated the whole thing: the confrontation, the hex-work beneath her skin, the fire she'd pulled out of herself. Mom would take her home, and the house would still be there, the bone-white paint peeling away. Nothing would be different, because nothing *could ever change*.

Then she noticed two things: First, her mother smelled like smoke, strong enough that Madelyn caught it at the other end of the room. It was the stench of charcoal and burned plastic particular to house fires. And secondly, her mother wasn't burned, but she had changed: dark streaks bruised the skin around her fingertips, the nail beds turned bluish-purple, like they belonged to a corpse's hands.

Madelyn put a hand to her chest, touched the rounded corners of the staples in her skin. Things had changed.

"What did you do to them?" she asked. Riley hadn't moved at all. Madelyn hadn't realized how fidgety Riley normally was, how she kept in constant motion. Seeing her so still was eerie and unnatural. Toby was slumped over in his chair, eyes closed, but he was breathing. She was glad that Sam at least was still upstairs, but what could she do if her mother decided to bring Riley's sister downstairs?

"He's sleeping, Maddie. It's fine. The little girl upstairs is too. I don't know why you sound so accusatory."

She didn't dignify that with a response, too busy trying to see what Mother had done to Riley. A charm had been wound around Riley's neck: a long cord of braided fibers, interwoven with dried belladonna fruits and flowers, tiny mouse bones, and beads of obsidian shards. The cord seemed to bite into Riley's skin, tightening around it.

"What about Riley? What did you do to her?"

"Her?" Mother said, nodding at Riley's silent form. "Maddie, if I'd known you had some attachment to this girl, I would have—"

"Taken her sister?" Madelyn said.

"Or her uncle, or someone else in the woods," Mother replied calmly. "The person doesn't matter. What matters is keeping our covenant. What did you think was going to happen when you pulled a dead girl out of the ground?"

She thought of what she and Jane had talked about, standing together by Riley's grave. She wanted to be free. She wanted to break out of this cycle she was trapped in. Jane hadn't even understood the extent of it, but she had told Madelyn that undoing it started with Riley, and Madelyn had believed her. She still did, but she was wishing that Jane had been able to give her a few more details. Something resembling a plan, maybe.

"Maddie, sweetie," her mother said.

"Don't call me that," she snapped. "I don't like it."

Her mother had a habit of testing her. Well, now she was testing her mother. Laying out a rule and seeing if she'd break it. If she broke a little rule, it was a sign that she wouldn't honor the bigger ones.

"Madelyn," her mother said. She held up the photocopied newspaper article that Madelyn had been looking at earlier, the one from when Camille Voynich went missing. It had the same portrait that she'd seen in the barn last night: a man and a woman in old-fashioned clothes, seated in two chairs. A young girl—Camille Voynich—seated between them, facing the camera directly. Another older girl stood behind the woman's chair, her expression stony.

"You know, they had two portraits of us taken that day?" her mother said. "My parents had planned to do only one of the two of them with Camille, but she insisted. Said she'd only sit for a photograph with them if we did one of all four of us as well. The whole family together, though she was the only one who thought of us that way. She was such a beautiful soul," Madelyn's mother added, with genuine sadness. "Nobody else could have loved me the way that she did. And none of this would have worked if she hadn't."

"That's . . ."

"Your extended family." Mother slid the paper across to her, and Madelyn caught it instinctively. "I had the original print of all four of us tucked away somewhere, but I suppose it's gone now."

She said the last part archly, one eyebrow raised. Like Madelyn burning the house down with her mother inside it was a minor inconvenience, but a forgivable one. This from the same woman who had held Madelyn's face underwater for talking back to her about *Frankenstein*.

She couldn't think of a single intelligent thing to say. Madelyn's mind was full of static, thoughts racing too fast, barely sensible against the backdrop of the chorus, which had been so quiet all morning but was now crying and wailing and shouting warnings at her. It wasn't just the shock of seeing her mother alive, or the revelation that her mother was Lillian Voynich, and far older than she looked. It was like she was really seeing her mother for the first time—or maybe the opposite, that Mother was seeing her. Listening to Madelyn, instead of *telling* her.

In her most vivid daydreams, when she felt trapped and feverish, all the walls of the house closing in on her, Madelyn would imagine her and Mother down in the basement with their positions reversed. Her mother strapped to a table in a dark, overly warm room, and Madelyn holding the scissors, the needle, and describing to her in calm detail the many ways she'd hurt her. But Madelyn always shied away from imagining using the scissors or needle on her mother; what she wanted, more than anything, was to force her mother to *listen to her.*

And here she was. Waiting for Madelyn to speak, to do something.

Move, she told herself. *Move one finger. Peel open one of your scars and set her on fire again. Tell her you're not her daughter anymore. Tell her that you remember her needles under your skin, choking and suffocating and not knowing why, only that it had been her. Tell her that you listened to her screams as the house burned like it was the sweetest music you had ever heard, and the only comfort in the cold new world you were alone in now. Tell her you'll make her scream again. Tell her. Say something. Do something.*

When Madelyn failed to react, her mother spoke again. "Someone once said that doing the same things over and over again and expecting different results is the definition of insanity. And I think that might be the issue between us. I keep trying the same things with you and expecting different results."

Madelyn took a step closer. "You think *that's* the problem between us?" she asked. "You . . . you hurt me."

Mom stood from the table and started to walk toward Madelyn. "I know. I'm sorry. Is that what you want to hear?"

The words and tone were deeply familiar—an apology used as a bludgeon, rather than reconciliation. She'd hated hearing her mother say *I'm sorry* more than anything else. "You don't mean it," Madelyn said. "You never did."

Mom moved cautiously toward her. "Maybe not the way you want me to mean it. You're mine. I spun you out of a hundred harvested dreams and wishes, and I kept trying to make you perfect. I always wanted to be a mother, but I find it hard to live with my mistakes."

"And I'm one of your greatest mistakes," Madelyn said bitterly.

Her mother lowered her head. "I think we both said and did things yesterday that we regret."

"I don't regret anything about what happened yesterday," Madelyn said. That wasn't true. She regretted that she'd wasted time crying to Jane about what she'd done when she should have made sure that her mother was really dead.

"That's because you don't have the whole story," Mom said. "Which is my fault. I should have told you. I was trying to keep you innocent, I suppose." She reached forward, as if to touch Madelyn's cheek, and Madelyn let herself flinch away. Mom pursed her lips unhappily, and Madelyn waited for the inevitable accusations: that Madelyn didn't love her enough, that she was trying to hide something, that she wasn't a good daughter. But her mother pulled her hand back and said nothing.

She was, Madelyn realized, actually trying.

"I think we can start over." She smiled magnanimously. "Without, you know, starting all the way over."

There was a scene in the last season of *HMS Broomstick* where Peggy finally learned about the coven, understood her own magic as something that was hers, that she could control, and that she could use with her aunts to make it even more powerful. But she still had to make a choice about whether she wanted to wield it, join the coven, and live a half step outside the rest of the world. Madelyn had never understood that; given the chance to have magic and family, she would have jumped.

That seemed like what her mother was offering her, and some part of her ached to grasp it with both hands and say, *Yes, yes, a thousand times yes.* It was what she'd been waiting for forever.

She doesn't get a vote, Riley had told her. *She sucks.*

"Why should I trust you?" Madelyn asked.

Her mother pursed her lips, and Madelyn knew that Mom wasn't someone who was used to hearing that. "You don't think you hurt me as well? Maddie—Madelyn. You tried to kill me yesterday."

"But you—"

"And it wasn't even the first time," she said, speaking over her. "You always do this. I kept trying over and over because you always hurt me in the end. You lie to me, you run away, get these terrible ideas from going on the internet or reading books." She made a fed-up gesture toward Riley. "You sabotage me. Or you go the direct route and try to burn me alive. It all hurts, Madelyn."

Had she done all of that? Any of that? "I don't remember doing those things."

"Of course not," said Mom. "Why would I burden you with those memories?" She looked searchingly into Madelyn's eyes. "You're my daughter and I love you."

There was something wrong with this conversation, Madelyn thought. But it seemed so reasonable. Even so, the chorus of whispers in her head were spitting poison and rage, a warning not to trust her.

Her mother took a deep breath. "There's hurt on both sides, is the point. And I think we can move on, but we need to be more honest with each other. There are things that I need to show you," Mom said. "And a story you need to hear. I think it's time you actually meet Generous for yourself."

INTERLUDE: THE DEVIL

Excerpt from *Bury the Echo: A Local Historian's Perspective on Folklore, Forests, and Other Important Stuff, or So I'm Telling Myself (Working Title)*, by Toby Walcott

It should be noted that the Devil in theology is not the same as devils in Roscoe's local legends. In New England, Satan is rarely spotted outside white-steepled churches or the vivid imaginations of certain reactionary conservative neighbors with QAnon brain rot. No matter what people like Mrs. LaFontaine says (or paints on her unhinged yard signs), here's the truth: Satan wouldn't be caught dead in Roscoe. We only get the weird diabolical D-listers.

The devil (small *d*) in New England doesn't have grand plans for the apocalypse, definitely isn't leading sabbaths or cult rituals to sacrifice babies. Sometimes he stops for drinks in a tavern and leaves behind a singed handprint on a bar and the smell of brimstone. His famous bargains sometimes go his way; all that's left of a person will be a dried-up liver or half of a heart, an ax with a charred handle, etc. But the devil, like all tricksters, also exists to be tricked. (My favorite story about the devil literally getting more than he bargains for involves a haunted house, apples, and a farmer scaring the devil off by mooning him. It inspired my younger niece to say, "He's trying to scare the devil" anytime someone's pants are hitched a little too low.)

But this kind of Elmer Fudd devil is common across America, and maybe especially in Appalachia. In Roscoe, the one difference is the devil and its Witch. Sometimes the Witch and the devil are a team, sometimes they're at odds, sometimes they're tricking each other. They tend to reward certain kinds of cleverness and determination, and punish certain kinds of greed. They always bring a sense of wildness and wonder to this town on the edge of the deep, dark woods.

They have deep roots in the town and the surrounding forest. Such as in this story, supposedly the origin tale for the Witch of the Woods.

A logger named Jack met the devil in the woods. The devil offered him a deal: In exchange for his soul, he'd give Jack one wish, answer one secret of the world, and grant one boon in his time of need.

Jack, who lived in a logging camp filled with other men, wished for a beautiful wife. Lo and behold, a woman appeared in front of him. But while his new wife was as beautiful as promised, she was willful and sharp-tongued, quick to anger when Jack came home drunk or got handsy with the good-time girls at the saloon. She refused to wash his clothes or perform her wifely duties when she was mad at him, which was most of the time. Jack went back to the old wolf tree where he first encountered the devil, and asked for the secret of controlling his wife. Get her pregnant, said the devil. She's only like this now because she knows she could find another man who'll treat her better than you do. Get her pregnant and she won't have any option but to stay with you and make the best of it.

(Historical digression: Is this sexist? Of course. Also unfortunately true.)

Jack's unnamed wife did indeed get pregnant, and all accounts have her calming down while in her delicate state. For nine months, all was peaceful. (At least for Jack. I can't find any version of this story where we hear from this mysterious wife.)

When his wife's labor started, the midwife warned Jack not to come into his house. Jack stopped himself the first time he was tempted to enter, early on. His brother (or alternately, his neighbor or the local priest) stopped him from entering the second time, when he heard his wife cursing him. The third time, though, he heard her call his name. Not in pained anger, but in pure fear. No neighbor, brother, priest, or midwife could hold him back then. But when he entered the birthing room, Jack saw his wife's true form, which is usually either a catamount or a timber wolf, depending on the story. A nightmare in flesh and fur, giving birth. The sight of her husband, rather than calming her down, enraged her, and she attacked everyone in the room, killing the midwife, the neighbor/priest/brother. But when she tried to kill Jack, he called out for the devil to grant his boon and save him. His wife fled into the woods instead. Jack tracked her to a big old tree in the woods, and in a hollow among the roots, he found a newborn girl. His wife was nowhere in sight, and Jack had no desire to raise a wolf-born daughter.

Jack knew that his soul now belonged to the devil, and there was nothing to stop him from collecting it. He offered the baby girl as a trade: The devil would leave him be until the end of his natural lifespan. The devil gladly accepted this final bargain and raised Jack's daughter to become the first Witch of the Woods.

When they met again at Jack's deathbed, Jack asked the devil: Why did you give me a terrible wife?

And the devil, though owing Jack nothing, gave him this answer for free: I gave you a fine wife, but you were a terrible husband. Human misery only ever has human origins.

My sister Anna hated that story but quoted that last line all the time. She liked to call it Roscoe's official town anti-motto, since this town made a habit of blaming every bad thing on "some supernatural bullshit or other," as she liked to say. She thought that my interest (obsession, she called it) in the paranormal was just an escape.

And—of course it was. Voynich Woods is a place for all kinds of monsters, and that's what I thought I was. When we grew up, wanting to kiss a boy was an unnatural, ugly, monstrous hunger. I wanted to find some strangeness in a landscape scraped clean of wonder, to know that the world was bigger than our shitty small town. To make it worth staying in.

I found it, and Anna didn't. And only one of us is left now. I fucking hate it.

Anna should have gotten to see her kids grow up. She should have gotten to grow up too—figure out who she was beyond her anger and depression and terrible coping mechanisms. She deserved wonder too.

I want Riley and Sam to have handholds in that wonder. Riley especially, since it doesn't come as naturally to her, just like it didn't come naturally to Anna. She needs to know that there's something beyond human misery in the world.

All I can do is offer up these stories and hope she sees them for the maps that they are: tools for always finding her way back home.

Lillian had gotten too complacent. She could see that now.

She resigned herself to this little life in this little town, to gnawing loneliness. Lillian was the Witch of the Woods, and while she never announced the fact to Roscoe's people, they seemed to sense it: some whiff of supernatural power, the taint of the woods. Voynich Woods, now. Lillian's name was inextricable from the mystery and strangeness of them.

She missed Camille. Sometimes, she even missed her mother and stepfather. Lillian felt the most alive in her fantasies about the future, her chance at motherhood, to correct all the mistakes her own mother had made.

Pregnancy was not what she imagined. Motherhood even less so. Madelyn, from the very beginning, seemed determined to squash all her mother's dreams of a new family. She was a tiny force of chaos that only wanted to eat when it was time to sleep, only slept for twenty minutes at a time, cried whenever her mother held her, and only ever seemed happy when she was outside.

And now, Madelyn had magic. Not like Lillian's, which was careful, precise, and paid for dearly. She had stumbled into magic like it was a game, and Lillian had shied away from the sheer power Madelyn wielded like it was nothing. Their yard a riot of color, the garden overflowing with out-of-season blooms. Since returning home she maintained a single camellia shrub in one corner of the yard, though it was always sickly and rarely bloomed. Now it was drooping with heavy flowers, red petals falling to the grass like drops of blood.

She found her way to the Wishing Tree that night. Camille's usual fury was subdued by her most recent feeding. Lillian could feel Generous watching her, though, quiet and patient as always.

"What did you do to her?" Lillian demanded. "My daughter. She's not normal. She's like a changeling, a feral creature. You tricked me somehow."

"Did I?" Generous asked, and it was somehow a shock to hear it speak. It had been so long since she'd heard that low, curious voice. Before Lillian could answer that question, it added, "Even if I did, what should I do from here?"

In her darkest moments, Lillian had wondered if her mother had been right: She would never be fit for motherhood, and her parents had been right to have her sterilized. Something was rotten inside her, and that rot had somehow passed into her daughter, made her strange and unknowable. Lillian had always thought that having a daughter would be like having a little sister again: a confidante, a conspirator, someone who would love Lillian unconditionally. But Madelyn was a queer and uncanny presence, like the wilderness had invited itself into Lillian's home.

"I see your game," Lillian spat. "You think I'll free you? I'm sure your solution would just be another trick."

"Then why are you here?" asked Generous.

"A good question," she replied, and turned on her heel to return home. Lillian had her power, her magic, her cleverness. She had time as well. She would create the family she deserved, longed for, and for which she had condemned herself.

CHAPTER EIGHTEEN

Madelyn followed her mother up the paths through Voynich Woods, strangely numb. It was the same feeling she'd had back in the basement, like she was only loosely tethered to her body, and the connection was stretching farther and farther. It was better than panic, at least.

Riley walked silently behind them. She moved with a slow grace that seemed totally alien on her limbs. Madelyn was used to her twitching, fidgeting energy, her questions that Madelyn didn't know how to answer. Seeing Riley like this felt too close to the corpse she'd been when Madelyn first saw her.

Ever since she met Jane, the woods had been the only place that she could escape to. The trees sheltered her from her mother's constant surveillance. And even though she'd always had to return to her mother's house, it was the first landscape that she'd felt a part of. She belonged to the woods, and that kind of belonging felt so much better than the belonging her mother claimed over her. Her mother owned the woods, and in a way, she owned Madelyn, her creation. She thought she controlled them both, but her daughter and the woods that bore her family's name had their own secrets, and their own plans.

Madelyn had to hope that she could remember that.

At the Wishing Tree—no, the wolf tree, she reminded herself. It felt like a truer name. At the wolf tree, her mother stopped at the edge of the clearing, but Riley continued past her. Madelyn tried to catch her arm, pull her back, but her mother said, "Let her go. We'll follow her in a second."

Madelyn eyed the grave in the clearing where she'd first found Riley, an uneasy reminder of what her mother was capable of. But she allowed herself to be pulled aside.

Her mother adjusted her bag where it hung on her shoulder. "Didn't you ever wonder why I sent you in to gather Generous's tokens, instead of going myself?"

She had raised Madelyn very specifically never to question anything she did, and to punish her if she tried. So yes, Madelyn had wondered, and never asked.

Her mother must have seen the answer on her face. "You can feel it, can't you? The lines of power I put down in this place. The trap I wove to keep Generous here. The only other people who can cross it are the ones we bring here, the ones who are carried or called."

And once she pointed it out, Madelyn could feel it. There were four trees that looked particularly weather-beaten, on the edge of rot. A birch leaning at an angle, an elderberry bearing misshapen fruit, a holly, and a beech. She could feel magic tying them together, a net that stretched down into the earth and up to the canopy. It was similar to the wards Mom had stationed around the house: mixtures of living and dead things, treasures she'd gathered from the Wishing Tree. She remembered that Jane had brought her to the edge of the clearing but hadn't crossed it. Hadn't intervened in her and Riley's fight until they'd passed back out of it.

"It's all part of the same magic that's in you," Mom told her. "You can pass through it without weakening it."

"You can't?" Madelyn asked.

As if in answer, her mother stepped forward, past that invisible line of magic. The net . . . shifted. Like a spider's web after something flew into it, breaking some of the strands. Madelyn could feel parts of the net weaken.

"It's a risk," Mom told her. "The net's stronger when I'm outside of it. When I'm inside, it's unbalanced. But you need an explanation, so. Here we are." She stepped farther into the clearing, approaching the wolf tree. Riley had waited beside the tree, next to a hole in the trunk that Madelyn hadn't noticed before. At their approach, Riley dropped to her knees and started to crawl in.

Madelyn's eyes darted between her and her mother, wanting to yank Riley out, not quite able to turn her back on Mom. "It's fine," Mom said. "I need to show you what's down there."

This was a trap. All the voices in her head insisted on it— all those previous Madelyns who'd been torn apart and put back together under her mother's hands.

But what could she do? She followed Riley into the tree. The hollow tunneled into the earth, and after a claustrophobic squeeze, opened up into one of the caverns that riddled Voynich Woods. Her mother followed close—too close—behind her.

This cave was shaped like a wide bowl, lit by a narrow shaft of light from the same hollow that they'd crawled through. Tree roots, like pale, thin fingers, dangled down, or crept through the walls. There was a slab of rock in the center with a dead child on it, with the same wounds that Riley had described: spikes through her hands and heart, her throat opened with a ghastly wound. Dried flowers rotted around her, and the rocks and dirt were dotted with spilled wax from candles.

Some rich and rotten magic seeped from her: an old animal stink, alive and dead and everything in between. Madelyn's mother—who Madelyn had always believed to be the most powerful—contained only an echo of it. Madelyn recognized it, had tasted it like copper in the back of her tongue when she pulled fire out of herself.

Other bodies radiated out from the dead girl on the slab, half-hidden among roots and rocks. They weren't nearly as neat or well-kept as the corpse in the center. Madelyn recognized the same transformation that was overtaking Riley: skin hardened and peeling open from a central wound, dark lines branching off in dendritic patterns, and tendrils sprouting up from the skin. All the dead wore peaceful expressions on their faces, like they were dreaming about wonderful things. She looked closer at one of the more intact bodies, then stumbled back with a gasp. The person's eyes were heavy-lidded but open, their irises faded as if with cataracts; when Madelyn had come closer, the person's gaze had shifted to follow her movement.

"They're alive?" she asked.

"No," Mom answered. She came over and gently closed the person's eyes. "At least, not like you're thinking."

She swept away some of the dirt from beside the body, and Madelyn could see a web of tangled, delicate roots branching off the person's flesh, burrowing down into the dirt, the other bodies. Mom smoothed the soil back over, patting it fondly.

Then she stood up and cleared a little space next to the dead girl in the center, brushing the dead flowers away so she could sit next to the body.

"Once," her mother said, "a long time ago, something in these woods offered me a covenant. A wish granted, a secret given, and a boon offered. In exchange, I would take on the role of its witch. Protect it, bind myself to it, keep its cycles."

"You became the Witch of the Woods?" Madelyn asked.

In *HMS Broomstick*, witches were born, not made. But there'd been witches in Voynich Woods before her mother, hadn't there? Riley had talked about stories of the Witch of the Woods going back hundreds of years.

"There's always a witch in these woods," her mother said. "One dies, another takes their place. Generous's offer never changes. I thought to myself that it was old and I was young, and I would be a servant to nobody. So I wished—" Mother's breath caught, and it took a moment before she could meet Madelyn's eyes and finish. "I wished for a daughter. I wanted a child more than anything in the world, and . . . couldn't conceive in the usual way."

Was that why Madelyn could never satisfy her mother? Her conception was miraculous, something out of a myth, but Madelyn could never compete with what her mother had hoped for.

"Then I asked for the secret of the Wishing Tree's charms: how to use them to work my will on the world, shape spells, protect myself and the people I loved. To make life, or bring it back."

"And the boon?" Madelyn asked.

"I built a trap, and a binding, and asked for it to walk into both." After a second, she added, "I thought it was clever. But magic is sacrifice and negotiation. It's cutting out pieces of yourself—or other people—and offering them to something hungry."

Her words had the cadence of a fairy tale, and Madelyn wondered if she'd told this story before. Told it to Madelyn, even, before cutting the memory out of her.

"But Generous tricked me as well. It told me how to trap it, but not how to keep it. The cage I built for it and Camille broke down over time. It needed more sacrifices to keep it whole."

Mom tenderly touched the dead girl's face, brushing away some fallen dirt and rotting petals, then took out fresh flowers from the bag she'd carried with her—sunflowers, asters, and coneflowers, the unseasonable morning glory blooms, along with sprigs of rosemary and mint—and began arranging them around the corpse's face and arms. She smiled at Madelyn, and unlike her normal smiles, this one seemed shy, a little sad. She was touching this dead child with much more gentleness than she had ever shown Madelyn, and Madelyn realized: This was who she had been created to replace.

Madelyn said nothing, kept her face still. Her mother's love was capricious, smothering and sharp by turns. Camille had learned that first.

"It doesn't hurt," Mom said. "Not after the first cut. They're not suffering. Your friend wouldn't have suffered if you'd left her down there."

She stood up and came close to Madelyn. The cavern was low-ceilinged, almost claustrophobically so, and her mother had to hunch a little, bringing her face closer to Madelyn's.

"Maddie—Madelyn. See?" She smiled at her. "I am making

an effort. I don't know how you did it, but this disruption has put everything in danger. If we unbind Generous from Camille, our magic dies."

Our magic, she said. Madelyn remembered the dandelions again, asking them to grow. She thought of the scars on her throat, and chest, and hands. *It's a binding,* she'd told Riley and her family, and wondered how she'd known.

Her mother had made her with stolen magic, trying to create a perfect daughter. She had spent years shaping and cutting and sanding Madelyn down, because she didn't want *her,* not really. Mother wanted something that would fill the terrible hollow spaces inside her, carved out by rage and grief and greed.

You always do this, her mother had told her. Madelyn always disappointed and frustrated her, talked back, fought back; she wanted and needed to be free. Something in Madelyn would always rebel.

I will revenge my injuries; if I cannot inspire love, I will cause fear, she thought. No wonder her mother had gotten rid of *Frankenstein.*

Madelyn realized that she could hear water down here. There were caves underneath the woods, and the caves were mostly formed by water—the underground streams and springs that rose and fell beneath the mountain. She walked toward the sound of water trickling. There was a pool of water, hardly more than a puddle.

The only people who could cross the net her mother put up were the ones who were carried there. Or called.

"Maddie?" her mother said. There was a warning in her voice.

She knelt down next to the water and called out. "Jane," she whispered. "Jane, Jane—"

The scar on her hand opened, and blood trickled out. The water rippled as she pressed her hand into the puddle, and the blood dispersed. She'd never tried this so far from the well, but she remembered the little exhibit on the Dead Girl in the barn: Any body of water in the woods would do. Jane was her first friend, and the one who maybe understood her best. Jane had held all her secrets, even the ones Madelyn had kept from herself.

"What are you doing?" her mother demanded.

"Jane, please—" she said.

And there was a hand around hers, sharp points of bone pressing into her skin.

Take a deep breath, Jane instructed.

Madelyn barely had a chance to follow her instructions before she was yanked forward, into that smell of mud and muck.

CHAPTER NINETEEN

The ground beneath Voynich Woods was riddled with caves. They were among its most famous features. Toby would go on about the beauties of karst topography, soluble limestone, and hydrogeology, but everyone grew up with stories about an uncle or a cousin falling through the forest floor. There was a sinkhole in the woods that everyone called the Witch's Well, one that the forest service had actually come in and covered up, since it was too deep to fill and posed a real danger to hikers. It was deep and dark, and you could drop a stone down it and hear it fall for a long, long time.

When Ivy slipped the charmed necklace over Riley's neck, it felt like falling into a sinkhole; the ground beneath Riley's feet wobbled and gave, and she plunged down into the darkness, tumbling through it like a pebble.

She could fall forever, she thought. Whatever Ivy had put on her was a weight around her neck, dragging her down.

"Help me!" she screamed. Riley reached out, trying to find a handhold in the darkness. There was nothing, only smooth emptiness she could fall through forever. "Generous, help!"

Ask for your boon, Generous told her. Its voice had always been so calm, but now it sounded as panicked as she felt. *I can't help unless—*

She could feel the needle-sharp prickling of roots emerging from her skin and didn't fight it; they were as desperate as she was to stop her fall, find some way to climb back up.

"Fine!" she screamed. "I demand the boon you owe me. Help me!"

She didn't know what Generous was going to try, but for the first time, she let it take over. Ceded control. If nothing else, she knew that Generous wanted to live and be free. To do that, it would have to get them out of this trap.

When Generous had first started to consume her, it had met her in some kind of other space, something that looked like a memory but felt like a dream. So when she opened her eyes to the damp interior of a familiar car, the windshield fogged from three people's breath, and smelled the ocean drifting through the crack in the window, it wasn't a surprise. But that didn't stop her stomach from dropping, dread filling her.

Mermaid Day. The best day she'd ever spent with her mother and Sam, all together on a beach near Portsmouth. The worst night probably of her life. At least until this week.

She had a sudden, fleeting hope that she'd never left this place. She had gone to sleep five years ago in the passenger seat with a musty-smelling blanket covering her, and never woken up. Everything since then had just been an incredibly vivid nightmare.

The brief, vivid hope deflated when she looked over at Mom and saw Generous looking out through her eyes.

"No," Riley said. She tried to sit up, fighting with the reclined seat. "This isn't—I wanted to wake up."

"You wanted to stop falling."

"Not if you were going to bring me *here*," she spat.

"I'm sorry," said Generous, in her mother's voice.

"Fuck you," Riley said reflexively. She finally managed to get her seat up and looked around. Sam, barely five years old, was sprawled in a nest of blankets across the back seat. She had fallen asleep with her two fingers in her mouth, a habit that she'd given up years ago, and intense nostalgia hit Riley. "What happened? We were in the kitchen. And then it was like the floor fell from under my feet."

Generous smiled with Anna Walcott's mouth. Her teeth were rimed with purplish-black. "The Witch was cleverer than we were."

It was hard to look at Generous, especially here, wearing her mother's face. "Ivy's the Witch? Wait, Ivy is Madelyn's *mom*?" Riley felt anger flush her cheeks. She'd been so stupid.

"There's always a Witch of the Woods. They come, deal with us, stay for a while, then die, and eventually someone else becomes the Witch. But the Witch is supposed to protect the cycle. She stopped it. Broke the wheel. Trapped us."

Generous tapped its fingers against the ridges of the steering wheel, and Riley realized that her nail beds were dark blue. Cyanotic.

"Why are we *here*?" said Riley. She gestured around them: the Jeep, the empty beach, the ocean in front of them. "I never wanted to come back here."

"It's better than falling forever through a lightless void, isn't it?"

"Not really," Riley said. "This is . . ."

"The worst memory, isn't it?" said Generous. "The one you'd throw down the Witch's Well if you could." It reached forward to wipe away the condensation on the windshield. "It seems so peaceful, though."

Out in front of them, the Atlantic Ocean stretched across the horizon. Riley remembered a beautiful sunset, but now it was that cold period before dawn, where the world was drenched in dark, mournful blue. The sharp crescent moon was dipped low, almost touching the water. There'd been so many stars out that night, she remembered.

"Why do you do this?" she asked. "Why do you look like her? Why do you take me to the worst memories I have?"

"Because you're trapped in them too," Generous answered. "The Witch's magic always finds the things you can't let go of, that eat at you. She makes her victims help build their own snares and cages."

Riley opened her mouth to argue—she didn't dwell on these memories; if anything, she avoided them like the plague. But that was the same thing, wasn't it? Both gave them more power over her.

"Can't we just stop the memory here?" Riley asked. "Where I'm only half-awake and still think this is one of Mom's better bad decisions?"

Generous looked at her; it was terrible, because it was her mother looking at her, looking at Riley like she was really *seeing* her.

"You can escape a trap," said Generous. "But not if you're standing still. And besides, the world is still moving outside of us."

It nodded at Riley's chest. Riley looked down and saw that cracks had spread upward from the wound there, creeping across her neck and now down her arms. Some parts looked like the patterns she had seen in the locket, flowers and branching vines. Other parts looked jagged, ugly.

Riley thunked her head against the window, thought of a meme she'd seen: *There should really be ways out that aren't through.* If she lived through this, she'd definitely incorporate that into a tattoo.

Generous didn't wait for her to answer. She just mirrored Riley's pose, leaning her face against the window. Her breathing slowed down, and her eyelids lowered, and her gaze became unfocused. At some point, it was no longer Generous sitting in the driver's seat. It was Anna Walcott, and it was the worst night of both her and Riley's life.

"You know what sucks, Rye?" Mom asked, when she noticed her older daughter awake. "There's really no escape from your own bullshit. Not even out there." She nodded to the dark, shifting waters. The ocean's waters were restless, constantly shifting and refracting the light from the moon and the faraway cabins.

Her voice was slurring, and it was taking her real effort to speak. Riley felt a wave of disappointment, heavy and oppressive, because she knew what this meant. Mom had snuck out of the car at some point, taken something. Riley wasn't stupid, though Mom always seemed to think she was.

Riley, resigned to reliving this memory, answered her. "There might be."

She imagined a fantastical underwater world, or stealing a

boat and sailing off the edge of the map. She imagined a life without her mom, or with a mom who was different.

Anna mumbled something else, not quite audible, and then took a long, rattling breath. It didn't sound like her mother's normal snoring, but wet, almost painful. Riley sat up, looking closer at Anna.

"Mom?" she said.

Riley had tried hard to forget. Generous, though, was gifting this memory back to her. Like all of its gifts, it was fucking awful. She wanted to distance herself from it, but there wasn't any space between now and then. It felt as raw as living it had.

"Mom," she said again, louder. When Anna didn't respond, Riley shook her. Her mother's head lolled, and she slumped bonelessly forward. Foamy vomit tipped out of her mouth, and now that Riley was looking, she could see that her mother's lips had turned dark, tinted as blue as the waters in front of them. *Mermaid Day,* Riley thought hysterically. *She's turning into a mermaid—*

Riley shook herself. She picked up her mother's phone, but it was dead. Anna had remembered the auxiliary cord—she'd blasted old-school punk songs the whole drive here—but had apparently forgotten her charger.

"Wait here," she said. "I'll be right back."

Riley ducked out into the night. She was barefoot, and the sand was cold and damp. The nearest building was a boarded-up taffy and fudge shop with a big sign that said SEE YOU NEXT SUMMER! It was the off-season, and it was that time of night between too late and too early, where anybody with any sense was asleep.

"Hello?" Riley screamed, and the empty beach echoed it back to her, a cruel joke. "Is anyone there? I need help!"

Nobody answered, and Riley took another couple of steps forward. "Hello?" she screamed again.

Still no answer, and Riley was struck by how alone she was. Nobody knew where they were. Nobody knew where *she* was.

For one terrible moment, she considered running. Not going back to the car, but taking off instead. She didn't want to see her mother die. If Riley didn't see it, she wouldn't have to remember it, wouldn't have to *live* with it. She forgot about her sister, who was still sleeping in the back seat of the Jeep. She forgot about everything except herself, and not wanting to be in this story.

Is that what makes this the worst memory? Generous asked her. Not in her mother's voice—her mother was still dying in the car—but in its own, from the shard of it inside her.

Riley nodded. Bad enough to remember her mother's blue lips, vomit leaking out of the corners of her mouth. She wouldn't wish that on her worst enemy. But this moment of cowardice and selfishness—she'd tried to scrub it from her memory, and still it haunted her. She'd never be able to forget it, and she hated herself for it.

But you didn't run, Generous reminded her, at the same time that Riley forced herself to turn back to the car.

It didn't matter. Nobody should have to know how weak they were, how their worst impulses were waiting for just the right circumstances to trap them. And that in the end, it wasn't any particular kind of bravery that made her turn back to the car, but just the terror of being alone. She hadn't run away, but not out of any sense of duty, responsibility, bravery. She'd just been too scared to face the awfulness of the world alone.

Riley ran back to the car and searched her mother's bag. Maybe she'd find another charger somewhere, and she could call Toby and—

A little zippered pouch fell into her hand, and she almost flung it away, thinking it was her mother's drug kit. Then she saw the words OVERDOSE RESCUE KIT.

A few months earlier, at one of the NA meetings that her mother went to sometimes, some harm reduction organization had come and passed out these kits after the meeting, explaining how to use them. Anna had seemed uncomfortable, didn't take the kit the man held out to her, and hurried out of there with Riley and Sam. But she must have gone back for one, or gotten one at a different meeting, because here it was.

Riley fumbled it open, snatching up the pamphlet and holding it close to her face, trying to read it despite the darkness and the way her hands were shaking. She followed the directions, prying the cap off the plastic cylinder, plugging in the capsule and applicator, and then clambering over the car's console to get to her mother's face. She pushed her back, pressed the tip against Anna's nostril, and ejected the spray. Half in one nostril, half in the other.

In reality, her mom's breathing had sped up almost immediately, and a minute or so later she'd blinked her eyes open. Sam was awake by then, crying, and Riley had helped her mother move shakily into the passenger seat. Riley had driven them—slowly, jerkily, with Anna coaching her in a hoarse, crackling voice—to a truck stop, where she could call 911 and Toby and—

But instead, Generous blinked her mother's eyes open, and Riley remembered that Anna was gone. She'd saved her mother, and Anna had gotten sober and promised this time it was permanent. No more half-assed NA meetings, no more contact with her old friends who were still using, she'd pass the six-week rehab treatment with flying colors, she'd ask Toby for support when she needed it and not when it became an emergency, she'd cooperate with DCFS even though she'd rant about how terrible they were—

And then she had started using again. And then she had disappeared.

Riley slithered back to the passenger side of the car, dropping the empty naloxone capsule into the footwell. She felt empty. It made sense that her first encounter with Generous had left her with a gaping hollow in her chest. That wound had been there all along, and Generous had just made it visible to everyone.

"I don't know how that sucked more the second time around, but it did," Riley said. She got out of the car again, nearly falling out until her legs steadied. She leaned against the hood of the Jeep and stared out at the ocean, its waters black except where the ripples caught the light.

There, in the shallow waters, Riley saw the girl. Dead, an iron stave through her chest, another through each of her hands. She watched Riley curiously, like she had the first time Riley had met Generous.

"Who is that?" Riley asked.

The other door opened, and Generous got out. It walked with her mother's footsteps, and Riley turned away. She still wasn't ready to look at Anna, or the thing that occupied her body. "That's the creature I'm bound to. The witch's sister. She bound the girl to me."

"Why is she following me?"

"Hunger, probably. She's not used to missing her meals."

Riley stood a little straighter, alarmed. "Me?"

"Mm."

The girl was watching Riley with a particularly intent focus that, yeah, looked a lot like hunger. "I thought you . . ."

Generous shook its head. "It's an ugly, awful thing that was done to her. Her sister used her to pin me in place under my tree, but she didn't realize what it would do to Camille. Now she's a hungry little ghost."

Wheels. Cycles. Camille ducked down into the water, so that only her eyes showed. She watched them without blinking.

Riley glanced at her own hands. The patterns and cracks had spread down her arms. She touched her neck and shied away; the wound had risen as high as the hollow of her throat. *Time is running out,* she thought.

"A wish, a boon, and a secret," she said. "That was the deal, right?"

It should have been getting lighter; dawn should have been coming. But they were frozen in this time, the coldest hour. Generous nodded solemnly.

"I think I know what secret I need from you," she said.

Generous didn't ask her what she meant. It didn't answer at all. It just waited attentively.

"How do I unbind you from Camille?"

A long, gusty breath. She could feel Generous slowly sloughing off Anna Walcott's appearance; if Riley didn't look too closely, it seemed like her mother was still standing next to her. But the details were going looser, impressionistic, the height shifting, the shape of her features fading. This was what it would have been like: forgetting her. The sharpness of the details eroding away. Maybe this part, at least, was a gift.

"The iron staves," Generous said. "That's the easy part. You have to take them out of her."

"What's the hard part?" Riley shut her eyes, because she could sense the last pieces of her mother drifting away. Her deal with Generous was concluding: She'd received her wish to go home, a boon to stop falling endlessly through this darkness, and now the secret to what bound Generous and Camille Voynich together.

"It was a sister who did this to her. You have to be a sister to her to undo it." Generous leaned forward. It no longer looked like her mother, though it had kept her voice. It was tall in her periphery vision, its arms long. There was something adorning its head: horns or antlers or just long, twisting thorns. "You can't think of her as the thing that's killing you. Can't think of her as the thing that stole your mother from you, or could have gotten your sister. And you can't let her rage infect you."

Riley thought of the night before, transforming into something fueled by rage and cold fury. It had felt so good in the moment, to be consumed by the urge to destroy.

"You don't want to know what will happen if you unbind us?" Generous asked.

"The deal was only one secret, wasn't it?" Riley asked.

"It was," Generous said. It sounded sorry, for the first time. "I'm bound as much as you are."

Riley didn't mind. She suspected the answer to that question wouldn't be anything great, and it'd probably be easier to pull some crazy, desperate shit without knowing she'd die or break apart like a rotten log or whatever at the end of it.

The wind suddenly picked up, tossing Riley's hair. Thunder started a slow rumble, so low that Riley felt it more than heard it. The water rippled as well, wavelets kicking up and crashing across the dirty sand where Riley had danced with her mother and sister on the best and worst night of her life.

CHAPTER TWENTY

Cold water closed up over Madelyn's head. Her mother's voice instantly cut off, and Madelyn felt pressure against her ears as she was dragged down underwater by the sharp grip of Jane's hand.

Every time, traveling with Jane was the same: the shocking cold of the water surrounding her, that sense of pressure, and a sickening velocity as Jane tugged her along.

Until suddenly, they stopped.

Madelyn opened her eyes and Jane wasn't quite there. She wavered the same way light did when it hit the water, refracting into dancing points of light. They were in some deep place, far underground.

This was the part she never remembered when Jane took her by the water's ways.

You never asked what happened to me, Jane said. *Why I'm like this, or why I helped you.*

There was something pleading in her tone, a childish note. They were still floating in the water, and Jane looked so lost: sad enough to drown, angry enough to drown the world with her.

Madelyn shook her head. It hadn't occurred to her to ask. She had needed a friend, an escape, and a confidante. Jane had offered all three of them, and in exchange, only asked for—

Madelyn realized that she didn't know. She couldn't remember. She knew Jane had asked for something, but not what.

Do you want to know? Jane asked. It was so dark. There was a current around them, and Madelyn could feel it pulling at her. It was only Jane's strong grip on her hand that was keeping her where she was.

Tell me, she mouthed to Jane. She owed Jane that much.

Jane pointed upward. There was sunlight up there, broken and scattered across the surface of the water. *It's not an interesting story,* she said apologetically. *But I had a family once, and plans for the future, and a sister that I loved.*

There was a splash above them. Jane's face, real and whole and not wavering at all, was pushed underwater. Her dark hair floated around her as she whipped her head back and forth, mouth squeezed shut but her eyes wide open, wild with panic. She stayed there for long, panic-inducing seconds, struggling against whatever was holding her down, getting weaker and more panicked. Finally, she was hauled out of the water.

My sister came to me in a panic one day, because she had met the devil in the woods, and he had offered her a deal for her soul. And she was so scared. So I stayed with her, and I told her I wouldn't leave her.

Jane, above them, was plunged into the water again. Madelyn couldn't help it; she tried to swim up to her, the girl's panic mirrored in her own heart. But the other Jane, who had brought her here, still had hold of her hand and wouldn't let go, dragging her down deeper into the water.

And my sister took me to the woods, where she had trapped the devil, and she killed me, and bound the devil to me so she could use his power.

Madelyn could just barely see the hand holding Jane's face under the water. She fought desperately to get to the surface of the water. She could save the girl if she could get to her, she thought. Fight whoever it was who was holding her down—who was she kidding, she knew who it was. And she was ready now, she thought, to fight her mother. Wasn't that why Jane had brought her here?

But Jane kept a tight hold of her hand, dragging her farther and farther away from the surface, farther from the weakening struggles of the girl above them, until Madelyn thought her eardrums would burst from the pressure.

Let me go, Madelyn said.

Jane continued as if she hadn't spoken. *After the cruelty and the spectacle, she cut my throat. Iron through the heart, and then through the hands. That's how you shatter a soul, so it can be reshaped into a vessel where something like Generous can dwell for decades.*

An even bigger splash, and it wasn't just Jane's face this time. She'd been thrown bodily into the water. Ribbons of blood pumped out of her cut throat and left shadowy trails behind her hands.

Madelyn shaped the name carefully, still holding her breath. *Camille?*

Jane nodded. *I'm the broken pieces of her that escaped in the water.*

Madelyn had been so distracted by both of the Janes that she hadn't noticed what else was in the water.

They looked like tree roots at first, growing along the long iron stave that was impaling the girl's chest. As the girl's movements grew sluggish, something seemed to move in the darkness around her. The blood in the water grew muddier, coagulating into thick, twisting roots that pulled themselves toward her. Into her. They curled around the stave in her heart, the wounds in her throat, her hanging mouth. Camille's body twisted and contorted in the water as they took root inside her.

Madelyn was used to Jane, the terrible visage of her face. She hadn't realized that it was just an echo of Camille. Instead of teeth like Jane, this Camille had a hole that yawned sideways across her face, cutting off her mouth, part of her nose, most of a cheek. Dark roots pierced through her skin, trapping her in place even as they tore through her.

I slept a long time in the water. When I woke, I didn't have a name. I didn't have all of myself or my memories. I only knew that I had to find a way here, because something I needed was caged in the center of the forest.

But now? I'm afraid of her.

She's so hungry. *So* angry.

But if she's whole, your mother's net won't be able to hold her.

She remembered Jane telling her, *You want to be free*, reminding her, *You don't like where you are.* But Jane had needed her just as much. Why hadn't Jane asked for help? Madelyn would have done all she could to help her only friend.

Before she could ask, Jane floated away, her eyes glistening with darkness and fixed on Camille. Camille, for her part, was returning the stare. Her face was still blank, but her eyes were terribly alert. The two girls looked like distorted reflections of each other: same doll-like frame, same dark hair.

I wish I could have helped you, Jane said to Madelyn. *I'm sorry.*

Before Madelyn could stop her, Jane swam upward to Camille. They looked like dancers in the water, readying for a waltz. The roots and thorns in Camille shifted, reaching eagerly toward Jane. Jane's gaze didn't leave Camille, even as the roots dug into her arms, dragging her toward the yawning maw that ran from her throat to her chest. Jane seemed to lose substance. Her mouth moved, speaking words that only Camille could hear. But then she seemed to collapse, her body losing its shape, flowing into Camille and dispersing into the water around her.

Madelyn was still treading water, still trying to understand what had just happened. Had Jane betrayed her? Used her, certainly. But all Madelyn could think was that Jane hadn't said goodbye. Hadn't even looked back at Madelyn before disappearing forever.

Camille's gaze shifted down. She'd ignored Madelyn up until now, and part of Madelyn had believed she was somehow invisible.

Jane had said she wished she could have helped Madelyn. Camille didn't seem to have the same impulse. She glided toward Madelyn, all the little roots and tendrils propelling her through the water. Madelyn felt like a mouse who'd just seen the shadow of an owl passing overhead. She was an idiot, she realized, cold fear filling her stomach. No wonder Jane had apologized when she abandoned her.

She barely noticed the sting of her scars opening at first; she was filled with the pure need to get away, get out of the water, back to firm ground, and back to Riley. She felt a jerk beneath her sternum, then a nauseating shift in her gravity as her magic pulled her—not through the water, but out of it. She felt Camille's enraged scream rattle through her head, and then she was hitting the ground.

◆ ◆ ◆

Madelyn opened her eyes, and her mother's face filled her vision, staring down at her. She felt a jarring moment of dislocation: Was she underwater? In her bedroom? Had she reset back to her old life? Was her mother about to force her into a bathtub full of cold water?

No. She was underground, in the hollow cavern beneath the Wishing Tree.

"What did you do?" Mother demanded, grabbing Madelyn by the shoulders. "You . . . you wicked girl. Was this your plan? Supplant my deal with one of your own? Steal the magic I paid for?"

"No," Madelyn said, still groggy and disoriented. "I didn't—I only wanted—" Her mother clamped a hand over Madelyn's mouth, then another over her throat.

"This always happens," she hissed. "Why can't I make you good? You're always a thief, stealing my magic, my time, my energy. How much will you take?"

Madelyn wondered how long it would take her mother to regret what she'd done and find some way to rebuild her: a new daughter, once again, pondering who had left all those messages in the room beneath the basement stairs.

Madelyn closed her eyes; she didn't want to die looking at her mother's face, choked with rage and disappointment yet again.

There was a strange gust of air in the cavern, not from wind, but stale and humid as an exhaled breath. The pressure on Madelyn's throat vanished, and the hand on her mouth fell away. She opened her eyes. Her mother was staring at the decomposed body of Camille, whose arms had fallen from their carefully arranged position. Something moved in the corner of Madelyn's eye, and she turned her head; the corpse she'd seen before had its eyes open again, and its faded, scratched corneas were staring directly at her. As she watched, the corpse began to peel itself up from the dirt.

"What did you do?" Mother said again. Not angry anymore; pure horror drenched her voice. She slowly stood up from where she'd been crouching over Madelyn. She was looking all around the cavern, and as Madelyn got to her feet, her mother did the same. A few feet away, Riley lay still, but all around the cavern, the dead were moving. Twitching, pulling against the roots that held them down, breaking free with wet snaps. They crawled toward Camille's body, reaching for her.

The wind blew through again. A pause, and then Camille shrieked.

"Get out," Mom told her. "Get outside, get out of the clearing—Maddie!"

Madelyn had used her distraction to crawl over to Riley. The wound she had first seen on Riley's chest as a neat, bloodless hole was now a fissure cracking across her torso, long enough to extend over the bulge of her throat and reach toward her jaw. The edges Madelyn could see were a patchwork of textures: rough bark, the smooth flesh of a fungus, the segmented chitin of an insect.

Riley was still breathing, though it was slow and dragging.

"Madelyn!" her mother screamed, a warning.

Madelyn yanked the charm that her mother had wrapped around Riley's neck off and threw it as far as she could. Riley came awake with a gasp, and Madelyn thought, briefly, if this were an episode of *HMS Broomstick*, one or both of them would have something either very funny or very romantic to say.

As it was, Riley gazed wildly around, then her eyes narrowed in hatred when she spotted Mother. "Fucking Ivy," she growled, which was an odd curse, but Madelyn didn't have time to ask about it. The whole cavern was shaking around them. She pushed Riley to the hollow in the tree, shoving her out into the harsh daylight. She followed her through, and they collapsed onto the forest floor, catching their breath.

"Where's Sam? Toby?" Riley asked. "We were at the house, but then I—"

"It was my mother," Madelyn said. "But they're both fine. She left them behind and took us to the tree."

"Your mother is Ivy," Riley said. "She's been stalking me. She made me take a goddamn piss test."

No wonder Riley had dropped like a stone, Madelyn thought. Her mother's charms were a lot more effective if she had physical cast-offs from the person they were meant for.

Her mother emerged from the hollow beneath the tree and stalked over to them. She hauled Madelyn up roughly by the arms and shook her. "Tell me what you did," she demanded. Her eyes were wide with anger and—Madelyn was very good at reading her mother's emotions—shock at how this possibly could have gone wrong for her. A vicious satisfaction burned in Madelyn's chest to see her mother so panicked. "I heard you call someone's name. What did you *do*?"

How was she supposed to explain Jane? First friend, only friend for so long, who had told her that she could free herself, and then left her behind to die? "There was a voice in the well," she said haltingly.

"Get the hell off her, you wretched bitch," Riley said, struggling to her feet. She was furious, but Madelyn could see that the fury was draining her. "I'll kill you for real, you—"

Before she could continue, the ground bulged until the sod ripped. The wolf tree shook, dropping coins into the dirt around them. There was a muted crack as the dead wood in its trunk split, and it pitched toward the three of them. Madelyn managed to shove Riley away in one direction before her mother pulled her in the other, and the tree crashed between them. Branches whipped painfully against her arms, and one clocked her hard in the jaw, knocking her down and dazing her for a second. When she shook herself out of it, she couldn't see Riley.

Slowly, all the dead emerged from their prison beneath the broken tree, their flesh joined together in a single asymmetric arachnid body. Fungi and slime molds dotted decay-mottled skin, and uneven limbs protruded at odd angles, dangling roots and mycelia. It towered over them, nearly half as tall as the tree had been. In the center, she could see Camille's original body: the long iron rod in her chest and the smaller ones in her hands. Some flesh had returned to her face, and Madelyn wondered if that was Jane's doing: that her face had some skin on it, had more teeth than the skull of a young woman should, and something as luminous as swamp gas shone out of her empty eye sockets.

Riley's mother was in there somewhere, Madelyn thought, then wished she hadn't.

"Lillian," the voice screamed from a dozen mouths; voices it had devoured over the years echoed. Camille turned, slow and awkward, to face her sister.

The unease that had flooded the woods the night Riley died was back, but was now a thick and choking malaise. It wasn't just the smell of putrefaction and rot, though that was everywhere as well, crawling into Madelyn's sinuses and throat. It was cold fury, rage and betrayal and a deep, terrible sadness that made Madelyn want to crumple. She could feel Camille's long years alone in her shriek, and it made her want to beg forgiveness.

"Get up," her mother hissed. She was facing Camille but speaking to Madelyn. "The net is weak, but it hasn't broken," she said. "The wards are still in place. I can still fix this."

Her words were harsh, but the blood had left her face, and she looked deathly pale, almost as gray as some of the corpses that now made up Camille's body. Her hands were shaking, but they were moving, pulling charms out of her bag and onto the ground, long and complicated chains, jars full of murky liquid. Camille's movements were still slow and ungainly, and her mother's were quick and practiced.

"Go, Madelyn. Get out of the clearing and let me work."

Where was Riley? She looked but couldn't see her. Didn't know what to do. Couldn't shake how she'd felt down in the water, helpless and floating as Camille came toward her. *She's so hungry. So angry.*

Madelyn walked backward on shaky legs, too scared to take her eyes off Camille, but silently begging the dead girl not to notice her.

So of course she did. Camille's attention shifted from her

mother to Madelyn. She'd spent decades hating her sister. Maybe she thought that hurting Madelyn would hurt her sister more—but Camille should know better than anyone how much pain Mother inflicted on the people she loved.

Camille's enormous body shifted as her gaze did. She moved faster now, though in a way that was utterly alien, a half-hearted imitation of nature. Clumps of dirt, coins, wire, nails all fell as she bore down on Madelyn.

"Maddie, move!" Mom screamed, but freezing in fear was more deeply ingrained in Madelyn than pure obedience. She could only stare as Camille got closer.

And then her mother was between them. She didn't push Madelyn so much as fling her to the edge of the clearing, where that net of energy and power still held.

Madelyn tripped, falling painfully on the uneven ground. Terrified that she'd feel Camille's many hands grab her and haul her back, she crawled through the edge of the net to safety.

She let herself take one breath, then another, before she turned over.

She was just in time to see her mother die.

She had gladly watched her mother burn only yesterday, and believed her dead for a few glorious, confusing hours. She had told herself that her mother hated her, and that it was mutual, and that she'd only ever be free when her mother was in the ground. And maybe if her mother hadn't just saved her, she might have cheered Camille on, advised her to learn from Madelyn's mistakes and make sure Mother was dead before celebrating.

Instead, she looked into her mother's eyes as Camille curved two spiderlike legs around her and tore Mother into two dripping pieces. Like tearing a leaf in two, only with a lot more blood, which drenched Madelyn immediately.

A few seconds later, she felt her mother's magic die. First it died inside her, and there was a terrifying moment when she believed what her mother had told her: It was her covenant with Generous that powered her magic, of which Madelyn was only a by-product. Everything that bound her together would dissolve, and she'd be another pile of flesh and liquid in this clearing. Like mother, like daughter.

But after that horrible moment, her heart kept beating. Her skin stayed shut where Riley had helpfully stapled it, and she could still move.

And then her senses flooded with connections: She could feel the forest around her, the roots of the trees stretching down below, tangling together. Farther away, her awareness brushed against the caves crisscrossing the mountain beneath them, which kept the secrets of the past: faces carved into one rock, keeping watch. A half-dozen birds with outstretched wings carved on another. She could feel the movement of the water beneath them, the spring forcing it upward, gravity pulling it down in trickling seeps and creeks. It was like she'd found a working light switch after a lifetime in a dark room.

It took Madelyn a long moment to come back to herself, to her fragile physical body cowering in the dirt.

It was another moment after that when she realized that the net her mother had made, which had trapped Generous and Camille for so long, had evaporated as well.

CHAPTER TWENTY-ONE

Riley had watched the tree come down, seemingly in slow motion. Madelyn had shoved her aside in time to keep her from getting squished by the trunk or its thickest branches, but she couldn't get out of the way entirely, and she was knocked to the ground.

She was struck with the memory of dying here the first time: lying on her back and looking up into the branches moving gently in the breeze. History repeating itself. Cycles and broken wheels. She was tired of struggling, fighting so hard and still never getting ahead.

Riley had always been afraid of ending up like her mother, in one way or another. She wondered how likely it was that Toby and Sam would wake up at home and have to wrestle with another family member's absence. How long would they wait for her to come home? When would they allow themselves to mourn her?

Riley felt very young for a moment; something in her wanted to kick her feet and scream at how unfair this was. Someone had done something unimaginably awful, and so many people had paid the price for it, and now, it was up to her to fix it.

She suddenly remembered a day with her mother, in that

cautiously happy period after she'd finished rehab and regained custody of her kids. Riley had been whining about something a teacher had done, how unfair it had been. They'd sent her home with a note for Anna and everything, to encourage the punishment to continue after school.

So many people say life's not fair, her mom had told her. *Like that's just a fact and not something that people actively decide to reinforce.* She had slowly and deliberately crumpled the note from the teacher, thrown it in the trash, and missed. Anna had sworn under her breath, then gone to pick it up. *It's not fair,* she'd said, *but we don't have to accept shit. If the world tries to chew you up and spit you out, make it damn well choke on you.*

She'd used drugs to cope with how disappointing the world was, how painful it could be, and how utterly shitty the status quo was. It had never stopped her from refusing to accept that suffering was just inevitable for some people.

Right on cue, Camille shrieked in rage. The ground trembled beneath her.

Riley couldn't change history to make life fair for Camille Voynich. But she couldn't ignore a deep, burning anger over what had been done to Camille. Camille had been someone's little sister. She should have been protected.

Now Riley just had to find enough strength to actually get her ass up and do something about it.

Her arms were shaking, barely able to hold her weight. She could feel the wound in her chest now, where it had been numb before. A brutal emptiness at her core, an ache that sharpened when she moved. Her legs were shaking too, her feet sore and scraped—Ivy had made her walk barefoot up to this clearing.

Finally, she was on her feet, just in time to hear Madelyn

scream. The panic in the sound slid through Riley's skin like cold needles. Her brain shut down and her legs took over, pivoting around before she could think, moving on pure instinct, scrambling over the fallen tree.

"Wait, wait!" she said. She came up short when she saw Ivy, or what had been Ivy. Camille was crouched above the messy pile of blood and flesh that had been her sister and her tormenter. Madelyn was a few feet away, frozen in terror. At Riley's voice, the thing that Camille Voynich had become swung around to face her. Riley wanted to look away; it was covered in blood, and the individual bodies bound together were making tiny, abortive movements, opening their hands, their mouths, twisting their faces as much as they could to look at Riley. She forced herself not to look away. This had been done to Camille, she told herself. That was the real horror here.

Which sounded reasonable, up until she saw a familiar jawline, her mother's mouth—not open in laughter or frowning in frustration, but slack and loose and dead.

Riley shut her eyes and shoved down a scream. She looked instead with the sight that Generous had given her.

It showed her Camille as she had first seen her: small, scared, sporting wounds that were even uglier than Riley's own. The heaving breaths of the flesh-tree-fungus monster were sobs.

She had been so alone for so long.

Riley thought about how she would approach Sam during a tantrum, if Sam had suddenly been turned into the Thing— from the one horror movie she'd vowed to never watch again. Riley kept her eyes firmly shut but spoke quietly.

"Hi, Camille." She tried not to feel stupid, or imagine that she was about to end up like Ivy. "I'm . . . god, I'm really sorry for what she did to you. I'm sorry she hurt you, and kept you here for so long. She—she hurt me too. And Madelyn. And—"

Camille was listening, but Riley could feel her shifting restlessly, her rage only quieted a little, not gone, not even dissipated.

"I bet you were thinking about this for a long time." Riley remembered how she'd felt after burying her fists in Bancroft's chest. "And thought you would feel . . . better? After doing it? Maybe not better, but like, it would fix something in you that she'd broken. But everything still hurts."

In Generous's sight, the little girl nodded.

"Maybe I can try something," she said. "It might hurt at first, but you'll feel better afterward."

She felt Camille's predatory regard; smelled the meat and rot and mud of all her many mouths breathing in and out. She tried to fix the image of her as a small girl in her mind. A sister. Her sister.

"Riley, what are you—" Madelyn whispered, and Riley flapped an arm and shushed her. She felt Camille shy away for a second, and held her breath, inwardly begging her to settle, to let Riley help her.

The air shifted, and she felt Camille calm and lower herself closer to the ground. The air around her was still buzzing. Riley thought of how she had felt after spotting Mr. Bancroft— like enraged wasps were droning against her skull.

Now came the real test, because she couldn't do the next part with her eyes closed.

"Can you give me your hand?" she asked, and opened her eyes. She took in Camille, trying to look just at her and not all the rot and suffering she'd pulled around herself like armor.

After a long moment, Camille pulled out one withered hand and extended it to Riley. A thick iron nail pierced her palm, bleeding rust onto the surrounding skin.

"It'll sting," Riley said, the same way she did when picking a splinter out of Sam's finger. Quiet, comfortingly authoritative. Trustworthy. "And it might ache a little when it's gone, but it needs to come out."

She got her fingers around it as best she could. "Ready?"

When Camille nodded, she gripped it tightly and pulled steadily, not yanking it, and not stopping when Camille whimpered in pain. She didn't stop until it was out, and she dropped it on the ground, breathing hard. Camille pulled her hand back, and her enormous body shifted back and forth in the clearing, like she wasn't sure if she should flee or not. Madelyn had stood up, eyes darting nervously between Riley and Camille.

"It's okay," Riley told her. Madelyn fell back a little, though she was looking at Riley like she was insane for doing this. But then, Madelyn was an only child.

"Okay, other hand," Riley said, trying for that authoritative, big-sister tone in the face of Camille's reluctance. "That wasn't so bad, right? And it'll feel better once they're both out."

Camille hesitated longer this time, but then extended her other hand to Riley. Camille's skin was damp, leathery. It felt like a clearance-sale prop Sam would buy at the Dollar General the day after Halloween. Riley repeated the movement: the brace, the pull. And then it was out, and Riley let it drop into the dirt.

Camille looked at her hands: the fronts first, then the backs, slowly flexing her fingers.

"I told you, didn't I? That it would feel better."

She eyed the spike that had been hammered into Camille's chest. It was thicker and rougher than the nails that had been pushed through her hands. "I need my friend's help with this one," she said. She gestured at the ugly wound in her own chest. "I don't think I'm strong enough."

Camille shifted away, raising herself off the ground and out of Riley's reach. She loomed over her, and Riley had to swallow back a gag at the smell that wafted toward her again. But she didn't take her eyes off Camille's face. Riley met her suspicious glare calmly, trying not to betray any of the fear she felt. She put a hand out behind her and gestured for Madelyn to come forward. Madelyn stepped up next to her and whispered, "You're sure about this?"

"No," she told Madelyn, because what would lying or false bravado get her at this point? She had no idea what would happen after she pulled out this last piece of iron binding Camille and Generous together. "But she deserves to be free, right?"

Madelyn nodded, and they waited together. Camille, obviously agitated, paced back and forth across the clearing before reluctantly returning. Her legs folded underneath her, and she lowered herself down so they could reach the stave that pierced through her heart. Riley put her hands on the stave, and, moving much more slowly and cautiously, Madelyn followed her, fitting her hands between Riley's. Camille fidgeted, anxious and mistrustful. "Hey, hey, it's all right," Riley said. "You're okay. We're gonna be fine. We'll wait until you're ready."

Eventually Camille stilled. Riley leaned in close to Madelyn and whispered, "Don't stop until it's out, okay? No matter what."

Madelyn frowned at her. "I don't like that," she said.

"I don't either, but if we stop—"

If they stopped, Camille might kill them. Or kill someone else. Or just suffer forever until whatever magic and spiteful hurt was fueling her eroded away naturally.

"Fine," Madelyn said. "Fine." Her hand, with its broad scar across the palm, was so warm next to Riley's.

"On three?" she said, and at Madelyn's nod, she counted them off. "One, two—"

It wasn't like the spikes in the girl's hands. The pain was immediate and consuming, like Riley was pulling it out of her own chest, yanking it out of her heart and bones. Camille gave a low, pained cry.

Riley must have made some kind of noise of her own, because Madelyn's hand went slack next to hers. "Riley—"

"Don't stop," Riley gritted out, and when Madelyn didn't start pulling, shouldered her in frustration. "Come *on*," she said.

The pain didn't let up; if anything, it got worse, even as she felt the spike moving under her and Madelyn's combined strength. It stole the breath from her, but she kept pulling. Camille's cry turned into a guttural scream as they pulled it, but she didn't fight them, and Riley wondered at that, how even in the pain, she trusted them.

And then the spike was free. Attached to the end, dangling down and covered in a disgusting fluid that smelled like absolute death, was a familiar heart-shaped silver locket. Riley felt light, suddenly.

Camille was coming apart. The magic binding all those bodies together was leaking away, and Madelyn dragged Riley back as they started to collapse. She worried for a second that there'd be some *Evil Dead*-esque rapid decay, but Camille simply stopped moving and sank down onto the ground. Riley couldn't make out the expression on her face—if it was the relief that Riley had promised, or at least the rest that Camille deserved. Riley tried to look at her with Generous's sight, but she couldn't, and that was when she realized the magic was leaving her as well.

Her knees buckled, and she would have fallen if Madelyn hadn't caught her. "Ow," she said. Because the hole in her chest was no longer magical—her body had just received the delayed message that she was wounded, maybe mortally. "Ow, fuck."

Madelyn lowered her to the ground, and she was making panicked noises that Riley couldn't quite hear. Her hands were warm on Riley's skin, and she concentrated on that, because shit, when had it gotten so cold?

That was when Riley realized she was dying, for the second, and presumably last, time.

CHAPTER TWENTY-TWO

Madelyn, her magic unbound, could feel Riley's life slipping away. She grabbed what she could, because Riley deserved to live. She was funny and sarcastic and she cared about everyone, even monsters like Camille.

Even monsters like Madelyn.

And because the idea of being alone terrified her. Madelyn had lost her mother, and lost Jane, but she could save Riley. She could feel her magic flowing through her, natural as the air in her lungs. What was the point of having power at all if you couldn't save one stupid, headstrong girl who insisted you were a real person and insulted your taste in TV and stapled you shut when you needed it?

But she couldn't stop Riley's death. She didn't have her mother's control or knowledge. If magic was sacrifice, then fine; she'd do it, but she didn't know *how*.

She didn't notice the slow, heavy footsteps behind her until something bent down and spoke in her peripheral vision.

"Did your mother ever tell you about our deal?" it whispered.

Madelyn didn't—couldn't make herself look head-on at Generous. Why was it asking her this now?

"She wished for a child. I don't think she realized what she was getting, though—something shaped like her, but still one of ours. Tricky and too smart and a little too wild."

"So what?" Madelyn spat, even though she also wondered at that phrase: *one of ours.* But it didn't matter, because Riley's life was still leaving her, dissipating into the trees and the air around them. It'd stay for a while—*Dead but not gone,* Jane whispered from her memories—but it wouldn't matter. "I need to—"

"We don't use magic like a witch would," said Generous. "We make offers. Deals. Trick people, when they deserve it. Or get tricked, when we do," it added wryly. "Magic is—"

"Sacrifice," she mumbled automatically, a habit long-learned from her mother.

"Collaboration," said Generous. It stood again, its proportions strange, too tall and lanky to be mistaken for human, and Madelyn thought again of that phrase, *one of ours.* Wondered idly if she would grow to look like that: not exactly unnatural, but uncanny. If she would have by now if her mother hadn't constantly unmade and remade her.

"She'd make a good witch," Generous said, and then walked its careful steps away. Madelyn hardly noticed. Riley was barely conscious, eyelashes fluttering. Madelyn could feel her struggling to stay.

"Riley," she whispered down to her. "I—I have an offer for you."

She swallowed, wondering if Riley would refuse. "A wish, a secret, and a boon. If you'll be the witch. My witch."

Madelyn's magic had been spread out across the forest, nestled among the roots and leaves. Saying that drew it all together, snapping it into place.

Riley's eyes were open, focused on her, and her mouth worked, like she was trying to speak.

"What's your wish?" she urged. Madelyn could see the magic, burning threads that she could pluck and play like an instrument, but they'd do nothing without Riley saying—

"To live," Riley said. "I want to live."

♦ ♦ ♦

When Riley blinked open her eyes a while later, it was to see Madelyn passed out in the grass next to her, and both of them surrounded by the tall, bobbing heads of dandelions, which had been out of season for months.

CHAPTER TWENTY-THREE

If you weren't looking with a witch's eyes, the forest seemed still. It was early in the morning, barely an hour past the late December dawn, and the sun hadn't climbed high enough to shine through the barren branches. In summer, the area by Dyson Pond would shimmer with life: insects darting through the air or dancing across the water, birds and squirrels and chipmunks in the trees. Leaves rustling in the mountain breeze, whispering to each other. In winter, the woods felt barren, silent and still as the dead. Frost drew tiny patterns on the edge of Dyson Pond, limned the edges of the moss and lichens on the trees. The girl sitting by the pond was still as well, no different from the forest around her.

With a witch's sight, though, Riley could feel the subtle magics that thrummed through this place. Slower in the winter, sluggish. Riley decided that she preferred the forest in the winter. Maybe because there were no tours, no tourists, nobody trying to sniff around her town's sad, dark history. It was quiet instead. Contemplative. Looking toward the end of one cycle, and the beginning of another, the wheel of the year turning over again.

Something broke the stillness. Heavy breath fogged the air, and footsteps crunched through the leaves. She could hear

Sam coming a long way off, easily recognizable by the way she kept stopping and shuffling around, probably peering at some weird-looking moss or stuffing a rock into her pocket to show Toby later. Now that there weren't hidden creatures or myths to uncover, Sam moved through the forest differently. Less driven, more meandering.

"Still super weird to be chasing *you* down in the woods," Sam said, sitting next to Riley.

"Instead of the other way around?" Riley asked.

Sam pulled out the whistle that she still wore on a chain, an old apartment key next to it. "You'd come if I whistled."

"Always," Riley agreed. She patted the matching whistle she wore under her shirt. There was magic in those whistles too, she could see now. A spell of returning, far subtler and weaker than what Lillian would have made. *Come find me.* She wondered now if Bancroft had seen it, though, seen that in all the objects he stole from the missing.

Sam had huddled next to Riley for warmth. She was bundled up in her winter jacket, an old castoff of Riley's that she'd outgrown, and that Sam would outgrow herself before next winter, probably. "I don't like it when you're out here alone," Sam said.

"I'm not alone," Riley reminded her.

When she and Madelyn had unbound Camille and Generous, she'd hoped that Camille would be able to rest. To move on, find peace, whatever it was that dead girls were supposed to do. But she'd realized life and death weren't separate countries with a border between them. Parts of Camille lingered in the woods where she'd been trapped for so long. There were pockets of her cold, biting rage in the forest, shards of her loneliness nestled in the roots of certain trees. Pieces of her sister Lillian survived as well; Riley could feel her strangling presence sometimes. (Riley wondered if Lillian had understood the incredible irony in choosing that name: Ivy was an invasive, parasitic weed, starving and crowding out native plants.) Though Madelyn had worked to uproot those pieces whenever she could, or pull them down into the deepest caves and sinkholes, where none of them would have to feel her presence.

Riley wondered if other witches had done this: cleaned up the messes of their predecessors, magic that had backfired or, worse, worked as they'd intended and thrown things out of balance. Riley had mapped the places where the Voynich sisters' pain and anger still grew like kudzu in the woods, and Madelyn had closed them off as much as she could.

The other dead were here too. Sometimes, especially on mornings like this, cold and sharp, she could hear her mother's jagged laugh, tinged with regret. It was hard, and Riley had to hold herself still, let the wave of sadness and resentment wash through her, before she could just sit with the lingering echoes of her mother and feel grateful. It was its own cycle.

"Dead people don't count," Sam said. It was supposed to sound scornful, Riley thought, but there was an edge of longing as well. She couldn't hear their mother the way that Riley could.

Learning magic when there was no witch to teach her—just her non-witch uncle and sister, and the hundreds of stories collected by the two of them—was slow and frustrating, like waiting for spring to come when the snow refused to melt. She didn't want to make charms like Lillian had, even though Madelyn remembered some of the structures and principles. Besides, that had been Generous's magic, and it seemed to have vacated the forest as well, or else gone to sleep deep inside the mountain. Riley had instead channeled the power she could feel licking up from the ground into drawings. Transforming ink into a wish, or a little piece of power that she could share. Maybe something that would allow Sam to hear her mother's laugh whispering among the trees, something more solid than memories to hold.

She'd keep working on it.

"Have you thought about a new name for the woods?" she asked Sam. The proposal had come up in town. Toby claimed that he had no part in it, that someone on Roscoe's select board had put it forward. The old men at Dunkin', thrilled to have new rumors to chew on instead of old stories, said it was because of all the disturbing, unsettling, and possibly satanic things found in the burned-out remains of the Voynich house. Toby said it was more likely because Lillian Voynich had mysteriously avoided paying property taxes for decades, and nobody was sure exactly who owned the house now that she was gone.

"I wish we could name it for Mom, but that's not really fair to everyone else who disappeared," Sam said. "But we should definitely call it a forest, and not a wood, since the canopy density is totally different now."

"I'll fight for that," Riley said. "Not that I'll technically get a vote." Town Meeting Day, when people in Roscoe would vote on any proposed name changes, would happen before Riley's eighteenth birthday.

"That's stupid."

"Witch of the Woods isn't exactly a recognized legal title," said Riley. But there was the woods—sorry, the forest—and the town, and walking between them, the Witch. Who had to speak for both, protect both, find a way for them to coexist.

No pressure or anything.

She and Sam sat there a while longer, and it gradually grew lighter between the trees, but no warmer. When Sam's shivering grew impossible to ignore, Riley nudged her sister. "Head back to the house. I'll catch up in a second."

"Are you going to commune with the devil?" Sam asked teasingly, and laughed when Riley shoved her. "Tell Madelyn that she should come to breakfast," Sam called as she ran back down the path.

Riley shut her eyes, following her with her witch sight. Eventually, her mind opened to the slow conversation of the forest around her, sluggish in the dead of winter, and waited.

Unlike with Sam, there was no observable change when Madelyn stepped out from between the trees. Riley stood up to face her.

Madelyn, despite the cold, was in jeans and a T-shirt, her feet and arms bare. She had given up on baggy sweatshirts and too-large coats that swallowed her. She didn't notice the cold and felt better with the dirt under her bare feet, the air against her skin. (Sam and Toby liked to sing "Let It Go" whenever Madelyn showed up in a T-shirt when it was twenty-five degrees, and once they'd forced Madelyn to watch *Frozen*, she had started singing along.) Madelyn was part of the forest, or maybe it was more accurate to say that part of her *was* the forest? She was life and death, fire and dirt and water. There was a certain point where Riley gave up on trying to describe Madelyn or their connection with words.

"How's the sigil coming along?" Madelyn asked. She didn't say hello or goodbye, really, just picked up conversations like it hadn't been hours, sometimes an entire day or two, since they'd last talked.

"Not ready yet," Riley admitted. They had been experimenting with symbols drawn on the trunks of trees to repel anyone wandering into the places where Camille's or Lillian's energy still clawed out of the ground. It might have been easier to trap that energy, but some lingering connection to Generous made Riley shy away from that—things festered in traps, as Camille had proven.

"Did you hear us talking about the town's decision? Renaming the woods?" asked Riley.

Madelyn frowned. "Why do the woods even need a name?"

"They don't. People need one for it, though."

Riley put her hands on either side of Madelyn's face and kissed her on the lips. The press of Madelyn's mouth was soft enough that it almost tickled. Left her lips buzzing.

She grinned for a moment. *Communing with the devil,* she thought. "Good morning, by the way."

Madelyn pressed her fingers to her lips, half hiding the grin that mirrored Riley's own. Riley could see her, all of her: the parts her mother had constructed, broken down, and rebuilt; the delicate spells imprinted on her skin, some from her mother, and newer, gentler ones from Riley. And then there was the part of Madelyn that had come from somewhere deep in the forest that not even Riley was privy to. Something ancient and wild and impossible to contain. Riley worried that Madelyn would retreat fully into that part of herself, and maybe wouldn't blame her if she did. But she did her best to bring Madelyn back here, where she could see all of Riley in return.

Madelyn looked around at the frost lacing the edges of the pond and the tips of fallen leaves, the cold blue of the sky. "Yeah, it will be," she agreed. She stood up and looked down the trail. "Should we catch up with Sam?"

"In a minute," Riley said. The morning was too soft and sweet to hurry through.

ACKNOWLEDGMENTS

All my love and gratitude to my wife, Nibedita Sen—who loves me at my messiest, and whose belief in this story helped me believe in it too—and to Ellen Cipri, my mother, who supplied endless pet and garden pictures, cookies, and financial and emotional support. Leah Cipri was my constant childhood companion of getting up to stupid shit in the woods—Riley owes a spiritual and creative debt to Leah, coolest older sibling.

Thank you to Wendy Wagner, John Joseph Adams, and the editorial team at *Nightmare Magazine* for publishing the earliest version of this story in 2017, "Which Super Little Dead Girl™ Are You? Take Our Quiz and Find Out!" I wrote that story and the first version of this novel at the University of Kansas's MFA in Creative Writing program. Kij Johnson offered encouragement, handholding, and invaluable feedback. Thank you also to Giselle Anatol, Laura Moriarty, Darren Canady, and Marta Carminero-Santangelo for your teaching and knowledge, all of which fed into this book.

DongWon Song is a wonderfully supportive agent, who not only sold this novel, but also rescued it when I got lost in the weeds of rewriting. Thanks to Tiff Liao for acquiring and shaping *Dead Girls* with her feedback, and to Kat Brzozowski and Eleonore Fisher for their guidance and patience during the long rewrite process when my brain was broken. Gratitude to everyone at HHYR who had a hand in creating this book: Jie Yang, senior production manager; Mallory Grigg, senior art director; Lelia Mander, production editor; Ann Marie Wong, editorial director; Jean Feiwel, senior vice president and publishing director. Thank you to Jasper Read for an insightful authenticity reading, and to Valerie Shea for sharp copyediting. Awe and praise to Michelle Avery Konczyk for creating the most incredible cover art.

Writing (and life) would be miserable without friends. Queerplatonic lifemate k8 Walton answered one a.m. texts like "would you be able to see someone's heart if you removed the skin of their chest, or would it be hidden behind their lungs?" Jason Baltazar, Hannah Warren, Maria Dones, and Kyle Teller encouraged this book from the start. Thanks to Manish Melwani, Marty Cahill, Lara Elena Donnelly, Victor Manibo, Liz Tieri, and the good folks down at the pub who provided writing dates, safe places to vent, names for local cryptids and silly fake TV shows.

Some of the folklore in this book is borrowed from or inspired by stories I found in *Jonathan Draws the Long Bow: New England Popular Tales and Legends*, by Richard Mercer Dorson, published in 1946. It's long out of print but available to read online.

This story draws from my experience as both the child of an alcoholic father and growing up during the early 2000s opioid crisis in Vermont. I lost friends to overdoses and jail, or watched as they went through cycles of rehab and relapse.